This book is for Ann Weir

The Joy and Light
Bus Company

ALEXANDER McCALL SMITH

Little, Brown

LITTLE, BROWN

First published in Great Britain in 2021 by Little, Brown

1 3 5 7 9 10 8 6 4 2

Copyright © Alexander McCall Smith 2021

The moral right of the author has been asserted.

A CIP catalogue record for this book is available from the British Library.

Hardback ISBN: 978-1-4087-1444-7
Trade paperback ISBN: 978-1-4087-1443-0

Typeset in Galliard by M Rules
Printed and bound in Great Britain by Clays Ltd, Elcograf S.p.A

Papers used by Little, Brown are from well-managed forests
and other responsible sources.

Little, Brown
An imprint of
Little, Brown Book Group
Carmelite House
50 Victoria Embankment
London EC4Y 0DZ

An Hachette UK Company
www.hachette.co.uk

www.littlebrown.co.uk

The Joy and Light
Bus Company

By Alexander McCall Smith

Chapter One

Past-tense Men

It was a question to which Mma Ramotswe, like many women in Botswana, and indeed like many women in so many other places, gave more than occasional thought. It was not that she dwelt on it all the time; it was not even that it occupied her mind much of the time, but it was certainly something that she thought about now and then, especially when she was sitting on her veranda in the first light of the morning, looking out at the acacia tree on the other side of the road, in which two Cape doves, long in love, cooed endearments to one another, while for her part she sipped at her first cup of redbush tea, not in any hurry to do whatever it was that she had to do next. That, of course, is always a good time to think – when you know that you are going to have to do something, but you know that you do not have to do it just yet.

The question she occasionally thought about – the question in question, so to speak – was not a particularly complicated one, and could be expressed in a few simple words, namely: *how do you keep men happy?* Of course, Mma Ramotswe knew that there were those who considered this to be a very old-fashioned question, almost laughable, and there were even those who became markedly indignant at the assumptions that lurked behind such an enquiry. Mma Ramotswe, although a traditional woman in some respects, also considered herself modern in others, and understood very well that women were not placed on this earth simply to look after men. There were unfortunately still men who seemed to hold that view – they had not entirely disappeared – but they were fewer in number, she was happy to observe, and nobody paid much attention to them any longer. These men were called *past-tense men* by Mma Makutsi, Mma Ramotswe's friend and colleague – a vivid, if perhaps slightly unkind expression. If any man expressed such sentiments today, Mma Ramotswe reflected, he would have to face phalanxes of angry women challenging him in no uncertain terms. Mma Makutsi would not tolerate attitudes like that, and no man would get away with speaking like that within her earshot. And Mma Makutsi's hearing, for this and other purposes, was known to be particularly acute.

'Grace Makutsi can hear an ant walking across the ground,' Mma Ramotswe had once observed to Mr J. L. B. Matekoni. 'At least, I am told she can.'

Mr J. L. B. Matekoni had looked incredulous. 'I do not think so, Mma,' he said. 'Ants do not make much noise when they are walking. I think that even other ants do not hear them all that well. I'm not even sure if ants have ears, Mma.'

Mma Ramotswe had smiled. She had not meant her remark to be taken literally, but Mr J. L. B. Matekoni often took things at face value and was not as receptive to metaphor as he might be. This could be owing to the fact that he was a mechanic, and mechanics tended to think in a practical way, or it could just be the way his particular mind worked – it was hard to tell. But even as she smiled at his response, she found herself wondering whether it was true that ants made no noise. She had always imagined that they did – at least when there were enough of them engaged in the sort of joint activity that ants sometimes embarked upon, when they moved in an orderly column, like an army on the march, shifting any blades of dry grass or grains of sand that got in their way. Even tiny ants, acting together in such numbers, could be heard to make a rustling sound, as they went about their unfathomable business. And of course there were enough monuments to that business in those places where termites erected their extraordinary mud towers. Those were astonishing creations – high, tapering piles of hardened mud, red-brown on fresh creation but, when old and weathered, as grey as a long-felled branch or tree-trunk. There must have been some noise in the making of those strange, vertical ant cities, even if there was usually nobody to hear it.

But now she was thinking of that other question – that of how to keep men contented. It was, she thought, a good idea to keep men happy, just as it was a good idea to keep women happy. Both sexes, she thought, might give some thought to the happiness of the other. She knew that there were some women who did not care much about men, and who would not be bothered too much if there were large numbers of discontented men, but she did not think that way herself. Such women, she thought, were every bit as selfish as those men who seemed not to care about the happiness of women. We should all care about each other, she felt, and it made no difference whether an unhappy person was a man or a woman. Any unhappiness, in anybody at all, was a shame. It was as simple as that: it was a shame.

If you were to think about the happiness of men, and if you were to decide that it would be better for any men in your life to be happy rather than unhappy, then what could you do to achieve that goal? One answer, of course, was to say that it was up to men to make themselves happy – that this was not something that women should have to worry about too much, that men should be responsible for themselves. There was some truth in that, Mma Ramotswe thought – men could not expect women to run around after them like nursemaids, but, even then, there were things that women could do to help them to look after themselves and to make their lives a little bit better.

The first thing to do, perhaps, was to look at men and try to work out what it was that men wanted. All of us, Mma Ramotswe thought, wanted *something*, even if we were unable to tell anybody exactly what it was that we wanted. If you went up to somebody in the street and said, 'Excuse me, but what is it that you want?' you might be rewarded with a look of surprise, perhaps even of alarm. But the question was not as odd as it might seem, because there were many people who were not at all sure what they wanted in life, and might do well to ask themselves that unsettling question from time to time.

There were, it was true, some men who looked as if they knew exactly what they wanted. These were the men you saw moving quickly about the place, walking in a purposeful manner, or driving their cars with every indication of wanting to get somewhere as quickly as possible. These were men who were busy, who were going somewhere in order to do something they had already identified as needing to be done. But then there were many men who did not have that air about them. There were many men who just stood about, not going anywhere in particular, or, if they were, not going anywhere with any great appearance of purpose. Were you to ask some of these men what they wanted, they might answer that what they really wanted to do was to sit down. And that, Mma Ramotswe had to admit, was not a bad ambition to have in this life. Many people who were not currently sitting down wanted to do so at some stage in the future – and why not? There was nothing essentially wrong in sitting down and doing nothing in particular. If more people sat down, there would probably be less turmoil in the world – there would certainly be less discomfort.

But there was more to the needs of men than that, thought Mma Ramotswe. At heart, men wanted other people, and in particular women, to like them. Men wanted to be loved. They wanted women to look at them and think, 'What a nice-looking man that is.' Even men who were unfortunately not at all nice-looking – and there were men who could do with some improvement in that department – wanted women to think that of them. And they wanted women to think that the things they did were worthwhile, were important, and would not be done if they were not around to do them. Men needed to be needed. That was a simple and easily grasped way of expressing what it was that most men were after, in one way or another.

On that particular day, a day in the hot season before the coming of the rains, Mma Ramotswe happened to have been thinking about these things, and raised the matter with Mma Makutsi as they sat in their office, drinking their mid-afternoon cup of tea, and rather feeling the heat. The conversation had started with a sigh from Mma Makutsi, a way in which she often signalled that she was in a mood to discuss a big and important issue rather than engage in small talk. Small talk had its place, of course – discussion of who had said what about whom, or about what one was going to have for dinner that night, or about what sales were on in what shops – these were all worthy topics of conversation, but had their limits and occasionally made one wish for more substantial conversational fare.

And so it was that after a rather loud and drawn-out sigh from Mma Makutsi's side of the room, Mma Ramotswe announced, 'I've been thinking, Mma, about what makes men happy.'

Mma Makutsi took a sip of her tea. 'That is a very big question, Mma, and I am glad that you raised it. I am certainly very glad.'

Mma Ramotswe waited. Mma Makutsi had a way of preceding important observations with a general prologue, rather as a politician might announce a plan to build a new road or excavate a new dam only after making some high-flown remarks on the importance of roads and dams, and about how some political parties are perhaps less aware of this than others. Now, having prepared the ground, Mma Makutsi continued, 'I have thought of that in the past, and although I wasn't thinking about it right now, I am certainly prepared to think about it.'

Mma Ramotswe digested this quickly, and went on to say, 'I know that we women have other things to think about – in some cases we have a list of things as long as your arm.'

Mma Makutsi interrupted her. 'Oh, that is very true, Mma. If there is any worrying to be done – and there always is – who is doing the worrying? It is the women. We are the ones who do all the worrying. All of it. One hundred per cent. That has always been the case.'

Mma Ramotswe nodded. She was not sure that this was entirely true. She knew a number of men who appeared to shoulder more than their fair share of worrying – that man at the supermarket, for instance, whose job it was to make sure that the tinned food shelves were always fully stocked – he invariably looked worried as he surveyed the aisles of his domain. And one of her near neighbours seemed to be permanently worried, even when she saw him walking his dog in the evening. The dog looked worried too, she thought, although it was sometimes hard to tell with dogs.

She returned to the topic in hand. 'But we cannot think about ourselves all the time – every so often we should think about men.'

Mma Makutsi weighed this suggestion gravely. 'That is certainly true, Mma Ramotswe. Women must think about themselves and make sure that they get their fair share of everything . . .'

'. . . because if they don't, men will not necessarily give them their due,' prompted Mma Ramotswe.

It was exactly what Mma Makutsi had been going to say, and she nodded her approval. 'We women have so much to do,' she said. And then she sighed again. It was not the sort of sigh that was intended to stop a conversation from proceeding further – it was a sigh that suggested that there were deep issues yet to be plumbed.

'I suppose one way of looking at it is to think of when it is that men seem to be happiest,' said Mma Ramotswe. 'If you can work out *when* they are happy, then you should know what it is that is making them happy.'

Mma Makutsi looked thoughtful. 'Phuti Radiphuti always looks happy when he sits down at the table,' she said. 'He looks happy when his food is in front of him – particularly if it's something he likes.' She paused. 'And that's everything, actually, Mma. My Phuti eats everything that is put in front of him.' She paused again, before adding, 'Without exception.' And then adding, further, 'Except certain things that he does not eat.'

Mma Ramotswe knew from experience that this was true of most men. She knew very few men who were fussy eaters – in fact, she knew none – and it was certainly true of Mr J. L. B. Matekoni that a joint of Botswana beef would produce a look of sublime contentment on his face.

And yet she was uncomfortable about any conclusion that men were concerned only with their stomachs. That was unfair on men, she thought, as most men had other things in which they were interested and that could gladden their spirits. Many men enjoyed football, and were happy talking about it for hours on end. Charlie and Fanwell were a bit like that, and could be found sitting outside the garage at slack times, endlessly discussing the prospects of various football teams. Charlie occasionally demonstrated a tactical point to Fanwell, expertly sending an imaginary ball in the desired direction, watched with admiration by Fanwell, who was not quite as light on his feet as his friend. They were happy at such times, there was no doubt about it, and so that was one thing – football – that lay at the heart of male happiness. And yet there were men who did not take much of an interest in football – Mr J. L. B. Matekoni was one of them – and they must have things that filled the spaces between work and meals. She now asked Mma Makutsi what she thought these things might be, and Mma Makutsi, looking up at the ceiling for inspiration, as she often did, was able to come up with an answer.

'I think that many men are looking for friends, Mma. Friends are very important to them.'

Mma Ramotswe considered this. It was true, she thought, but then surely it was something that could be said of anybody, man or woman: friends were undoubtedly important. She expressed this view to Mma Makutsi, who agreed, but pointed out that there were special issues when it came to men and their friends.

'Many men have a big problem with friends, Mma Ramotswe,'

she said. 'They do not have as many friends as women do. We call this the "male friend deficit".'

Mma Ramotswe looked at her colleague with interest. She had noticed the way that Mma Makutsi occasionally used the expression 'we call this' when expounding on a subject. It was a curious phrase, one of those expressions that seemed to confer additional authority to a statement that was, after all, no more than a personal opinion. By saying 'we call this' something or other, Mma Makutsi seemed to be claiming some sort of scientific status for observation, much as a doctor might say to a patient 'You have what we call . . .' and then come up with a name that either made the patient feel a whole lot better, or a whole lot worse.

She was not sure where Mma Makutsi had heard about this so-called 'male friend deficit'; she rather suspected that one might look in vain for it in any textbook, but she had to admit that it sounded impressive. So she said, 'That is very interesting, Mma. I would like to hear more about it, I think.'

Mma Makutsi raised her tea cup to her lips. 'It is a big subject,' she said, and took a sip of tea.

'You must have read a lot about it, Mma.'

Mma Makutsi nodded. 'I have read about it in . . .' She waved a hand airily. 'In various places. In some books, and in some other places.'

'In magazines?'

This brought a nod. 'Yes, in magazines, too. It is something they occasionally talk about in magazines – when they are writing about the problems of men.'

Mma Ramotswe knew that Mma Makutsi subscribed to a number of magazines that she received by post and that were sometimes brought into the office. Left lying on her desk, they were sometimes spotted by Charlie, who would hover over them, squinting at the covers and the indications they gave of the contents within.

'These magazines have many articles about men,' he once observed. 'Look at this one. It says, *Inside: special feature on how men think.*' He smiled. 'So who are these people, Mma Makutsi? Who is writing this stuff that you're always reading? How do they know how men think, if they are not men themselves? How can they tell what is going on in men's heads? Have they got special X-ray vision or something?'

Mma Makutsi gave a tolerant smile. 'These articles are written by *experts*, Charlie. These people know what they're talking about – that is why they are called experts.' She paused. 'You are not an expert, Charlie.'

This stung. 'I am not an expert, Mma? You're saying that I am not an expert?'

'That is more or less what I am saying, Charlie.' She paused. 'I am not saying that you know nothing. That is not what I am saying. You know some things – not many, perhaps, but some. All that I am saying is that there is nothing special on which you can be said to be an expert. That is all.'

Charlie stared at her resentfully. 'I know a lot about cars,' he said. 'And football.'

Mma Makutsi smiled tolerantly. 'Yes, you may know something about those things, but so does just about every other man. But those are not subjects on which magazines want to publish articles. Do you see any articles entitled *What the Zebras should be doing this weekend*?' The Zebras were the main football team in Botswana and the subject of great pride.

She answered her own question. 'Look at any of these magazines and you will not find an article like that. Nor will you find anything about spark plugs or suspension or . . .' She waved a hand in the air, having exhausted her grasp of mechanical terminology.

Charlie laughed. 'That is because those magazines you read are for women, Mma. They are not for men.'

'Then why do you always pick them up and read them when you find them on my desk?' Mma Makutsi challenged.

Charlie looked sheepish. 'They have pictures of pretty women in them, Mma. That is why. I do not read the words, but I like to look at the pictures of women.'

'You see,' said Mma Makutsi, as if Charlie's answer somehow proved everything she had said at the beginning of the exchange.

Mma Ramotswe had decided to intervene. 'I do not think that this discussion is going anywhere,' she had said, and now she remembered the resentful silence that had followed the termination of the argument. She wished that Mma Makutsi and Charlie would not rub one another up the wrong way – that had been getting better recently, but they still had a tendency to look for areas of disagreement rather than agreement. Perhaps they needed this apparent antipathy: although Mma Ramotswe disliked conflict, she was aware that some people appeared to require what they called creative challenge – what she would call niggling – to keep themselves on their toes.

Now Mma Ramotswe remembered that conversation as she and Mma Makutsi continued with their tea break and considered the interesting question of men and their friends.

'They are definitely different from us,' Mma Makutsi ventured. 'Women have many friends because we look after our friendships.'

Mma Ramotswe nodded. She thought that was true. Women tended their friendships as a gardener might nurture a delicate plant, providing water and shade as required. Men were far more casual about their friends – in general.

'Let me ask you this, Mma,' Mma Makutsi began. 'How many of the men you know do anything about their friends' birthdays?'

Mma Ramotswe looked up at the ceiling. She tended to do that whenever she had to address a difficult question, although this question was not really difficult. She already knew the answer to this question even before she thought about it: none. She did not know a single man, not one, who marked a friend's birthday; or even knew when such birthdays were, come to think of it.

'You see?' said Mma Makutsi. 'You see what I mean, Mma? They do not care about these things.'

'But that does not mean that they don't care about their friends,' objected Mma Ramotswe. 'Maybe it's just that men think of these things in a different way.'

Mma Makutsi's rejection of this was adamant. 'No, Mma, that is not so. Men don't think about their friends very much. They don't seem to take much notice of them.' She paused. 'In fact, most men couldn't care less if their friends got up and walked off, Mma.'

She saw the incredulity in Mma Ramotswe's expression. Mma Makutsi was far too hard on men; far too hard. You could not write off men in quite the way that Mma Makutsi did, thought Mma Ramotswe. Men were a large tribe, and you should not generalise, especially when your generalisations were so dismissive. Men were half the world, after all – although perhaps slightly less than half because they had a lower life expectancy than women, and so there would always be more women than men.

Mma Makutsi shook her finger. 'No, I mean that, Mma Ramotswe. If their friends got up and walked off, most men would say, "I think my friend has gone." They would not wonder what had happened. They would not try to find out what their friend was thinking; they would simply say, "I think my friend has gone. That is it. He has gone."'

Mma Ramotswe looked doubtful. She would never deny that there were differences between men and women – of course there were – but she had never been comfortable with any suggestion that men were in any way inferior to women. To say that, she felt, was every bit as bad as saying that women were inferior to men, and nobody would stand by and let that be said today. There had been a major change in attitudes – thank heavens – and the idea of equality was now widely accepted, even if there were still some of these past-tense men to whom Mma Makutsi had referred. But even if it had been necessary to expose and challenge the hurtful and false beliefs of the past, it was wrong, she thought, to make belittling remarks about men in general. Mma Makutsi was slightly inclined to do just that, she felt – not all the time, of course, but every so often, and Mma Ramotswe thought that perhaps she herself should be a little bit more forceful in standing up for men – for the good men – who otherwise might be unfairly bundled up with all those past-tense men. There were times when we had to speak out, even if it involved questioning, or even refuting, things said by our friends and colleagues.

She took a deep breath before she spoke. 'Well, Mma, that's very interesting,' she began.

'Yes,' said Mma Makutsi, perhaps more firmly than was strictly speaking necessary. 'It is.'

Mma Ramotswe persisted. 'I'm not sure if you're entirely right about men and their friends, Mma.'

The light flashed from Mma Makutsi's large, round spectacles. This was a warning sign.

'Oh yes, Mma? Well, I would never say that I am one hundred per cent right about everything – I have never said that, Mma.'

Ninety-seven per cent right, thought Mma Ramotswe, seditiously, doing her very best to prevent herself from smiling.

Mma Makutsi was looking at her, waiting for further elucidation, and so Mma Ramotswe continued, 'I think that many men are good with their friends. They may not buy them birthday presents, but that does not mean that they have no feelings for them, you know, Mma.' She paused. 'Some men like their friends, you know. They like to spend time with them.'

Mma Makutsi took off her spectacles and began to polish them. That, too, was a bad sign, and usually meant that a devastating riposte was about to be made.

'You may be right, Mma,' said Mma Makutsi. 'But let's just take Mr J. L. B. Matekoni as an example. How many friends does he see in the average week, I wonder? Five? Or maybe a few more? Ten?'

Mma Ramotswe looked up at the ceiling once more. The answer, of course, was, in the average week, none. And yet to give that response would be to suggest that Mr J. L. B. Matekoni had no friends at all, which was simply not true. He was a much-loved man, who was very much appreciated by so many people whom he helped with their cars. Those were his friends. And what about Mma Potokwani? She was his friend, and she often spoke with gratitude about the help he had given the Orphan Farm over the years, fixing its ancient and temperamental water pump and persuading their rattly minibus to continue to operate well after its biblical mileage had been clocked up – twice. When it came to Mr J. L. B. Matekoni's funeral – and everybody hoped that would not be for a long, long time – then she was sure that the whole country – or at least the whole southern part of the country – would be there. That was the test of how many friends a person had – that was always the real test. And yet, she could not remember when Mr J. L. B. Matekoni had gone to visit a friend, or a friend had come to visit him.

Mma Makutsi sensed Mma Ramotswe's hesitation. Now her manner changed, and became conciliatory. She liked and admired Mma Ramotswe, and she would never willingly do anything to cause her discomfort. 'I'm sorry, Mma,' she said. 'That is perhaps an unkind question. I know that the answer is probably zero. I am very sorry.'

'It's different with men,' said Mma Ramotswe. 'They don't go and have tea with their friends, as we do.'

Mma Makutsi was quick to agree. 'You're quite right,' she said. 'Men do have friends, Mma, but I think they handle friendship in a different way.' She paused. 'And perhaps we should talk about something else.'

Mma Ramotswe took a last sip of her tea. 'There are many things to talk about,' she said.

But for some reason, neither of them could think of anything, and so the tea break came to an end and they returned to what they had been doing before this awkward, and somewhat unresolved, conversation about men and their friends had begun.

Chapter Two

Where Is Your Business Going?

Neither Charlie nor Fanwell was at tea that morning in the office of the No. 1 Ladies' Detective Agency. Charlie was on paternity leave, his new wife having given birth to a son the previous week. The idea of paternity leave had come from Mma Ramotswe rather than from Charlie himself, and had been enthusiastically supported by Mma Makutsi, who thought that giving men paternity leave was a good way of showing them just how demanding it was to look after a new-born baby.

'Many men,' she observed, 'have no idea how much work a new-born baby is, Mma. They go off to work and don't think about it until they come back in the evening, when the baby is all fed and settled. Then they think: this baby business is not all that hard – what's all the fuss about?'

Mma Ramotswe nodded. She agreed – up to a point. There

were many men, nowadays, who *did* know what it was like to look after a baby – and many of these men were prepared to share the burden – but she was not sure if Mma Makutsi would be prepared to accept that.

'There are some men these days, Mma,' she ventured, 'who are very good with babies—'

Mma Makutsi cut her short. 'Very few, Mma. Maybe one or two modern men, but most men are not modern.'

This statement was delivered with a challenging stare, and Mma Ramotswe had changed the subject. It arose again, though, when Mma Ramotswe suggested paternity leave for Charlie.

'Such a good idea,' said Mma Makutsi. 'That will show him.'

'But more than that,' Mma Ramotswe argued, 'it will give them time to get together as a family. It will be good for all three of them.'

Mma Makutsi grudgingly accepted this, although she added the qualification that the paternity leave should be no more than ten days, as she was sure that Charlie's wife, Queenie-Queenie, would be keen to get him out of the house after a while. 'You do not want men in the house, you know. Men get in the way if you let them stay in the house.'

'Oh, I don't know,' Mma Ramotswe began. She rather liked having Mr J. L. B. Matekoni in the house, which was one of the reasons why she so enjoyed the weekends. He did not have to be doing anything – it was perfectly all right for him just to be there, sitting quietly in a chair. His presence, though, was somehow reassuring.

Mma Makutsi had more to say on the subject.

'I have a cousin, Mma,' she went on. 'She lives up at Mahalapye. She has built a separate house for her husband, in the yard. It is a small rondavel, actually – just one room – but that is where he has to go during the day.'

Mma Ramotswe drew in her breath.

'That seems a bit harsh, Mma. Men have their feelings and I—' She did not finish.

'He is very happy,' Mma Makutsi interrupted. 'She says that she does not hear from him very much until it is time for dinner. Then he is allowed back and they can talk about the things that happened during the day. She says that it is far easier for her if he is not in the house during the day.' She paused. 'He is very small, that man. Just this high, Mma. Not much more.' She demonstrated. 'He does not need much space.'

'And your cousin, Mma?' asked Mma Ramotswe. 'Is she small too?'

Mma Makutsi's answer did not surprise her. 'No, Mma. She is not small. She is a very large lady.' Then she added, 'She has always been large.'

Mma Ramotswe pictured the large cousin and the small husband, and tried not to smile.

'So,' said Mma Makutsi. 'This paternity leave will be a good thing for Charlie. It will teach him a lesson, I think.'

Charlie, of course, was employed by both Mr J. L. B. Matekoni, for general garage work, and by Mma Ramotswe, as an assistant detective, or an assistant-junior-detective, as Mma Makutsi put it. Fanwell, by contrast, had remained fully employed by Tlokweng Road Speedy Motors, Mr J. L. B. Matekoni's garage, with which the No. 1 Ladies' Detective Agency shared premises. On that morning, he was in sole charge of the garage, as Mr J. L. B. Matekoni was spending the day at the President Hotel, attending a course for small businesses organised by the local Chamber of Commerce. The course was entitled *Where Is Your Business Going?* and it was offered, for a small fee, to anybody employing between one and ten people. The publicity for the course had studiously avoided the term 'small business', even if that described exactly the attending firms. Reference was made, rather, to 'growing businesses' – a description that Mr J. L. B. Matekoni thought might be misplaced, in some cases at least. His own business was a case in point: it had, if anything, contracted slightly over the last year, and could not therefore be described as a growing business.

Mma Ramotswe, though, had encouraged him to attend.

'It is a long time since you were on a course,' she said. 'Many years, in fact.'

Mr J. L. B. Matekoni looked at her. He had *never* been on a course, he thought – unless one counted the advanced-driver skid-patch sessions organised by the Gaborone Police Traffic Department, or the lecture he had attended three years earlier on First Aid in the Workshop – a lecture that had to be terminated unexpectedly when the lecturer tripped and fell, cutting his head rather badly on the sharp edge of the podium.

'I'm not sure that this course is really meant for businesses like mine,' he said. 'I'm not sure if I want to go anywhere in particular.'

Mma Ramotswe laughed. 'Every business is going somewhere, Rra,' she said. 'Even if it is standing still. Standing still is actually going down. If you stand still, then you are in decline. That is well known, Mr J. L. B. Matekoni.'

He had looked at the programme, as it was advertised in the *Botswana Daily News.* The day would begin, it said, with a talk entitled 'Do You really Want to Get Somewhere?' given by one Mr Elton Dlamini, described as a 'major figure' in southern African motivational circles. Dlamini was a Swazi name, Mma Ramotswe knew, and his origins were confirmed by a biographical note at the foot of the programme. 'Mr Dlamini,' the note read, 'is the founder of 123 Drycleaners, headquartered in Manzini and now operating through southern and central Africa. Following the success of his own firm, Mr Dlamini has made it his life's work to pass on his motivational secrets to those struggling to find a path ahead for their business. This is a talk that takes no prisoners and will set the tone for a day of discovery of the mindset that will enable you to more than match the efforts of some of the most successful and innovative entrepreneurs of our time.'

Mr J. L. B. Matekoni wondered what was the significance of this reference to the taking of no prisoners. Did it suggest that those who failed to pay attention to the speakers would find themselves in trouble? It hardly bore thinking about, especially as he often found it hard to stay awake when listening to somebody talking at length about something. This had often been the case in church, when Mma Ramotswe was regularly obliged to give him a gentle dig in the ribs during the sermon, in case he should snore. A few weeks previously, during a pause in the preaching of a particularly long-winded sermon by a visiting clergyman, snoring was heard coming from four or five places in the congregation, and was so unmistakable and so audible that many had found it impossible not to burst out laughing. The preacher had been embarrassed and had brought his sermon to a premature halt, leaving the congregation with no answer to a particularly challenging question that had just been posed. 'What are we to do in the face of indifference to the plight of others? To whom are we to turn?' They would have to wait for their answer, if it were ever to come – a great pity, observed Mma Ramotswe, as life was challenging enough without important questions like this being left hanging in the air.

But now, glancing at the list of sessions that would follow this opening talk, he thought that there would be little danger of dropping off to sleep at the wrong moment. There was to be a talk on making the most of your working capital; a talk on quick ways to make customers pay up on time (that would be interesting, thought Mr J. L. B. Matekoni, who always found slow payers hard to deal with); a talk on planning expansion and taking advantage of new opportunities; and finally one on how to deal with difficult people – among both your employees and your clients. That made Mr J. L. B. Matekoni think of his years of dealing with his two apprentices, Charlie and Fanwell. He had become fond of them both, and was a sort of father figure to the two young men, but there had been times when his patience had been tried. And as for difficult customers, there were some people who believed that anything that happened to their car was the fault of their mechanic, even if the car was over twenty years old, or had rarely had an oil change, or had been used, as in one case, to provide temporary accommodation for a flock of chickens. All of these presented challenges for a garage business, and he would be interested to hear how he might deal with them.

He had signed up for the course in good time, and had been assured of a place. But then doubts had surfaced – not so much about the expense, since the Chamber of Commerce was bearing most of the cost, but more about the prospect of leaving the garage in the hands of Fanwell for an entire day. Although the young mechanic, unlike Charlie, had completed his apprenticeship and was therefore fully qualified, Mr J. L. B. Matekoni had always been around to be consulted should any problems arise. And Fanwell was not slow to ask for advice, even if he was engaged in an entirely routine procedure.

'Will you be all right, looking after things all day?' Mr J. L. B. Matekoni asked. 'The course begins very early, you see, Fanwell, and I won't be able to get away until after six. That makes it a long day for you.'

Fanwell did not seem perturbed. 'I'll be fine, boss. No problem. You leave everything to me.'

Mr J. L. B. Matekoni bit his lip. We all have to fly by ourselves sooner or later, he thought. We leave the nest and set forth. We cannot have somebody by our side forever.

'Are you sure, Fanwell?'

'One hundred per cent, boss. No drama.'

Mr J. L. B. Matekoni looked at the diary – an exercise book covered with oily fingerprints. There were three jobs listed for the day in question. His heart sank as he saw the first on the list. 'That car,' he muttered. 'That very bad car.'

Fanwell looked over his shoulder. 'Oh, I know that one, boss. That is the car that belongs to that person whose wife went off with that man who drove his truck into a ditch out on the Lobatse Road. Remember? He was carrying goats and they all escaped. You went to tow the truck in. Remember? He went off with that woman just a few weeks later. And that man – the man with that bad car – he went and met a lady who won a beauty competition by putting on so much make-up that you couldn't see her face. She looked like somebody else, boss. Underneath, she was nothing special, you see. That new lady of his tried to take over his car – the bad one. She went off in it, but it kept breaking down and she gave it back to him. She made him buy her a new one, which she used to run away with a guy who was only eighteen at the time – eighteen, Rra! He played a guitar, that one, and all the girls thought he was great. I didn't. He only went off with that woman because of her car, boss.'

Mr J. L. B. Matekoni stared at Fanwell. His two young mechanics lived in a completely different world, it seemed to him. This was not the world that he and Mma Ramotswe inhabited – a world in which people went about their business in an orderly way, drank tea at regular intervals, and retired to bed before nine-thirty at night. Yet there was a parallel universe in which people drove trucks into ditches, played the guitar, and went off with eighteen-year-olds. For the most part, these separate worlds never met, but every so often the inhabitants of each would look across the fence at one another and wonder how the people on the other side could live their lives as they did.

'We're thinking of the same car, I believe,' he said to Fanwell.

Fanwell made a face. 'I like Peugeots. But that car is a very old one. No French people are driving round in those cars any more, boss.'

'There are many people who like French cars, Fanwell,' said Mr J. L. B. Matekoni. 'But they can be tricky.'

He gave Fanwell an anxious glance. Would he be able to cope if inspection of the car revealed anything out of the ordinary?

But the young man seemed quite confident. 'I took that phone call,' said Fanwell. 'He said that the engine keeps missing. He says that he gets jolts and a loss of power.'

Mr J. L. B. Matekoni nodded. 'And what does that suggest to you, Fanwell?'

'One of the spark plugs is not firing – and so one of the cylinders isn't working.' Fanwell paused. 'If you want my diagnosis, boss, I'd say that his high-tension leads are breaking down. They don't last forever and once they start to go rotten . . .'

Mr J. L. B. Matekoni nodded his approval. 'You're probably right, Fanwell. The rubber rots and then the wire gets damp. And then you have problems.'

'So I would order some replacements, boss. Then I'd put in a new set of spark plugs – just to be sure.'

'You can never go wrong if you put in new spark plugs,' said Mr J. L. B. Matekoni. 'When I was an apprentice myself – a long time ago – we were taught at the Mechanical Trades College: if in doubt, replace the spark plugs. I have never forgotten that.'

'And I'd take a look at the points,' Fanwell added.

Mr J. L. B. Matekoni gave him an admiring look. 'Very thorough. Yes, the points.'

Fanwell pointed to another item noted down in the diary for that day. He left a small, greasy fingerprint on the page. 'And this other job booked in is a brake matter. That truck – we've fixed it before. There'll be oil in the brake drum – definitely, boss. Definite, definite.'

'You're probably right.'

'So I'll take a look at that and put in a new seal. That's what I'll do, Rra.'

It was the perfect answer, thought Mr J. L. B. Matekoni, and it reassured him that Fanwell seemed so confident. 'You can call me if there's a problem,' he said. 'I can always come and sort things out.'

'There will be no need, boss,' said Fanwell. And he said this with such authority, such self-assurance, that Mr J. L. B. Matekoni smiled. I have done this, he thought. I have made a confident and well-trained young mechanic out of raw material that I thought at times would never come to anything. If we all have one or two small achievements in our lives, then this is mine. This is what I have done: this, and marry Mma Ramotswe. Two good things, both very much worth doing.

It was that morning, then, with Fanwell looking after the garage single-handed, that Mr J. L. B. Matekoni nosed his truck into a shady spot under a tree not far from the side entrance to the President Hotel. He had not been sure how to dress for a course, and had almost donned the blue suit he wore on Sundays, when Mma Ramotswe had suggested that a smart white business shirt, well-pressed slacks, and a tie would easily meet whatever sartorial standards were expected, and would be more comfortable, too, in the warm weather they were experiencing. The rains were late, and the heat had built up steadily, as if goading the sky and land on their dryness. That could change – and do so within the space of a few hours once the rain clouds gathered – but until then, cool clothing would be the order of the day.

Even a tie could be dispensed with, she said, as the number of men wearing ties was getting smaller and smaller every day. But that was a step too far for Mr J. L. B. Matekoni who felt that if men could not wear ties, then they would have few opportunities to show any colour at all. He had several red ties, one broad blue one, and a tie that featured the crest of the Botswana Motor Trades Association. It was this last tie that he chose for the course, as he thought there might be others there wearing ties that proclaimed membership of a profession or business, and he would not want the motor trade not to be represented.

Now, making his way round to the front steps of the hotel, he looked up at the raised veranda on which he and Mma Ramotswe had enjoyed lunch together on birthdays and anniversaries. It was on that veranda, too, that Mma Ramotswe occasionally had working lunches with a client, or a social lunch with Mma Potokwani, who had a particular fondness for the President Hotel's generous, all-you-can-eat curry buffet. On those encounters there was no doubt as to who got the better side of the bargain, as Mma Ramotswe reported that her friend succeeded in piling her plate with such heaps of curries, poppadoms and nan bread that there was barely any room for chutney or desiccated coconut. Lunch would be provided for the delegates, Mr J. L. B. Matekoni had read, and this, the organisers hoped, would provide 'ample opportunity for the sort of networking so vital to any business'. He had been concerned by that: should he be networking? As far as he knew, he was doing no networking at all – indeed, he was not at all sure how one went about networking – and if everyone at lunch was going to be networking, he might be a bit conspicuous in his failure to join in.

He put these thoughts aside as he made his way up the stairs and into the entrance lobby of the hotel. There he saw the course registration desk, behind which two smartly dressed young women sat checking names off a list. Neatly laid out on another table were rows of white name badges for those attending, arranged alphabetically, according to the name of the business.

'You must pick up your badge, Rra,' said one of the young women as she handed him his folder of papers.

He thanked her and reached for the badge on which 'Tlokweng Road Motors' was printed in large red letters. He noted the omission and turned to the young woman who had just ticked off his name.

'I do not like to complain, Mma,' he said, showing her the badge. 'But the name of my business is Tlokweng Road *Speedy* Motors.' And then, noticing something else, he added, 'And my own name is not Mr J. B. L. Matekoni, it is Mr J. L. B. Matekoni.'

The young woman took the name badge from him and examined it closely. She passed it to her colleague, who glanced at it and then looked up at Mr J. L. B. Matekoni.

'We can change it for you,' said the first young woman. 'I have a marker pen.'

Before he could say anything, the young woman had produced a stubby black pen and made a crude addition to the business title – which now read 'Tlokweng Road Spedy Motors'. And then, with an additional flourish, the initials 'J. B. L.' were transposed so as to read 'B. J. L.'. 'There,' she said, handing the badge back to him with a smile. 'That is all in order now, Rra.'

Mr J. L. B. Matekoni frowned. 'Speedy is spelled with two "e"s,' he said. 'It is *Speedy*, not *Spedy*. You have written *Spedy*.'

The young woman looked at him defiantly. 'It says *Speedy*, Rra. It definitely says *Speedy*. And we cannot sit here all day and argue about what is on your name badge. There are many important people at this meeting today – you are not the only one, Rra.'

This was delivered with a sternness that rebuffed any response, and so Mr J. L. B. Matekoni, pinning his incorrect name badge onto his shirt, moved off towards the crowd of participants who were settling into the rows of chairs set out in the hotel's main dining room, converted for the day into a conference room. He looked about him. There were various people he knew, and others whom he vaguely recognised. There were several of his clients, one or two of whom waved a greeting. In spite of the bad start, with the first session about to begin, Mr J. L. B. Matekoni began to feel more confident. These other people seemed to be just like him – not high-powered big businessmen, diamond merchants and so on, but ordinary people working in ordinary firms, struggling to keep solvent, battling with all the issues that beset the small fish in the large economic sea. He would enjoy himself, he decided, and at the end of the day he might even learn something. There was also the lunch to look forward to, with its promise of networking opportunities. It had been a good idea to sign up for this course, he decided, and if this worked out as he hoped, there might even be further courses in the future. One could perhaps attend a course every month or so, which would result in an impressive collection of certificates and might even make a difference to his business. But what could that possibly be? People kept going on about the need for a business to get bigger, but what if your workshop was already as full as it possibly could be with spare parts, grease guns, and cans of motor oil? Further branches, perhaps? Francistown Road Speedy Motors, Mochudi Speedy Motors, and so on. All Botswana Speedy Motors. There was a lot to think about, and now here was the first speaker, and it was clear to Mr J. L. B. Matekoni that here was a man who was confident in himself and in what he had to say – you did not have to be Mma Ramotswe to work that out. Dressed in a lightweight linen jacket, the cuffs of his shirt protruding just enough to reveal large gilt cuff links, he held himself erect, his gaze boring into those in front of him. *This man is an eagle*, thought Mr J. L. B. Matekoni. He was not sure why he should think that, but that is what came to mind. *He is an eagle soaring above the rest of us.*

Fifty faces watched the speaker in rapt attention.

'Why are you here, ladies and gentlemen?' he began.

The question was a rhetorical one, but he let it hang in the air long enough to suggest that he was expecting an answer.

Somebody coughed, and heads turned round to see if the cough would mature into a response to the speaker's question. But it did not. A few feet shuffled under chairs. Then came a voice from the back. 'To learn how to take our businesses to new heights.' And then, mumbled, 'I think.'

The speaker punched the air with delight, the gold cuff links catching a ray of the sunlight coming in the windows. 'Exactly right, ladies and gentlemen. That is exactly why you are here. Because you're *hungry.*'

Mr J. L. B. Matekoni thought of the networking lunch ahead of them. He was sure it would be good, because it would be provided by the President Hotel, but it was a good four hours away and he began to wonder if he should have had a slightly larger breakfast. And if lunch was to be occupied with networking, as had been promised by the organisers, would there be enough time to eat?

And then he asked himself whether the answer given by the voice at the back had anything to do with hunger, as the speaker suggested. Taking a business to new heights may have nothing to do with an appetite for more money – you might want to do that because what you were doing was, in itself, worthwhile. Or you might do it because you wanted to hand over a successful business to your children. Or you might do it because the people who worked for you needed their jobs and you were the only one who could keep the firm going. There might be buyers circling, with plans to get rid of the existing employees once they had acquired the business – there were many examples of that having happened, Mr J. L. B. Matekoni thought – and this was not the sort of thing that he would ever countenance.

The speaker continued very much in the way in which he had begun, peppering his talk with questions, with pregnant pauses, and with passionate assertions of how, if only one is determined enough, anybody might achieve anything. 'You will have heard the well-known saying,' he intoned, 'that you can't make a silk purse out of a sow's ear. You will have heard that, ladies and gentlemen – people are always saying that. Well, I can tell you that these people are wrong. *They* may not be able to do that, but that does not mean that *you* cannot. I have seen many cases where that is exactly what people have done – that is what I have to say to you today.'

Mr J. L. B. Matekoni's head began to hurt. He was not sure that he could take this rapid-fire list of things that he should be doing, and now, with this statement about silk purses and sows' ears, he found himself closing his eyes and imagining some of those present returning home via the butchery, collecting on the way a large sow's ear. He saw them sitting in their kitchens, frowning with concentration as they tried to sew the ear into the shape of a silk purse, while their wives and husbands stood in the background shaking their heads at the futility of the exercise.

The opening speaker eventually reached the end of his talk, and the next topic was introduced. This was more down to earth, being concerned with loans and how one might use a loan to increase turnover. Mr J. L. B. Matekoni listened carefully, taking note of various suggestions, but he was generally unenthusiastic about debt, and wondered whether there was much point in burdening a debt-free business with debt, even if there was a chance that this might lead to an increased turnover. There were more important things than turnover, he felt, and one of these was the feeling of being unencumbered by loans. He could look his bank manager in the eye – at any point – whereas he knew some in business who would cross to the other side of the street rather than come face to face with their bank manager.

As lunchtime approached, he felt that he had learned a little, although not very much. He was hungry now – not in the sense in which the opening speaker had spoken of hunger, but looking forward to having something to eat, especially since he could smell a President Hotel curry being prepared somewhere in the background. If there was a buffet, he would go straight to that, he decided, and leave any networking that needed to be done until after he had finished a plate of curry, and perhaps even treated himself to a second helping.

Now it was time for the last speaker of the morning to give his presentation. Mr J. L. B. Matekoni glanced at the programme as the speaker came to the podium. 'Mr T. K. Molefi,' he read, 'is an entrepreneur of broad experience. From small beginnings in door-to-door sales, he progressed to the post of regional manager of a leading personal products distributor. That was followed by a spell at business school, where he graduated with an MBA in sales. Mr Molefi then founded his own firm, Forward Planning Solutions, which has met with considerable success in the catering industry and which is planning to introduce a transport division in the near future. Mr Molefi is the author of *Ten Secrets of Business Success* (forthcoming). He is in wide demand as a motivational speaker and business adviser.'

Mr J. L. B. Matekoni frowned as he read this. Molefi? T. K. Molefi? Molefi was a familiar enough name, especially around Mochudi, where Mma Ramotswe had spent her childhood, but there were Molefis everywhere, now that the old, local associations of names were fading. And Molefi could be a first name or a family name, which made it even more likely to seem familiar. But T. K. Molefi?

And then, as the speaker placed his notes on the lectern and looked out over the audience, it dawned on Mr J. L. B. Matekoni that he knew exactly who this was. This was the boy he had known as T. K. at school, all those years ago. This was the T. K. Molefi who had sat in the desk next to his and who had regularly found himself in trouble for shooting small pellets of blotting paper at other members of the class with a catapult made of rubber bands. This was the T. K. Molefi who had brought a snake to school one day and who had fished it out of its box, explaining to horrified onlookers that it was not a poisonous species and it was quite safe to handle it. This was the same T. K. Molefi who had then been bitten and whose hand, the site of the bite, had swollen noticeably. He had been driven to the hospital by the deputy principal, who had then addressed the whole school on the need not to do anything foolish, such as bringing a snake to school. 'Not that I am thinking of anyone in particular,' she had said. 'I am not suggesting that anybody in this school would be so foolish as to do a thing like that.'

31

He had lost touch with T. K. Molefi after they had both left school. He thought that he had seen him once in the street, walking arm in arm with a woman wearing a red dress and red hat, but he was not sure. There were many people you knew in childhood who simply faded away. You might find them if you looked – few people disappeared without leaving some trace behind them – but in general you thought nothing further of them until suddenly, in the street, perhaps, or at a filling station, or in a supermarket car park, suddenly they were there; older, of course, and often stouter, but nonetheless there. And you hesitated because the years can create a gulf that is hard to cross, but then you decided to speak to them. And after the initial pleasure of recognition there would be curiosity to find out how much of the person you had once known was still there – because we all changed, and sometimes that change was so great that there was very little of the earlier person left, and it seemed there was an entirely new identity within – one that you barely knew.

As the talk began, Mr J. L. B. Matekoni sat up straight, watching the speaker intently, listening to the intonation of his speech. The T.K. Molefi he knew had had a slight lisp – something for which he was teased by other boys. That was because boys in those days were quick to laugh at anybody who was slightly different, or who had some cross to bear in this life; except for Mr J. L. B. Matekoni, of course, who had been kind, because he saw no reason to be otherwise. He had understood that at a very early age; he had grasped that unkindness or cruelty, along with just about every other vice, simply rebounded on those who practised such things. A bully would eventually encounter a bigger, more brutal bully, and would learn a salutary lesson in that way; a liar would eventually be told even bigger lies by others; the disloyal would themselves be betrayed, and so on. He had understood all that, it seemed, without ever even having to be told it. Such was his nature.

So he had not laughed at T. K. Molefi's speech impediment, and as a result had been rewarded with the other boy's friendship. T. K., as he was known, seemed to have money when nobody else had any, and as a result Mr J. L. B. Matekoni had benefited from his largesse in the form of fat cakes, biltong, and fizzy drinks – all things for which the boyish heart yearns. T. K. had also given him a penknife and a cap with the name of a football team of which he had never heard embroidered on the peak. Then they had lost touch, and Mr J. L. B. Matekoni rarely had occasion to think about his boyhood friend. Somebody said that T. K. had taken up a job over the border, in Mafikeng. Another said that he was running a stock-food business in Serowe. Yet another said that he had seen him fishing at the dam, but after turning his back for a few minutes and looking back at the spot where he thought he had seen him, there was nothing.

'Perhaps it was a ghost,' this person said. 'Or perhaps a crocodile seized him in the time I was looking away.'

Well, now everything was made clear, and here was T. K. Molefi, smartly dressed in a light grey suit, giving everybody the benefit of his views on the running of a business. When he began to speak, any doubt as to his identity was removed: the lisp was much better now, although there were traces of it on the occasional sibilant sound. This was definitely the man who had once been that boy.

Mr J. L. B. Matekoni closed his eyes. He was back in that classroom, on one of those warm afternoons of childhood, when the sluggish air became heavier yet with the effort of learning. Before the board stood the man who taught them physics, a tall figure with a look of resignation on his face, and a quiet, soporific voice. He was explaining about pulleys, and their efficiency, and about how to calculate mechanical advantage, and T. K. Molefi was tearing up a small piece of blotting paper to make missiles of it, and he was smiling at Mr J. L. B. Matekoni, conspiratorially, as if to involve him in the catapult barrage. And the world was so much simpler then, and so much easier, in a way, because the future was not something that fourteen-year-old boys needed to worry about. It would take care of itself and arrive in its own time. And its face, if one bothered to look at it, was never threatening.

He felt a sudden wave of nostalgia. So much had changed since those days; so much had gone of that old intimacy that bound people together simply because they were the same people, all 'me's in the same 'us'. The comforting assumption that everybody knew exactly who everybody else was had been replaced by doubt as to the identity of so many others. Who were all these people you met on the road today? Did they even have a village to which they could return from time to time? Did they put their savings into cattle, as all reasonable people did, and keep a cattle post somewhere, or were they people who thought only of money in the bank? Money in the bank did not have to be fed and watered, nor given salt lick. Money in the bank did not need a herd boy to move it from place to place, nor have cattle bells strung about its neck ... Cattle bells ... He opened his eyes, and looked directly at Mr T. K. Molefi, at this holder of an MBA degree, this successful entrepreneur who had even written a forthcoming book; and Mr T. K. Molefi, from behind his podium, paused briefly in mid-sentence, and smiled at him, with a smile that said, *I see you, Mr J. L. B. Matekoni.*

Chapter Three

Calm and Inner Peace

The following morning, shortly after she arrived in the office and was enjoying the first morning cup of tea – Tea Break No. 1, as it was called – Mma Ramotswe announced to Mma Makutsi that she thought she might absent herself for the rest of the morning. Mma Makutsi did not object – after all, Mma Ramotswe was the senior member of the firm – its owner, in fact – and as owner she could do whatever she liked without getting permission from her junior colleague – or business partner, as Mma Makutsi had taken to calling herself. Her natural curiosity, though, was piqued and she asked, as casually as she could, whether Mma Ramotswe needed her help. 'If there's anything, Mma, in which I might be of assistance . . .'

'That is very kind of you, Mma,' replied Mma Ramotswe. 'This is not something which needs your help.' And then she added, quickly, 'Not that your help is not always very helpful, Mma. There are many occasions on which your help is crucial.' And then, after a short pause, 'Not this time, though.'

Mma Makutsi took a sip of her tea. 'That is what I am here for, Mma – to help.'

'That is what we are all here for,' Mma Ramotswe agreed. 'We are definitely on this earth to help other people.'

'And those other people?' asked Mma Makutsi. 'What are they here for then?'

Mma Ramotswe hesitated, and then laughed, as did Mma Makutsi.

'So I hope this appointment of yours goes well,' said Mma Makutsi, adding, 'Whatever it is.'

This was as obvious an enquiry as it could be without being a direct question, which might have seemed a bit prying, and after she had posed it, Mma Makutsi looked unconcernedly out of the window, as if the answer were not really that important.

But Mma Ramotswe could tell how keen Mma Makutsi was to find out where she was going, and did not wish to disappoint her. 'Actually, Mma,' she said, 'I am only going to see Mma Potokwani. That is all.'

This was a disappointing answer from Mma Makutsi's point of view. She had been hoping for something more interesting than that: a visit to Mma Potokwani was nothing special, as it always involved very much the same thing: tea and fruit cake, followed by a discussion of what was going on at the Orphan Farm. 'I see,' she said, the disappointment registering in her voice. 'Well, I shall look after things here while you and Mma Potokwani are gossiping.'

Mma Ramotswe caught her breath. If Mma Makutsi thought that she had nothing better to do than to exchange gossip with Mma Potokwani, then she would need to be disabused of the notion.

'It will not be gossip, Mma,' said Mma Ramotswe. 'I am going there to seek her advice.'

This was more interesting, and Mma Makutsi sat up to attention. 'Very wise, Mma. Mma Potokwani is very helpful on these matters ...' She realised that she did not know what matters were involved, but this was a broad enough phrase to encompass most things.

Mma Ramotswe sighed. 'I am a little bit worried about Mr J. L. B. Matekoni,' she said.

Mma Makutsi sat even more erect. When women were worried about their husbands, it was usually because their husbands were showing signs of wandering. Was Mr J. L. B. Matekoni doing that? It seemed most unlikely. If ever there was a man to remain on the straight and narrow, it was Mr J. L. B. Matekoni. And her own husband, Phuti Radiphuti too: he was a man of the utmost probity who would never behave in the way some men did when they entered that trying stage that so many men seemed to encounter in their forties. Neither Mr J. L. B. Matekoni nor Phuti Radiphuti was ever likely to be difficult, in that sense, she thought. In the case of Phuti Radiphuti, he had survived a blatant attempt by Violet Sephotho to turn his head, and if a man could survive Violet Sephotho, the husband stealer *par excellence* on an all-Botswana scale, then he could survive any challenge or temptation.

Mma Makutsi waited. Now that Mma Ramotswe had mentioned her concern, there was no reason for her not to explain it further. Indeed, she should do that if she wanted to avoid Mma Makutsi's jumping to the wrong sort of conclusions.

And it seemed Mma Ramotswe thought the same way.

'You may remember, Mma,' she began, 'that some years ago, Mr J. L. B. Matekoni became depressed. You remember that, don't you, Mma?'

Mma Makutsi nodded. 'It was very strange, Mma. I remember that he stopped eating. You told me about that. And if a man shows no interest in food, Mma, then there is very good reason to worry.'

'Yes,' said Mma Ramotswe. 'And his sleep was disturbed. That is another sign, I think.'

'You went to Dr Moffat, didn't you?'

'I did. And when they gave him some pills he became better. They have very good pills these days for that sort of thing.'

Mma Makutsi looked thoughtful. 'Perhaps you should get him some more of those pills,' she suggested. 'You could put them in his tea so that he wouldn't know he was taking them.'

Mma Ramotswe stared at her colleague. 'I don't think so, Mma. I don't think that is a good thing to do.'

The objection surprised Mma Makutsi. 'I don't see what's wrong with it, Mma. As long as the pills do not cause a reaction. If somebody needs something, then why not give it to them? Sometimes they refuse and that is because they don't know what's good for them.' She paused, as if about to impart a confidence. 'I give Phuti pills in his tea. It is the simplest way of treating your husband.'

Mma Ramotswe gazed at Mma Makutsi, trying to conceal her astonishment. 'Regularly, Mma?'

Mma Makutsi shrugged carelessly. 'I am giving him vitamin pills,' she said. 'I know that chemist in town. He has given me these pills and I am giving them to Phuti. He would not take them if I asked him to. Men can be funny about pills. They think they are so strong and that vitamins are only for ladies and for men who are weak.'

Mma Ramotswe's eyes widened. She thought about what she might say about this, and decided that it was best not to say anything. Mma Makutsi had firm views, and any discussion as to the rights and wrongs of secretly dosing one's husband with vitamins would not be an easy one.

'I am glad that you agree,' said Mma Makutsi. 'Men need these things, Mma, and it is our duty as women to make sure that they get them.' She paused, and then, leaving the subject of vitamins, she returned to Mr J. L. B. Matekoni's health. Was he getting enough to eat? she asked. And what about exercise? Men never walked if they could avoid it, and that, she felt, was not at all good for them. Was she giving him butter, rather than margarine or one of those other spreads? Because it was well known, she believed, that men became depressed if you started to give them spreads rather than butter.

Mma Ramotswe explained that she did not think this was a dietary problem. 'There is something worrying him,' she said. 'He came back from that business course of his looking very low. Depression can start very quickly, I'm told. I am worried that something happened there that has tipped him into this state.'

Mma Makutsi shook her head. 'Perhaps he shouldn't have signed up for that course. Perhaps it has given him ideas, Mma.'

This last suggestion was made with a gravity that almost became foreboding, and although Mma Ramotswe did not respond to it, it worried her. She would talk to Mma Potokwani about all this, and would mention Mma Makutsi's views, and see whether the matron, with all her experience of the world, could propose something – even if only a small amount of reassurance. We all need reassurance, she thought. We all need people to tell us that everything is going to be all right, even when it is not, and that we should not worry, even when we clearly need to be concerned about something. We are only human, after all, and that is why reassurance is so important to us. That is undoubtedly well known.

Mma Ramotswe sighed. 'Well, Mma, I did not mean to burden you with this. You have your hands full with Phuti and I do not expect you to deal with my problems. I shall see what Mma Potokwani has to say. Her views are always worth listening to.'

Mma Makutsi finished her tea. 'She has been a good friend to you, Mma. You are very lucky.'

Mma Ramotswe agreed. She had been lucky with all her friends, but she knew that of all of them, the friend who was most valuable to her, and most beloved, was Mma Potokwani. She was wise – it was as simple as that. She had that greatest of all things, wisdom, and that was a very important thing to possess in a world that seemed to be losing the respect it had always had for wise people. Wise people had been replaced in the public estimation by that curious category of people – celebrities – who were, for the most part, shallow people not known for their wisdom. Where were the Nelson Mandelas of this world of celebrity? Where were the Gandhis? Where were the Seretse Khamas?

She thought of the wise people she had known personally. There was Mma Potokwani, of course. There was Professor Tom Tlou, now late, but at one time a great expert on the history of Botswana and its people; a kind man, too, in his dealings with others – as great men often are. And then, of course, there was her late daddy, Obed Ramotswe, who may not have had a long education, whose name may never have appeared in the newspapers, but who had a wisdom far exceeding that of many a more strident public figure. His wisdom came from deep wells – from the things that had been known to the generations that had gone before him. It was fashionable to put all that knowledge behind us, to think that only our modern understanding counted for something, but that, she thought, was so wrong, so wrong. We were not the first people to tread where we now trod; countless ancestors had come exactly this way. And although their footprints might have been blown away by the wind, we could sense their presence if only we opened our eyes and ears to it. And we could hear their voices, too, if we listened hard enough. We could hear their warnings, their encouragements, their advice – if only we turned our heads to the wind and heard the voices, faint and distant, that the wind carried. We could hear.

Mma Potokwani was busy with one of the housemothers when Mma Ramotswe arrived at the Orphan Farm, but told her visitor that she would not be tied up for more than ten minutes. Mma Ramotswe occupied that time inspecting the garden that had been planted around the small tin-roofed building that housed Mma Potokwani's office and that of her book-keeper and store-man. A couple of sweet-thorn trees had seeded themselves in this garden, and were now in blossom, their miniature yellow flowers like tiny tufted balls alongside their curved green seed-pods. At the foot of one of these trees was a plant that Mma Ramotswe recognised only because she had recently seen a picture of it in a magazine – Madagascar periwinkle. She had liked the name and had written it down, but had not seen it before. Now here it was – planted, she imagined, by Mma Potokwani, who had an interest in plants and who liked small flowers that you might walk past without noticing, unless you were looking for them.

It was while she was bending down to examine the periwinkle that she heard Mma Potokwani calling her from her veranda. 'The kettle is boiling, Mma Ramotswe. I am waiting for you now.'

She made her way into her old friend's office, feeling the

breeze from the ceiling fan that Mma Potokwani had installed above her desk.

'It must be good to sit under a breeze,' Mma Ramotswe observed. 'We need a fan in our office, but these things are very expensive.'

Mma Potokwani felt she had to explain that the fan had been a gift from one of the orphanage's supporters. 'He is a man with a great deal of money,' she explained. 'Looking at him, you would not think he is rich. He wears very simple clothes and does not drive an expensive car. He is not one of these Mercedes-Benz types.'

'Not all drivers of Mercedes-Benzes are bad people,' said Mma Ramotswe.

'Oh, I would never say they are bad,' said Mma Potokwani. 'But I think that if you drive a Mercedes-Benz you have a duty to do something to make up for it.'

'Is that what you told him?' joked Mma Ramotswe.

But Mma Potokwani was not joking. 'Exactly,' she said. 'I told him that God had a list of people who drive Mercedes-Benzes, and He checks to see if they have made up for it by being kind to people.'

Mma Ramotswe's eyes widened. 'And, Mma? What did he say to that?'

'I think he was worried. I don't really think there is a such a list, but once this rich man had heard that it existed, he was very worried and came to ask me if there was anything I needed for the Orphan Farm. I told him, yes, there was a great deal we needed, starting with a new fan for the office. He noted this down, and three days later a man came to install this fan. That rich man is a very good man, I think. He will certainly fit through the eye of a needle on a camel, if it comes down to that. But others need to be reminded of that story – in case they forget to give to good causes …' There was a short pause. '… such as our children out here.'

'I don't think they will forget about that,' said Mma Ramotswe, recalling that the story of camels and needles was slightly different from the tale that Mma Potokwani appeared to have in mind.

'Don't be too sure,' said Mma Potokwani, as she began to pour out tea for herself and her visitor. 'Rich people are always forgetting that they are only rich because of the work of others. They do not dig their money out of the ground, you know, Mma.'

'That's true,' said Mma Ramotswe. And then she made the observation that there was enough to go round if people were prepared to share. Mma Potokwani agreed with that, and, as if to emphasise the point, extracted a quarter of a fruit cake from a tin and cut it into two large slices. She put one of these on a plate and passed it to Mma Ramotswe, who received it reverentially, as one might receive a gift of great value.

For a couple of minutes they sat in silence, drinking their tea and eating the fruit cake that Mma Potokwani had made from her famous recipe. Then Mma Potokwani said, 'You told me that there was something you wanted to discuss, Mma. Is it one of your cases?'

Mma Ramotswe occasionally confided in Mma Potokwani about her cases, and had received useful advice on how to make progress in a stalled investigation or how to deal with a particularly difficult person. Mma Potokwani was not only a competent matron, she was also a natural psychologist, with a good understanding of human behaviour, and an ability to come up with novel ways to deal with recalcitrant or obstructive conduct. But now Mma Ramotswe explained that it was not a professional matter that she wished to raise, but a domestic one.

'I am worried about Mr J. L. B. Matekoni,' she began. 'Ever since that last time when he became depressed, I have been watching for any signs. I was warned that it could happen again, and I should be on the lookout. Well, he seemed to be in a very quiet mood last night. And again this morning, when I made him his breakfast, he ate it without saying anything very much. He usually talks to me in the kitchen while I am making breakfast for everybody. He talks to the children. He talks back at the radio. But no, he said nothing, and just looked out of the window, as if he was thinking about something.'

'Sometimes they do that,' said Mma Potokwani. 'Sometimes men think.'

'I know that,' agreed Mma Ramotswe. 'There are many men who think, Mma.'

Mma Potokwani looked thoughtful – as if she were weighing the truth or falsity of what had just been said. But she decided not to add anything to that particular side of the discussion, and waited for Mma Ramotswe to continue.

'But when I asked him whether he was thinking about something,' Mma Ramotswe continued, 'he just shook his head and said something like *oh*. That's all he said, Mma. Just *oh*.'

Mma Potokwani frowned. 'That is very strange, Mma. I do not think that it can be a very good sign when a man just says *oh*.'

Mma Ramotswe explained about the course, and asked Mma Potokwani whether she thought Mr J. L. B. Matekoni's behaviour could have something to do with that.

'I can't see why going on a business course should have that effect,' said Mma Potokwani. 'Unless . . .'

Mma Ramotswe looked at her expectantly.

Mma Potokwani lowered her voice. 'Unless he met somebody there.'

'What do you mean, Mma? That he met a . . .' She hardly dared say it. Was it possible that Mr J. L. B. Matekoni had met another woman and that he was behaving exactly like all those other married men who suddenly met a woman and became distant and moody and dissatisfied? That was how men behaved at the start of an affair – she had heard that from so many of her clients who had come to her to ask her to investigate their errant husbands. It was one of the first and most obvious symptoms of the male menopausal affair.

'I don't think so, Mma Potokwani,' she said firmly. 'Mr J. L. B. Matekoni is not the type to do that sort of thing.'

Mma Potokwani might have disagreed, had they been talking about any man other than Mr J. L. B. Matekoni, but she thought that Mma Ramotswe was probably right: Mr J. L. B. Matekoni was the very last person she would suspect of infidelity. Men were weak – everyone knew that – and nobody should be surprised by what they do, but somehow it seemed impossible that Mr J. L. B. Matekoni would have his head turned in the President Hotel of all places, while listening to a talk on how to improve one's business.

She had an idea. 'Of course, those courses can be unsettling,' she said. 'He might have been somehow persuaded that he is a failure. Or he might have met all sorts of big, successful people there and drawn the conclusion that his own business was never going anywhere. He might well have been upset by that.'

Mma Ramotswe thought that this was possible. 'But what should I do?' she asked.

'Give it a day or two,' advised Mma Potokwani. 'If he is still like this after two days, maybe, then you should talk to him. Ask him what's bothering him. And if he is still quiet and moody, take him to the doctor. Insist. Take him to see somebody. Nip whatever it is in the bud.'

Mma Ramotswe found this conversation helpful. Mma Potokwani may not have said very much, but what she had said seemed like good sense to Mma Ramotswe and made her feel less anxious. So, once they had finished talking and the last crumbs of fruit cake had been consumed, she decided to ask Mma Potokwani if she could visit one of the housemothers and perhaps talk to some of the children. Mma Potokwani readily agreed.

'We have a new child here,' she said. 'She's not one of the smaller ones – she's thirteen, although we can't be absolutely sure, as she has no birth certificate and we don't know anything about her family. The doctor who treated her said he thought thirteen would be a good enough guess.'

'Treated her?' asked Mma Ramotswe. 'Has she been ill?'

They were walking over to one of the small bungalows in which housemothers lived with a group of five or six children. Mma Potokwani bent down to pick up an empty bottle that somebody had tossed away. 'We tell the children not to litter,' she said. 'We try to drum it into them every single day, but sometimes things go in one ear and out the other.'

'This girl?' prompted Mma Ramotswe. 'Was she very ill?'

Mma Potokwani shook her head. 'No. It was not illness.' She hesitated. It seemed that what she was about to say was painful. 'She had been treated cruelly, Mma. Somebody had broken her wrist. And she was very frightened.'

Mma Ramotswe looked into Mma Potokwani's eyes. She knew that her friend often saw things that many others were spared. Her job was to look after children who had had a bad start in life in one way or another – as orphans, or as children whose parents had abandoned them. That was the greatest loss anybody could have, she thought: not to have a mother or father, or other adult to look after you – to be on your own when everybody else had somebody to love them and protect them from the dangers that the world held for those with nobody at their side.

They reached a small cottage-style building. On its front veranda – a cramped enclosure bounded by a low, mud-stained wall – a chair and table had been placed. A cardboard box had been left on the table, and Mma Ramotswe saw that it was filled with freshly pulled carrots still covered with clumps of crumbling soil.

'The children grow their own vegetables,' Mma Potokwani explained. 'It reminds them where food comes from.' She looked at Mma Ramotswe, and smiled. 'People may forget that, Mma. You and I, we don't, but sometimes children these days think it comes from cans. Not that we can blame them . . .'

Mma Ramotswe laughed. 'We can all forget these things, Mma.'

The housemother, a comfortable woman of traditional build, appeared at the door, and clapped her hands in delight at seeing Mma Ramotswe. This was Mma Molebatsi, who had worked with Mma Potokwani for years and whom Mma Ramotswe had met several times. They exchanged traditional greetings, and Mma Molebatsi then led them into the room that served as the house's kitchen and living room.

'You always come before I have had a chance to tidy up,' said Mma Molebatsi. 'And when I have everything spick and span and polished – no visitors. It is always like that.'

Mma Ramotswe assured her that this was a universal rule, and that no apology was required. 'The house is very clean, Mma. I can see that.'

'It's the houses with the very small children that are the ones that are difficult,' said Mma Potokwani. 'You tidy up with them, and then the next minute, everything is all over the place. These older children are neater.'

'Not all of them,' said Mma Molebatsi.

They sat down while the housemother made tea. She had some fat cakes and offered one to her visitors, who accepted, purely out of politeness. And also because nobody could resist a fat cake, even after having recently eaten a large slice of Mma Potokwani's rich and filling fruit cake. But that was not mentioned, as there was no need to do so.

'I was telling Mma Ramotswe about your new charge,' said Mma Potokwani.

'About Keitumetse?'

Mma Potokwani nodded. 'That's right. Is she around?'

Mma Molebatsi looked over her shoulder. 'She is with some of the smaller children. She is helping with them, I think. She is a very helpful girl.'

'And then there is her name,' said Mma Ramotswe. Keitumetse meant *I am happy*.

'She's happy enough,' said Mma Molebatsi. 'Now that she is here, she is happy. Before that . . .'

'Could you call her to say hello to Mma Ramotswe?' Mma Potokwani suggested.

Mma Molebatsi went to the door and shouted an instruction to a child who was filling a bucket with water from a standpipe. The child went off, and a few minutes later Keitumetse appeared hesitantly at the front door.

'You can come in, Keitumetse,' said Mma Potokwani. 'There is a lady here who wants to say hello to you. She is my friend.'

The girl, who was wearing a faded blue smock dress – a very obvious hand-me-down, Mma Ramotswe thought – gave a small curtsy in her direction.

'Have you started at school yet?' asked Mma Potokwani.

The girl inclined her head. 'I have started, Mma.'

'She is learning to read very quickly,' contributed Mma

Molebatsi. And to the girl she said, 'You will soon be reading books, I think. And the newspaper. Everything.'

The girl spoke quietly, keeping her eyes fixed on the floor. 'I hope so, Mma. There is so much to read.'

'And I have heard that you are good at mathematics,' said Mma Molebatsi. 'How much is two hundred and one hundred and then one hundred and fifty?'

Keitumetse did not lift her gaze. 'It is four hundred and fifty, Mma.'

Mma Ramotswe chuckled. 'That is very good. I would have to write that down on paper and add it all up.'

That was not true, of course. Mma Ramotswe had been taught her sums by her father, even before she started school, and she had never forgotten.

'These days children use calculators,' said Mma Potokwani, disapprovingly. 'It is good to see that there are still children who can add. Calculators make us lazy.'

'All machines make us lazy,' said Mma Molebatsi. 'Calculators. Machines that mix food. They will soon be making a machine that will tie your shoelaces for you.'

Mma Potokwani smiled at Keitumetse. 'I think you can go now, Keitumetse,' she said.

The girl nodded in Mma Ramotswe's direction and left.

'She's small for her age,' said Mma Ramotswe, once she had left the room.

'Not enough to eat,' said Mma Potokwani, grimly. 'Wrong food. Violence. Fear. All these things stop a child growing.'

'That is true,' said Mma Molebatsi. 'That girl has been badly treated.' She shook her head sadly. 'It is a scandal, Mma Ramotswe. It is a big scandal. Those people should not be allowed to get away with it.'

Mma Ramotswe frowned. 'Which people, Mma?'

Mma Potokwani raised a hand. 'We must be careful, Mma Molebatsi. We must be careful what we say.'

Mma Molebatsi pursed her lips. 'Careful, careful, careful. That's the problem, Mma Potokwani. Everybody is so careful when there are important people involved in something. Rich people. Oh my goodness, Mma, we must be careful not to upset rich people. They do not like it. Oh, no, they do not like that, Mma.'

Mma Ramotswe was surprised by the tone of the house-mother's voice. The Orphan Farm housemothers were usually women of an equable temperament, chosen for their patience and calm. It was unusual to hear them speak as directly, and as disapprovingly, as Mma Molebatsi now did.

Mma Potokwani glanced at Mma Ramotswe. 'Mma Molebatsi here is a bit upset about this child, Mma Ramotswe,' she said. 'It has been hard for her.'

Mma Ramotswe assured Mma Molebatsi that she understood. 'I am the same, Mma,' she said. 'Sometimes I see things in my work that make me feel very angry. I think: this is very unjust, because somebody who is rich or powerful is getting away with something while there is some poor person who is suffering as a result. It is hard to accept that sort of thing, Mma.'

And as she spoke, she reflected on just how hard that could be. You saw things that were so obviously unfair – you saw unkindness and thoughtlessness; you saw downright cruelty; and yet so often you had to bear mute witness because you were unable to do anything about it.

Mma Molebatsi was pleased with the support Mma Ramotswe voiced. 'I'm glad you feel the same way, Mma Ramotswe. I would not have expected anything else.' She turned to look at Mma

Potokwani. 'It doesn't matter who those people are, Mma. They should not be allowed to get away with it.'

Mma Potokwani hesitated. She felt the reproval in what Mma Molebatsi said, and she knew that she could not leave the issue where it was. 'Mma Ramotswe,' she began, 'it might be best if you heard the whole story.'

Mma Molebatsi nodded vigorously. 'It would definitely be best, Mma Potokwani. Mma Ramotswe may even be able to do something. That is her business, I think.'

'I cannot always be a help,' Mma Ramotswe protested.

Mma Molebatsi was tenacious. 'But I have heard that you help people.'

'I do – if I can. But the No. 1 Ladies' Detective Agency is a small business, Mma Molebatsi. We do what we can, but we cannot set the whole world to rights.'

'No,' said Mma Potokwani firmly. 'And I don't think we should burden Mma Ramotswe, Mma Molebatsi. She can't do everything.'

'Tell me,' said Mma Ramotswe. 'Let me decide.'

Mma Potokwani took the initiative. 'That girl was brought to us by a lady in town,' she said. 'She saw her outside one of the shops. She was nursing a sore arm and she looked as if she had been crying.'

'The lady took her to the hospital,' Mma Molebatsi interjected. 'They dealt with her wrist and then said that she was free to go home. But when the lady asked her where her home was, she said that she did not know. She said that she had been living with a family and that she was working for them. But she said that she did not want to go back there.'

'She was frightened?' asked Mma Ramotswe.

'Yes,' replied Mma Molebatsi. 'She was very frightened.'

51

'So she was brought here?'

'Exactly, Mma. And we found out about what had happened to her. She told us.'

Mma Potokwani raised a finger. 'We have only the girl's word for it, of course.'

Mma Molebatsi snapped back, 'Are you saying she is making it up, Mma Potokwani?'

Mma Potokwani was placatory. 'No, Mma, I am not saying that. All I am saying is that children – young people, I suppose – can get things wrong. They can add to the truth, so to speak. Or they can take away from it. They are not always reliable.'

'Keitumetse is not making anything up,' said Mma Molebatsi. There was defiance in her voice, and once again Mma Potokwani sought to play down any suggestion that the girl was not to believed.

'I'm sure that she is telling the truth, Mma Molebatsi.' And to Mma Ramotswe, she explained, 'She told us that she had been living in a village with an aunt, because her parents were late. She said that the aunt drank heavily and sold her to a man when she was eight – not to be taken advantage of in that way, Mma, although terrible things like that do happen, but rather to be sold as a domestic worker.'

Mma Ramotswe gasped. 'Oh, Mma, that is terrible. A child . . .'

'Yes,' said Mma Potokwani. 'It is very terrible, Mma Ramotswe.'

Mma Molebatsi took up the story. 'She was taken to another village. She said that there was a large house there – it was a farm, really – that belonged to people from Gaborone. She was made to work there for four years. She did not go to school. She just had to work.'

Mma Ramotswe shook her head. She could well believe this story.

'And then, about a year ago,' Mma Molebatsi continued, 'she was brought down to this family's main house, here in Gaborone. There was much more work to do there, and she often had to work from six in the morning until eight at night. Every day, Mma.' She paused. 'And without pay.'

'Slavery,' said Mma Potokwani.

Mma Ramotswe closed her eyes. Mma Potokwani was right. We thought that slavery was a thing of the past, but that was not true. There were slaves right under our noses – everywhere – all over the world, in spite of all the efforts of governments. Of course, they were not in chains, as they used to be, and the servitude in which they lived was never imposed in the open, but it was there nonetheless, and for those who suffered under it, the absence of chains was a minor detail.

'We know these things happen,' Mma Potokwani said quietly. 'But we don't expect them to be done by one of the wealthiest families in the country.'

She gave the name, and for a few moments Mma Ramotswe imagined that she had misheard it. But then Mma Molebatsi echoed what the matron had said, and Mma Ramotswe knew exactly why they had been so shocked.

Then Mma Molebatsi spoke with feeling. 'We went to the police. We told them the full story. But you know what happened, Mma? Nothing.'

Mma Ramotswe's eyes narrowed. 'Surely not.'

'Well, not exactly nothing,' Mma Potokwani corrected. 'You should tell Mma Ramotswe that the police went round there. They were reluctant to go, but they did. And they found nothing.'

'I know that, Mma,' said Mma Molebatsi. 'They went there because we had passed on what the girl had told us – that there were two other children there. But, of course, there was no sign of them, and so the police said there was nothing more they could do. They were very unwilling to take matters any further, anyway, because that man is so influential. Money, Mma – that is what counts in this life.'

Mma Ramotswe asked about the two other children, and was told that Keitumetse had told them of a girl and a boy who were also being used as domestic workers by the family in question. She said that they were a year or two older than she was. She also said that there were others who were being made to work for some connections of the family.

Mma Ramotswe shook her head. 'Those people can afford to pay,' she said. 'Why do they do that sort of thing?'

'Because they are greedy,' Mma Molebatsi answered quickly. 'That is how they became rich, and that is how they continue.'

Mma Potokwani had to agree. 'Mma Molebatsi feels very strongly about this,' she said. 'But she's right, I'm afraid. These people ...'

She did not finish. Mma Molebatsi was staring at her, and Mma Ramotswe became aware of an uncomfortable chill in the atmosphere. Looking out of the window, she made an attempt to change the subject. 'There are some clouds in the sky, I see.' She pointed. The clouds were there, but were barely detectable. Perhaps they were just a smudge on the window; that was always possible. 'That may mean rain before too long ...' She trailed off; it was not working, for Mma Molebatsi now said, 'You have taken money from those people, Mma Potokwani. You should tell Mma Ramotswe that.'

Mma Potokwani looked down at her hands in embarrassment. Mma Ramotswe felt a surge of sympathy, of love, for her old friend. None of us is perfect, she thought; and as she thought this, she gave a reproachful glance in Mma Molebatsi's direction. What was the housemother trying to do? To embarrass a woman who spent her entire life looking after other people? If Mma Potokwani had taken money from those people, it would have been for one purpose only, and that was to benefit the children. That was what she did: she cajoled, she pushed, she shamed people into donating money to the Orphan Farm. And she did that, Mma Ramotswe imagined, whether the target of her campaigns was the deserving or undeserving rich. What mattered was that the children should benefit – that was her only concern.

'I am sure that Mma Potokwani has nothing to apologise for,' said Mma Ramotswe.

For a few moments, Mma Molebatsi was silent. Then she made a strange clicking sound with her tongue – a sound that was difficult to decipher. It might have been disapproval, and it might have been directed against Mma Potokwani or Mma Ramotswe – it was difficult to tell.

'Perhaps it is time to go,' said Mma Potokwani at last.

Mma Ramotswe looked intently at Mma Molebatsi. There was something biblical that she could say, she felt, but she could not quite bring it to mind. It was something to do with throwing the first stone, or it was maybe something different. That was the problem with biblical quotations: when you needed them, they tended to merge into one, or you might find that you remembered the first half, but not the second. In such circumstances, it is best to finish your tea and go. Quotations would also come back to you on your way home – too late, of course, but ready, perhaps, for use when the occasion next arose.

As she walked back to her van with Mma Potokwani, the words came back to Mma Ramotswe.

'Let him who is without sin cast the first stone,' she said aloud.

Mma Potokwani gave her a sideways look. 'What is this about stones?' she asked.

'I was just thinking,' said Mma Ramotswe. 'Mma Molebatsi should not have said what she said, I think.'

Mma Potokwani stopped. 'Oh, but she should,' she said. 'She had every right, Mma – every right.'

As they approached the van, Mma Potokwani explained to Mma Ramotswe what had happened. At the end of her explanation, Mma Ramotswe reached out and took her friend's hand.

'You did nothing wrong,' she said. 'You do not need to reproach yourself, Mma.'

Mma Potokwani gazed at her. 'You are very kind, Mma Ramotswe.'

'I am nothing,' said Mma Ramotswe, shaking her head. 'You are the kind one, Mma.'

She opened the door of the van and began to get in. Mma Potokwani stopped her.

'One last thing, Mma,' she said. 'I meant to tell you back in my office, but it slipped my mind. It's about Mr J. L. B. Matekoni.'

Mma Ramotswe waited. The sun was beating down. She felt it on her skin, like a hammer.

'Yoga,' said Mma Potokwani.

Mma Ramotswe lifted a hand to shade her eyes. 'Yoga, Mma?'

'Yes. Get Mr J. L. B. Matekoni to do yoga. I have been trying it myself, Mma.'

Mma Ramotswe could not conceal her surprise, and Mma Potokwani smiled when she saw the reaction.

'Yes, Mma, even the traditionally built can do yoga.'

'Of course,' said Mma Ramotswe quickly. 'But do you think it will help him if he is beginning to feel a bit low?'

'Yes, I do,' said Mma Potokwani. 'There is a class every Monday night. At Maru-a-Pula School. It is open to everybody.'

Mma Ramotswe eased herself into the van. 'I shall think about it, Mma Potokwani. But it certainly sounds like a good idea.'

'Yoga brings calm and inner peace,' said Mma Potokwani.

Calm and inner peace ... The words stayed in Mma Ramotswe's mind as she drove back along the Tlokweng Road. Yes, calm and inner peace were undoubtedly important, but did you need to practise yoga to achieve such things? Or was it enough just to be here in Botswana, which was a country of peace, and a country of calm, too? Was it enough to walk along one of those paths in the bush, with the acacia trees on either side of you, with cattle bells sounding somewhere far off, with the sky above you so wide and so understanding of all it witnessed? Surely that was enough. Surely there was enough calm and peace in this land to bring quiet and healing to every heart that was open to it? Surely. And yet, now she suddenly saw Mr J. L. B. Matekoni standing with arms stretched out above his head, one foot off the ground, a benign smile on his face. It was a wonderful image, and she laughed out loud at it, causing her tiny white van to swerve slightly before she corrected its course. She would speak to him about it, she decided, and even encourage him. She was not planning to do yoga herself, of course, as there were limits to what she could fit into her life. Some things had to be forgone, and imagined rather than experienced. Yoga, she thought, was probably one of those.

Chapter Four

Mr T. K. Molefi, Successful Man

That evening, in that precious half-hour between day and night, when the sun is low above the horizon and the sky is filled with flocks of settling birds, Mma Ramotswe went out into her garden to inspect her beans, her tender lettuce, her three beds of tomato plants. The beans were mostly for her – Mr J. L. B. Matekoni had never liked them – and the tomatoes were exclusively for him. He could eat tomatoes with anything – on the side of his plate with his breakfast egg, sandwiched between slices of bread at lunchtime, and made into a pasta sauce for dinner. They should have been easy to grow, as they had more than enough of the sunlight they needed to ripen, but for some reason they did not thrive particularly well in Mma Ramotswe's garden. Now, as she strolled past the vegetable beds, a mug of redbush tea in hand, she peered at the flowers that should in due course bear fruit, and

58

shook her head. Perhaps there were people who were simply never destined to success with tomatoes; perhaps she was one such. In a way, it was like any limitation; you accepted what you could do and not do, and thought no more of it.

Her beans were a different matter. Their pods curled thick and heavy from the stem, and now were almost ready for harvest. She loved the task of splitting the pods and encouraging the beans to pop out. She loved adding butter and salt to them once they were cooked, and eating them by themselves, a course in their own right, in the knowledge that there was nobody who could shake a finger at you and accuse you of taking unhealthy pleasure in something that was not good for you. So many foodstuffs, it seemed to her, had their enemies now: butter was meant to be too fattening, bacon too full of whatever it was that bacon was said to be full of; even bread, that most innocent and ubiquitous of staples, was accused now of being too full of carbohydrates and therefore bad for you, especially if you were a traditionally built person, which of course she was.

But there was nobody to make you feel guilty about eating beans, even if you added a good dose of forbidden butter to them. Beans had plenty of fibre – and fibre, everybody said, was a good thing. Fibre kept you regular, which, even if we did not like to talk about it, was so important, because not being regular always made people look unhappy. Mma Ramotswe could tell – she could always tell, just by looking at people – whether they were regular or not. There was a politician, for example, somebody who was always in the newspapers and on the radio, who had that irregular, unsatisfied look about him. He was always arguing against spending public money – unreasonably, thought Mma Ramotswe – and that, she imagined, might well have something to do with his not being regular. If she ever met him, perhaps she would be able to tell him about the advantages of being regular and how it led to a more generous view of life. She could recommend more fibre, perhaps, but would have to do so tactfully. There were some people who did not like to discuss these subjects and one had to be careful not to upset them.

She knew exactly where her love of beans had come from: that was from her late daddy, Obed Ramotswe, who had taught her to enjoy a plate of beans fried in butter and then salted, or perhaps served with gravy. He had acquired his taste for beans in his mining days, when the men had been fed on high-protein diets to give them strength for their long, dusty shifts. Down in the tunnels of the gold mines, deep in the hard rock that lay below, the temperature quickly rose, and men would sweat profusely from the physical challenge of the work. For this reason, they needed a lot of salt in their diet, and were given it on these fried beans.

'There is no taste like it,' he said to the young Precious. 'And every time I eat beans – every time – I think of being down there, down in those rock tunnels, and then coming up into the light, which was so bright after the darkness, and picking up the smell of the food from the mine kitchens.'

She looked at her bean plants, with their elaborate watering system. A hosepipe had been strung across the top of the plants, and in this pipe tiny pinholes had been drilled. From these, lines of thin thread were dangled, to reach the soil around the stem of the bean plant. Small drops of water made their way down this thread, ending their journey precisely where they were needed. No water was wasted on the surrounding ground: every drop was directed to the roots.

Satisfied with the beans, she made a quick inspection of her lettuce plants, which had been attacked, since she had last looked at them, by caterpillars or snails. She sighed. Any battle against nature was bound to be a losing one. You could try to defeat whatever natural enemy had chosen to show itself, but in the long run you would always fail. The answer, then, was to live with whatever it was that was competing with you.

She smiled as a memory came to her. As a girl, she had been responsible for tending the small field of maize that Obed Ramotswe had planted on a stretch of communal land allocated him by the Chief Linchwe. As the crop matured, it became increasingly attractive to a troop of baboons living on a small nearby *kopje*. They were a ragged bunch, presided over by a large and ill-tempered male who was blind in one eye and who bore a large scar on the side of his snout. Obed had called him One Eye and had an intense love-hate relationship with him. He was angered by the troop's thieving, but he admired the old baboon for simply hanging on that long, and for surviving whatever misfortune had lost him his eye and given him his scar. That, he suggested to Precious, might be the result of a fracas with a leopard. Baboons feared and hated leopards, for whom they were a great delicacy, and it was high on the job description of the lookout baboon to watch for any sign of leopards. Occasionally, though, a leopard would approach with sufficient stealth not to be detected, and would drag off a young or vulnerable baboon before the troop could do anything to defend itself.

The local troop of baboons liked nothing more than fresh maize, and would suddenly materialise on the boundary of a maize field, barking and shrieking as they plundered the unprotected crop. It would have been bad enough had they merely taken what they could carry, but the eventual damage was exacerbated by their fevered picking of maize cobs, tucking them under an arm, and then lifting the same arm to pick another cob. That meant that the ground was soon littered with dropped and wasted

maize, left behind when the baboons grew tired of their ineffi-
cient harvesting and moved on.

She had felt some sympathy for the baboons, and the vestiges of
that early feeling were still there, as she could not bring herself to
punish the snails or caterpillars for their depredations. They were
her fellow creatures, after all. They had not asked to be snails or
caterpillars, and they needed to eat, as we all did. So she accepted
that her lettuce leaves, when eventually she picked them, would
be punctuated with holes and ribbed with nibbled edges.

Her inspection completed, Mma Ramotswe made her way
back to the house. Mr J. L. B. Matekoni was working late – a
recalcitrant delivery van, he explained, that had defeated several
attempts to fix an electrical problem – and she was contemplating having an early dinner with Motholeli and Puso rather than
eating with him later in the evening. The children were busy with
their homework, but would appear in the kitchen, ravenous on the
stroke of seven, for their meal. She liked to sit with them at the
table and talk about the day's events, although those occasions
were often one-sided conversations, the children being unwilling
to say much about what had happened during the day. She was
used to that, of course, and was even amused by their desire to
keep the world of school private. She remembered doing that
herself when young – rarely telling her father about the arguments
and jealousies, the hopes and passions of that intense world from
which adults were excluded.

But now, as she reached the veranda, she saw Mr J. L. B.
Matekoni's truck arrive at the gate and she watched as he climbed
out of the cab, opened the gate, and then drove up to his parking
place at the side of the house. He would be tired, as he always
was after a long day in the garage, and she would pour him a
glass of cold beer that he would drink as he talked to her on the

veranda. It was an important time for both of them: a time of sitting together, talking if the spirit moved them, but also being perfectly happy saying nothing if there was nothing to be said. And that was often the case. There were times when nothing was to be said because the world was simply behaving in the way in which it had always behaved, and there were no surprises. What could one say about that, other than something like, 'There it goes again!' or 'I knew that something like that would happen'?

She had his beer ready for him.

'You will be tired,' she said, as he sat down next to her and reached out for his glass.

Mr J. L. B. Matekoni took a sip, followed by a longer draught. 'There is a very difficult van,' he said. 'And the people who own it think that I am a magician, Mma Ramotswe. They think I can fix it by magic. All the wires are rotten – all of them.'

She shook her head in sympathy. 'That is very sad, Rra. When things get to that stage . . .'

She did not finish. 'When things get to that stage, Mma Ramotswe,' said Mr J. L. B. Matekoni, 'it is best to say *finish*. There comes a time when people should buy a new van. It's as simple as that.'

She agreed, but then, almost immediately, realised that this was dangerous territory. Her own van was hardly in the first flush of youth, and Mr J. L. B. Matekoni was firmly of the view that it should be replaced. But she did not want that. She loved her van, and as long as it did what vans are meant to do – which was to travel between the start of a journey and its end point – and as long as it could do that without breaking down, then she saw no reason to go to all the trouble of buying a new vehicle. A new van might be bright and shiny; it might have more buttons and switches, it might even have something called *climate control*, but did any of these things make it better in any real sense? What was this *climate control* anyway? Could you not control the climate in a van by just opening the windows? Was that not enough for anybody? There were many expressions used these days, she thought, that were simply old things dressed up as new, and people fell for them, and willingly paid money for something that they already had – if only they knew it.

Mma Makutsi might do well to reflect on that, Mma Ramotswe thought. She had bought a battery-operated pencil sharpener of which she was inordinately proud, having believed the claim on the box that this was something that would 'transform productivity in all business situations'. What did that nonsense mean? And the sharpener itself was very bad at getting a fine point, requiring Mma Makutsi surreptitiously to finish off with an old-fashioned pencil sharpener no bigger than a walnut. Mma Ramotswe had observed that, but had said nothing, because in her experience people who bought new and useless things were usually rather embarrassed when they discovered that the things they had bought were not nearly as good as the old things they had had before. We should look after old things, she said to herself; we should love those familiar things we have that have done us well for year after year. We should not forget them.

She glanced at Mr J. L. B. Matekoni, hoping to reach some conclusion as to his mood. He did not look depressed, she thought, but he had not looked depressed on the earlier occasion when depression had been diagnosed. Depressed people, it seemed, could look quite normal, even cheerful, while within themselves they felt defeated and despairing.

'Apart from that van,' she ventured, 'has everything been all right today?'

Mr J. L. B. Matekoni did not answer immediately, but after a few moments' thought he said, 'Well . . .'

She waited, before eventually prompting, 'Well, Rra? Well?'

He picked up his glass and took a sip of beer. 'There is something I wanted to talk about, Mma.'

'I am listening, Rra. I am listening.'

Now, she thought, I shall find out.

'That course I went on,' he began.

Yes, she thought: that was the problem after all. Dissatisfaction. Failure.

'I met somebody there.'

Her heart stopped. That was the precise possibility that she had so confidently dismissed.

She could only stutter, 'Somebody?'

'A man I was at school with.'

She recovered. 'I thought you were going to say you had met a lady . . .'

He laughed. 'It was mostly men. There were one or two ladies there, but it is mostly men who go to that sort of course.' He paused. 'Apart from Violet Sephotho, of course.'

Mma Ramotswe drew in her breath. Violet Sephotho was Mma Makutsi's arch opponent, the Great Husband Stealer of Gaborone, the woman who was to be found at the heart of virtually every scandal or piece of skulduggery, the manipulator *par excellence*, the intelligence behind every plot or underhand connivance; the woman who, in spite of graduating from the Botswana Secretarial College with a final mark of barely fifty per cent, had nonetheless talked her way into a series of highly paid jobs, while Mma Makutsi, with her ninety-seven per cent, had struggled for every small advance – that Violet Sephotho.

Mma Ramotswe managed a cursory, 'So she was there. Hah!'

and then went on quickly to ask which of Mr J. L. B. Matekoni's school contemporaries had been on the course.

'T. K. Molefi,' he replied. 'We called him T. K.'

'I have never met him, Rra. Nor heard of him, I think.'

'He has been very successful, Mma. Very successful indeed. That was why he was speaking on this course.'

There was a note of sadness in his voice, and Mma Ramotswe thought that her original conclusion was probably correct. He had been unsettled by meeting somebody whose career had obviously been so much more successful than his own. That is what had made him feel low – it was perfectly understandable. Many men, for all their toughness and bravado, were at heart uncertain of themselves. Mr J. L. B. Matekoni might appear secure, she thought, but could there be a little boy within – a boy who, when he looked about him, saw only those who had done better than he had?

She felt a sudden desire to embrace him. She felt that she should lean over and put her arm around him and tell him that he should not worry about what other people thought about him, about what other people had done. She wanted to say to him, 'Mr J. L. B. Matekoni, you are the finest man I have ever known; you are worth more, far more, than any of these people you see driving around in their expensive cars, living ostentatiously, throwing their money around to impress the easily impressed.' She wanted to say that what Botswana had achieved since that windy night in 1966 when its flag was first raised in freedom, all that was built not on the machinations of boastful businessmen, but on the exertions of ordinary, hard-working people of integrity – 'people like you, Mr J. L. B. Matekoni,' she wanted to say.

Before she could do any such thing, however, or make any such pronouncement, he turned to her and said, 'T. K. is coming to see me tomorrow, Mma. He has a business proposal for me.'

She drew in her breath. 'That is very interesting, Rra.' She might have said it was alarming rather than interesting, but she kept her reaction in check. He was not his normal self – she was sure of that – and she would need to handle this carefully.

She saw that he was watching for her reaction.

'Yes,' he continued. 'T. K. has been doing very well and he said that he thought I could do rather better than I have been doing so far.'

So there it is, thought Mma Ramotswe. This Mr T. K. Molefi had undermined him: nothing could be clearer.

'How does this Molefi know how you have been doing?' she challenged. 'What does he know of your business, Mr J. L. B. Matekoni? Has he been to Tlokweng Road Speedy Motors? Does he even know where it is?'

'He has driven past.'

'Driven past?' Mma Ramotswe exploded. 'I have driven past the Bank of Botswana many times, Rra. And the Diamond Office too. And do I know how much money is in the bank or how many diamonds are in the Debswana safe? I do not; you need to do more than drive past a building to know how the business inside it is doing.'

She weighed her own point. What she had said was true – but only up to a point. There were many businesses that might easily be assessed after a single drive past. The No. 1 Ladies' Detective Agency, for instance, would hardly be mistaken for anything but a tiny business with a very small turnover. The state of the sign on the front of the building would probably be enough to justify that conclusion: she had meant to have it repainted the previous year, and the year before that, but the painter had given such an expensive estimate that she had put it off. And then there was her tiny white van, widely to be associated with the agency: for all its character, for all that it was loved, no business that was making a healthy profit would wish to be associated with such an aged vehicle. And what went for the No. 1 Ladies' Detective Agency went too for Tlokweng Road Speedy Motors, with its old yard full of rusty mechanical bits and pieces and cut-off oil drums. There would be no confusing that with the well-ordered forecourt of a large and profitable garage, as grease-free and antiseptic as an operating theatre. If this Mr T. K. Molefi – she could not bring herself to think of him as T. K. – had correctly summed up Tlokweng Road Speedy Motors for what it was, purely on the basis of a single drive-past, then it would be difficult to gainsay him.

'You say that he has a business proposal for you, Mr J. L. B. Matekoni?'

He nodded. 'That is why he is coming to see me. He wants to talk business.'

She thought for a few moments. 'But why, I wonder, Rra? Why would this Molefi want to discuss a business proposal if he knows that you ...' She paused. But then she realised that there really was no way round this, and she would have to be direct. So she continued, 'If he thinks you have not been a big success, then why would he bring you a proposal? Surely he would take his idea to somebody who has shown that he can succeed in business.'

Even as she said this, she realised that it was a mistake. She saw Mr J. L. B. Matekoni's face fall, and she tried immediately to repair the damage.

'What I meant, Rra,' she said, 'is that he might think that you will have your hands full trying to improve your existing business, rather than taking on new proposals. That is what I meant to say. I did not mean to suggest that he thinks you are a failure.'

'But I think he does,' said Mr J. L. B. Matekoni. 'I believe that is exactly what he thinks, Mma Ramotswe. But he wants to give me the chance to stop being a failure.'

'But why, Rra?' she protested. 'Why would he want that? Even if he did think that you are a failure – which I'm sure he cannot, because you are *not* a failure – not by any standards I know of. In fact, you are the opposite. You are a big success.'

'You are very kind, Mma. You have always been kind to me. But if I am realistic, then I must say that I have only a small business, and it does not do very well.' He looked down at the floor of the veranda. This was painful to him, she thought. 'Part of the trouble, Mma, is all these modern cars. They do not have proper engines – not engines you can fix. If you go to one of those big garages, what do they do, Mma? They plug your car into a computer and it tells them where the fault is. Then you take out the part – you do not fix it – and you throw it over your shoulder and put in a new one. Anybody could do that. You could do it; Mma Makutsi could do it; Mma Potokwani's husband could do it; Mma Potokwani herself. Anybody, Mma. It is not skilled mechanics, it is nothing at all, really. A robot could do it, Mma. Maybe they already are. Even an apprentice robot.'

She knew that he was right. She had heard him talk of this before, and she knew how painful it must be for him. His mechanical skills had been honed over the years; he could listen to engines and hear what they were saying to him; he could coax them and tune them and make them sing in the note that a happy engine knows is just the right note. He could do all that, and now those abilities were being steadily overshadowed by these new tricks that relied not at all on any human skills. Oh, that must be a hard thing to stomach, she thought – as hard for him as the invention of a detective machine would be for her. You would switch on such a machine and let it get on with the job of detection. It would hum and whirr and produce the answer in a matter of minutes, along with all the necessary proof. It would leave nothing for a human detective to do: no patient observation would be necessary, no enquiries, no intuition, no judgement.

She took a deep breath. 'May I ask you something, Mr J. L. B. Matekoni?'

He smiled. She had not expected that, and for a moment she was not sure whether to proceed. But then she said, 'You aren't feeling a bit low, are you? It's just that . . . well, do you remember when you had that bad spell all those years ago? They said that you should watch out in case it happened again.'

He looked at her with a mixture of surprise and amusement. 'Low, Mma? Oh, no. I'm not feeling low. That was quite different.' He paused. 'Do I *look* low? Is that what you're telling me?'

She shook her head. 'No, it's just that you were a bit quiet last night and now you're talking about being a failure. That's a sign of depression, I think.'

He smiled again. 'No, Mma, you need not worry. I assure you, I am not feeling low. I remember what it was like when I was depressed. That was a bad, bad time, Mma. I do not feel like that at all – not now.'

She thought that what he said sounded completely rational. Perhaps she had been too quick to reach her conclusion. 'You would let me know if you did feel a bit . . . a bit low?'

'Of course I would, Mma. No, it's just that this course yesterday made me think about things. And then when T. K. and I had a talk, it struck me that perhaps I should do something about my life.'

'But is there anything wrong with your life, Mr J. L. B. Matekoni?'

'Nothing actually wrong, Mma. It's just that I don't think I'm reaching my full potential.'

My full potential . . . She recognised this as the sort of expression

70

that would be used on a course like that. People were always going on about full potential and about how everybody should try to reach it. Well, she, for one, was not going to sit there and think about her full potential, whatever her full potential might mean. Doing more? Worrying more? Spending more time working and less time walking in her garden and looking up at the sky and thinking how good life was?

But this was not the time to engage with Mr J. L. B. Matekoni on a deep discussion of what the aims of life should be, and so she simply asked, 'What is Molefi's proposal, Rra?' She still called him Molefi; she could not yet use this T. K. name.

'He is starting a bus company,' said Mr J. L. B. Matekoni. 'He says that there are great opportunities in transport, and setting up a bus company is exactly what we should all be doing.'

She resisted the temptation to laugh. How could we all do that? How could *everyone* set up a bus company? Who would travel on the buses if everyone had their own bus company?

With a straight face she asked, 'So he wants you to be involved, Rra? Is that what he wants?'

'Yes, that is so, Mma Ramotswe.'

She pursed her lips. 'Bus companies sound expensive to me. What does a bus cost? A lot of money, I imagine. And where would that money come from? Has this Molefi got a big pot of money somewhere?'

'We would be joint partners,' said Mr J. L. B. Matekoni. 'I would put up half, and he would put up the other half.'

Mma Ramotswe digested this information. 'And where would you get your half from, Rra? I don't think there is much in the garage account, is there? Not last time I looked, anyway.'

Mr J. L. B. Matekoni had the air of one who had anticipated an objection – and was ready with a response. 'We are going to buy an old bus to start with, Mma. I shall fix it up and then it will be ready for use. He has located a bus for sale. It has done one hundred thousand miles, but that is not much for a big diesel engine. They can go on forever, Mma.'

'But it will still cost *something*, Mr J. L. B. Matekoni. Even an old bus costs something. And you will need money to pay the driver and advertise and print the tickets and so on. None of that is free. You will still need to find your share of the capital.'

'I know that,' he said. 'I shall get a bank loan.'

Mma Ramotswe rolled her eyes. 'Rra, a bank loan is a big thing to take on. You know the rate of interest banks charge. And would they lend it to you for a new business? New businesses are always a bit of a risk.' That, she thought, was true. You did not have to go for a day-long course at the President Hotel to know that new businesses had a habit of losing money and going under within months of their having been started. That, she told herself, was as well known as any fact in the world of business.

But he was undaunted. 'They will lend me the money on the security of the garage,' he said.

She stared at him wide-eyed. 'You'll mortgage the garage?'

'Yes,' he said. 'This is a big opportunity for me, Mma Ramotswe. And if I don't take a risk with this, then I may never get another chance.'

Chapter Five

Mr Baboloki Mophephu

O ver breakfast the following morning nothing was said of the conversation that Mma Ramotswe and Mr J. L. B. Matekoni had had on the veranda. Mma Ramotswe had lain awake for hours the previous night, worrying about what she had been told, with the word *mortgage* sounding in her mind like a dreadful, tolling bell. By contrast, Mr J. L. B. Matekoni seemed to sleep well, with the result that when she saw him off in his truck, he seemed cheerful and optimistic. She would see; presumably nothing had been signed yet, and she would have a chance to dissuade him from taking matters further. Perhaps Mma Makutsi would be able to help: she could speak to Phuti, who could perhaps have a word with Mr J. L. B. Matekoni on a businessman-to-businessman basis and warn him of the consequences of investing in companies one knew nothing about. Phuti had always been successful in business, and a word from him might help; on the other hand, it might not. Mr J. L. B. Matekoni could be stubborn, and once he had decided on a course of action he was not easily turned.

She decided that she would discuss the matter with Mma Makutsi, perhaps over mid-morning tea, which was always a suitable time to bring up matters that needed careful consideration. Before that, there was work to do, and money to be earned, particularly if Mr J. L. B. Matekoni was about to take on a ruinous bank loan. She sighed as she sat down at her desk and looked at her diary. There was an appointment for ten minutes' time and she would have to clear her mind before the client arrived.

A few minutes later, Mma Makutsi came into the office and flung her bag down on her desk.

'Really, Mma,' she said. 'This traffic is getting me down. I spent fifteen minutes waiting to get onto the Tlokweng Road. Fifteen minutes, Mma, with all sorts of people trying to push in ahead of me.'

'Very bad,' said Mma Ramotswe. 'There are too many cars now. They are like ants, I think, Mma.'

'You're right, Mma Ramotswe. And I do not think that all of them have any business being on the road. People are just driving round for no good reason. The government should put a stop to it.'

Mma Ramotswe looked at her watch. 'We have somebody booked in, Mma. You took the call, I think.'

Mma Makutsi looked at a file on her desk. 'That's right, Mma. I have opened a file for the case. It has no papers in it yet because I do not know what it is about.'

'They did not say anything on the phone when they made the appointment?'

'They did not, Mma. All that he said was that it was very important and he wanted to see you as soon as possible.'

'And who was this *he*, Mma?'

Mma Makutsi consulted the label on the file. 'He is Mr Baboloki Mophephu, Mma. That is what he said he was called.'

Mma Ramotswe made a note on a scrap of paper. 'I have not heard that name, Mma Makutsi. Have you?'

Mma Makutsi shook her head. 'It is vaguely familiar, Mma, but I cannot place it. I knew a Baboloki up in Francistown, but this is not the same person.'

'Well, we shall soon find out, Mma Makutsi. We shall find out how important – or otherwise – this is.'

'We need a big case, Mma,' said Mma Makutsi. 'We need a big case with large fees.'

Mma Ramotswe almost said that yes, this was important in view of the proposed bank loan, but did not. There would be time to discuss that later on.

Mr Baboloki Mophephu arrived exactly on time, knocking at the door just as Mma Makutsi finished applying fresh lipstick. She rose from her desk, straightened her skirt, and admitted him to the office.

'What shall I say your name is, Rra?' she asked.

Mr Baboloki Mophephu looked momentarily taken aback. 'Say to who, Mma?' he asked, looking across the room towards Mma Ramotswe's desk. 'To that lady over there?'

'That is correct,' said Mma Makutsi primly.

'But she can hear everything we're saying,' he pointed out. 'You don't need to repeat it, surely.'

It was a very inauspicious beginning, and Mma Ramotswe was on the point of intervening when Mma Makutsi said, 'There is a correct way of doing things, Rra. We always do things correctly in this business and will not compromise on standards.'

Mr Mophephu raised an eyebrow. 'You can tell her that I am Mr Baboloki Mophephu.'

Mma Makutsi turned to face Mma Ramotswe. 'This is Mr Baboloki Mophephu,' she said. 'He has an appointment, I believe.'

Mma Ramotswe rose from her desk and pointed to the client chair. 'I thought it might be you, Mr Mophephu. Please sit down in this chair.'

Mr Mophephu sat down, glancing at Mma Makutsi as he did so. 'Please thank your secretary,' he said.

Even if there had not been that bad beginning, this made the situation beyond rescuable.

'There is no secretary in this room,' said Mma Makutsi icily. 'I do not see a secretary, Rra.'

Mma Ramotswe attempted to smooth things over. 'We do not have a secretary as such, Rra,' she said quickly. 'These days, things are different. And . . .' She paused, trying to convey to him with a meaningful look, that nothing short of a full apology would restore the temperature to normal. 'And Mma Makutsi is, in fact, a colleague. She is a—'

'Senior co-managing director,' interjected Mma Makutsi.

This was a new claim. Every promotion Mma Makutsi had enjoyed thus far had been at her own instance. She had been an assistant detective for a relatively short time and had then become an associate detective. Then she had become a co-detective and joint partner and various other things, but never a senior co-managing director. That was definitely new.

Mr Mophephu grinned. 'I am very sorry, Mma,' he said. 'I should not mistake the boss for the secretary. I shall not do that again.'

'I am not the head boss,' said Mma Makutsi. 'I am a co-senior boss. That is different.'

'Well, I apologise anyway,' said Mr Mophephu. 'All these titles are too much for my small head, Mma.'

Mma Makutsi grudgingly accepted the apology and returned to her desk.

'Well, there we are,' said Mma Ramotswe with forced cheerfulness. 'That settles that. Now you have my full attention.'

From behind Mr Mophephu's shoulder came a quick, 'And my attention too.'

'Yes, and Mma Makutsi is listening too,' said Mma Ramotswe. 'We work together.'

'Jointly,' said Mma Makutsi. 'As a closely knit team.'

Mr Mophephu absorbed this. 'That is always best. Work together, I always say. Work together and succeed together. That is another thing I say.'

'That is very true,' said Mma Ramotswe. She had been studying her visitor while this exchange had been taking place. There was a great deal you could learn from a person's clothes, and from Mr Mophephu's turn-out she had garnered clues enough to place him. This man was a fully paid-up member of the Botswana upper-middle class – a man who was one clear generation away from the relative simplicity with which everybody had lived in the first part of the twentieth century, in the days of the Protectorate. He would have been at Maru-a-Pula School, perhaps, and then at the university. His father would have had to have had a bit of a head start to afford the school fees, and so that meant that his grandfather was probably the first man of any real substance in the family.

Mma Ramotswe reached for a pen. It was a sign that the consultation could start, but it also gave her something to do with her hands as the client spoke.

'What can we do for you, Rra?' she asked. 'The No. 1 Ladies' Detective Agency is at your disposal.'

Mr Mophephu crossed his legs, and Mma Ramotswe noticed that the creases of his trousers had been carefully pressed. He would not have done that himself, she told herself; men relied on others for such things. His manner was very self-assured, she thought, and that was because of a number of things: his education at Maru-a-Pula; financial security; from knowing who he was. All of these things could combine to give confidence in one's dealings with others. Of course, one had to be careful not to become *too* self-assured – the boundary between what people found acceptable and what they found irritating could be a narrow one. At present she was not quite sure which side of the divide Mr Mophephu was on.

He smiled. 'I wondered a bit – before I came here. I asked myself: is this a detective agency just for ladies, or are male clients accepted too?'

The answer came from behind him.

'We do not discriminate, Rra,' intoned Mma Makutsi. 'We are here to help all sorts and conditions of people. We are an inclusive agency.'

Mr Mophephu nodded as he absorbed this. 'That is good,' he said. 'These days everything has to be open to everybody. That is the law, I think. Anybody can do anything – or they think they can. There are still plenty of people who can do nothing, in my view.'

Mma Ramotswe had been writing the date at the top of a blank sheet of paper. She looked up sharply.

'You think there are some people who can do nothing, Rra?'

She became aware that Mma Makutsi was following the conversation closely. She would have to be careful not to draw Mma

Makutsi in too much, as any discussion in which she became too involved could turn heated in moments.

Mr Mophephu uncrossed his legs. 'Yes, that is what I think, Mma. I know that you aren't meant to think these things these days, but I think that there are a lot of rubbish people in this town. You see them. Look for them, and you will see them. They are sitting around doing nothing because they know that there are plenty of people doing a lot. So they think they don't have to do anything because other people will do all the work.'

Mma Ramotswe listened courteously. This was a familiar complaint – she had heard other people make the same point, but, when challenged, they found it a bit difficult to refer to actual people who fell into the category they were attacking. In Mma Ramotswe's view, the overwhelming majority of people were not only prepared to work, but were anxious to do so. And it was not the fault of ordinary people if there was not enough work to go round. There never would be enough work to keep everybody employed – that was a hard fact of life.

'I think that most people want to work,' she said, mildly. 'We often get people knocking on our door asking for a job, don't we, Mma Makutsi?'

Mma Makutsi answered quickly. 'All the time, Mma. All the time.'

Mr Mophephu looked unconvinced. 'Work as detectives? Is that what they want to do?'

'Yes,' said Mma Makutsi, a bit defensively. 'Detective work is very skilled work, Rra – and prestigious.'

'Oh, I don't doubt that,' said Mr Mophephu, half turning to speak to Mma Makutsi at her desk behind him. 'But I imagine that these people who knock on your door are not seriously thinking you will have anything for them. I suspect that they are knocking on your door precisely because they know that they will not be able to be taken on as detectives. Yet they can claim that they have been asking everywhere and knocking on every door.'

'Oh, I don't know, Rra,' said Mma Ramotswe. 'I think that many of them really imagine that—'

She did not finish. There was a loud expostulation from Mma Makutsi. 'That is nonsense. Not you, Mma Ramotswe, but Mr Mophephu. With the greatest of respect, that is nonsense. These people who knock on our door are doing so because they have heard of Mma Ramotswe – and heard of me, too, if I may say. They have heard of us and they think: we could be like those ladies over there. We could be leading that interesting life if only we got a job in a detective agency. That is what they are thinking, Rra.'

Mma Ramotswe felt that it was time to move the conversation on to the purpose of Mr Mophephu's visit.

'Be that as it may, Rra, perhaps you could tell us what it is that you wish to consult us about?'

'It is a family matter,' said Mr Mophephu.

Mma Ramotswe made a note on her sheet of paper. 'May I ask, Rra – is it a divorce issue?'

'If it is, you have come to the right place,' said Mma Makutsi. 'We are the number one experts in divorce and how to get husbands to pay their fair ...' She stopped as it dawned on her that Mr Mophephu was probably a husband.

Mma Ramotswe covered Mma Makutsi's embarrassment. 'We mostly work for wives,' said Mma Ramotswe. 'Mma Makutsi was not intending to be disrespectful of husbands in general. We believe in justice for all: wives, husbands, children – everybody.'

'Especially wives,' said Mma Makutsi.

'It is not divorce,' said Mr Mophephu. 'I am very happily

married.' He sighed. 'And I think my wife is happily married too – to me.' He sighed again.

Mma Ramotswe watched him. She was charitable in her view of people and always gave others the benefit of the doubt, but there was something about Mr Mophephu that she found unappealing.

'I see,' she said. 'Well, perhaps you could tell us a bit more.'

Mr Mophephu cleared his throat. 'I should start with myself, Mma. You may know my name, but I do not think you know where I am from or anything else very much about me.'

'It would be helpful to know,' Mma Ramotswe encouraged.

'My father is Fidelis Mophephu,' he began. 'He was—'

Mma Makutsi cried out. 'Oh, that Mophephu! I know who you are, Rra. I know all about your father. There is a school named after him, I think. He had stores, didn't he? All those hardware stores all over Botswana. There was one in Bobonong . . .'

'She is from Bobonong,' explained Mma Ramotswe.

'It is a very fine place,' said Mr Mophephu. 'I have always said that people from Bobonong are among the most intelligent people in the whole country.'

The effect of this remark was immediate – and profound. Mma Makutsi's hands shot up to frame her face, which was a perfect picture of unalloyed delight. Her eyes widened and her mouth fell open at the same time – a seismic change in facial topography. And then, from Mma Makutsi's lips, came a sound that, if one were to hear it with one's eyes closed, would most likely be iden-tified as a feline purr.

The ensuing silence was broken by Mma Makutsi, her voice quivering with emotion. 'It is very interesting to hear you say that, Rra. You are very kind.'

Mr Mophephu was matter of fact. 'Well, I think it's true, Mma.

I have met some very accomplished people from Bobonong.' And here he mentioned a couple of names that had Mma Makutsi nodding in vigorous agreement.

'Yes,' she said. 'That one is a very smart man, Rra. Some call him a genius, in fact. And that other one is said to have one of the best memories in the country. He remembers everything he reads. Everything, Rra.'

'Perhaps there is something in the water,' said Mr Mophephu, laughing. 'Either that, or genetics.'

'There are many things that are genetic,' said Mma Makutsi.

Mma Ramotswe had recovered her composure after the initial shock caused by Mr Mophephu's remark. She was still wary of this man, in spite of his extraordinarily well-judged compliment. Was he a flatterer, perhaps?

'So that is your father,' said Mma Ramotswe. 'I think that my own father knew him slightly, Rra. I remember he mentioned him sometimes. You are fortunate, Rra. There are many people who would dearly love to have a father like that.'

Mr Mophephu gave a satisfied grin. 'I was lucky in having the father I have had. He was a very important influence on me.'

Mma Ramotswe could identify with that. Her own father, the late Obed Ramotswe, had been a similar influence on her. He, of course, had not met with the financial success that had visited the older Mophephu, nor had he had a school – or anything, for that matter – named after him, but he had been a fine judge of cattle and much respected for his integrity. She could be every bit as proud of him as could Mr Mophephu of his illustrious parent.

'Did you work in the family business, Rra?' she asked.

Mr Mophephu nodded. 'I did, Mma. For many years, I had a hands-on role in that. Ask me anything you like about hardware – nails, power tools, corrugated iron – anything. You ask me, Mma, and I will be able to tell you.'

Mma Ramotswe laughed. 'I am not very good at that sort of thing, Rra. I am married to a mechanic, you see, and if you are married to a mechanic, you do not have to bother about that side of things.'

'I can understand that,' said Mr Mophephu.

'You are no longer in the business?' she asked. And then added, 'Is your father late, Rra?'

He shook his head. 'He is not late, Mma. He is very old now, but not late.' His expression became serious. 'And that has something to do with my reason for coming to see you.'

Mma Ramotswe waited. Through the open window, she could hear the sound of birds in their acacia tree – a squabbling noise, the soundtrack to one of the constant territorial disputes in which birds engaged.

'My father is very old,' Mr Mophephu repeated. 'But in spite of that he is as bright as ever up here.' He tapped his forehead. 'In fact, Mma Ramotswe, I think he gets even brighter every day.'

'There are many senior people like that,' said Mma Ramotswe. 'It is a mistake to assume that your mind fades as your legs get weaker. That is often just not true.'

'My grandmother is still alive,' chipped in Mma Makutsi. 'Nobody knows how old she is – maybe one hundred, maybe a bit more – but she still knows exactly what is going on. She has forgotten nothing, I think.'

'She must be from Bobonong,' said Mr Mophephu, over his shoulder. 'Like you.'

Again, this brought a warm response. 'Yes, Rra, perhaps it is further proof of what you said.'

Mma Ramotswe smiled. The atmosphere between Mma

Makutsi and Mr Mophephu was beyond cordial now, but she wanted to hear more about what had brought Mr Mophephu to their door.

'Of course, my father is not running the business any longer,' said Mr Mophephu. 'We have good managers for that. We don't have to do very much at all.'

Mma Ramotswe made a note on her sheet of paper. 'I see.'

'And he has retired to his farm off the Lobatse Road. It is quite near Kgali Siding. He has a very fine house there – you might have seen it.'

'I have,' volunteered Mma Makutsi. 'You see it from the road there, don't you? It has a thatched roof.'

'That is the one. My father had it built about ten years ago. He has lived there ever since.'

Mma Ramotswe said that she thought the father must be a happy man. 'It is good land there,' she said. 'And it is attractive, too. There are those hills.'

'He likes those,' said Mr Mophephu. 'Some of them are on his land. He looks out over them from his veranda.'

'Does he live by himself?' asked Mma Ramotswe.

Mr Mophephu frowned. 'That is the problem, Mma. He does not.'

Mma Ramotswe thought she could tell what was coming. There would be a second wife – or somebody with ambitions to become a second wife. Their visitor would be the son by a wife who was now late, and he was concerned that his father was threatening to get married. A marriage contracted in old age always, always set alarm bells ringing amongst family members. This was a matter of property – as so many matters revealed themselves to be, under the surface, when you scratched at them.

'Is there a girlfriend?' Mma Ramotswe asked. It was a rather direct question, but the relationship between private investigator and client could, at times, be like the relationship between doctor and patient: one had to probe.

To Mma Ramotswe's surprise, Mr Mophephu said that there was nothing of that sort, as far as he knew. 'For many years,' he began, 'my father has not been interested in that sort of thing.' He paused. 'I do not wish to go into details, Mma, but he told me that those things are in the past for him.'

Mma Ramotswe looked away. She had led the discussion in this intimate direction, but she was not sure whether she wanted to go any further into such matters.

Mr Mophephu sensed her embarrassment. 'You must see a lot of that sort of thing in your work,' he said.

It was Mma Makutsi who confirmed that this was so. 'Oh, every day, Rra,' she said. 'You should hear some of the things we hear – right in this office. Shameless things, Rra. Oh yes, I could tell you things that would shock you, Rra—'

'But of course Mma Makutsi will not do that,' interjected Mma Ramotswe. 'She fully understands the requirements of professional confidentiality.'

Mr Mophephu looked a bit disappointed – as if he had been cheated of some juicy bit of information. But he said, 'Yes, obviously you cannot speak of these things.'

Mma Makutsi had a parting shot. 'That's quite right. So I won't tell you, Rra, about the man who was seeing four women at the same time, Rra. Four! Sometimes all on the same day, if you can believe it. I shall not tell you about him.'

Mma Ramotswe cleared her throat loudly. 'Do other members of the family live there on the farm with him, Rra? Do you have brothers and sisters?'

'I have two sisters, Mma Ramotswe. One is called

Keabetswe – we call her Betty for short. The other is Masego. She answers to the name Maisie. These are their pet names – but everybody uses them now. I like the Tswana names, but you know how things are. People like to take short cuts in the way they speak.

'Maisie,' he continued, 'is three months younger than I am.' He paused, watching as Mma Ramotswe wrote on the piece of paper in front of her.

She looked up. 'Three months younger?'

Mma Makutsi joined in. 'That is very unusual, Rra, to have a sister who is so close in age.'

'Yes,' said Mr Mophephu, but added nothing.

'And the other sister?' asked Mma Ramotswe.

He seemed surprised by the question. 'You don't wish to ask more about Maisie?' And then he grinned. 'That was a bit of a test, Mma. I wanted to see what sort of detective you were – whether you would spot anything inconsistent in what I said.' There was an air of challenge in his voice.

Mma Ramotswe met his gaze. She tapped her pencil on her piece of paper. 'I have written *half-sister* here, Rra.'

Mr Mophephu seemed disappointed. 'I was not trying to trip you up, Mma. Yes, she is my half-sister – my sister by a different mother. My father is her father, though. She is his daughter by the lady who was his secretary at the time. He was very kind to her, and when she had his baby, he said that the baby could come and live under his roof.'

Mma Ramotswe saw a small flash pass across the ceiling. This was the reflected light from the window, caught by Mma Makutsi's large round spectacles. It was usually a bad sign.

'What about the mother?' Mma Makutsi asked. 'What did she think of that, Rra?' The friendly tone of voice, a response to the remarks about Bobonong, had been replaced by something rather different.

'That lady? The secretary?'

'Yes, Rra,' said Mma Makutsi. 'I am thinking of Maisie's mother.'

Mr Mophephu shrugged. 'I think that she had another husband. I am not sure what happened to her.'

'And Maisie herself?'

'She is a teacher, Mma. She taught Setswana, but is now a principal in a junior school. Her husband was a very good runner in his day. He ran for Botswana, but he never came first in any international competition. He went to a competition in Namibia and came second. He said that he had a sore stomach at the time because of something he had eaten. He often came third. Then he stopped running. They have two children, both boys. The first born is showing signs of becoming a good runner himself. They live in Lobatse, near the hospital there. They are very happy, I think, although who knows what goes on inside people?'

Mr Mophephu seemed keen to expand on this side of the family. 'He works for a company that imports kitchen equipment – big stoves, and things like that – for caterers and hotels. He has done quite well, but he is greedy. For food, I mean. He eats far too much, that man, although he never puts on weight. They came for a barbecue with us and he ate two pieces of steak – large pieces, Mma – and five of those large boerewors sausages, Mma. And they were big.' He paused. 'We get on well enough with them, but we do not see them very often.'

'It's hard to keep in touch sometimes,' said Mma Ramotswe. 'We try, of course, but I suppose everybody is so busy.'

'Precisely,' said Mr Mophephu. 'It is very hard.'

Mma Ramotswe cleared her throat again. 'These things happen. Sometimes people's private lives become complicated. What about Betty, Rra?'

'She is married to a man who works in the Bank of Botswana, here in Gaborone,' said Mr Mophephu. 'He is an economist. They have four children – two twins, and then two who are not twins, but who look very like one another. In fact, all those children look the same – I cannot tell which one is which. They all have very big noses, which they get from their father. He has one of the biggest noses in the country, Mma.'

Mma Makutsi's voice came from behind him. 'That is genetic, I think.'

'It is definitely genetic,' agreed Mr Mophephu. 'You get your nose from your ancestors.'

'There was a man in Bobonong who had three nostrils,' said Mma Makutsi. 'His grandfather had the same thing, I believe. I remember seeing him once – he was pointed out to me, but I wasn't able to get close enough to take a good look and—'

'So neither of your sisters can live with your father?' asked Mma Ramotswe.

'They have asked him to go and stay with them, Mma. And my wife and I have done the same. But he does not want to leave the farm. He is very happy there, and I can understand why he wishes to remain. He has said to me that that is where he would like to die. He said that he would like to die in his own bed, looking out of his own window, at his own land.'

Mma Ramotswe nodded. She felt moved by what he had just said, and her feelings towards him, which had been ones of slight wariness, seemed to be changing.

'I can understand that,' she said. 'Everybody has their place, and would like to be in that place when their years are running

out. That is quite understandable, Rra. But he must have somebody there, surely . . .'

'Oh yes, there is somebody, Mma. And that is why I have come
to see you. There is somebody who looks after him. She is a nurse,
and I think . . .' He hesitated before continuing, 'I think that she
is a very wicked woman.'

In the silence that ensued, Mma Ramotswe watched
Mr Mophephu closely. He had become tense, and she noticed that
his right fist was clenched. His sentiment for his father, expressed
in such a tender way, was now overshadowed by a quite different
emotion. This was anger.

'Tell me about this nurse,' said Mma Ramotswe quietly.

This, she thought, is a familiar story, and I suspect that I shall
have heard the very same story before – in a different setting,
of course, played out amongst different people, but at heart
identical. Human avarice, human jealousy, human resentment:
these never changed, but did their unsettling work in ways
that were recognisable and predictable to anybody whose job
it was, as it was Mma Ramotswe's, to sort out the problems of
others. There was rarely anything new in life, she thought – but
it was not just human failings that repeated themselves: so too
did those things that were positive. They recurred, which was
a good thing, in a way, as familiarity brought with it a certain
comfort. So it was reassuring when people followed routines
that you had seen them follow countless times: without pattern
the world could be a perplexing and frightening place. That was
why Mma Ramotswe liked the old ways; that was why she appreciated it when people greeted you in the traditional manner, or
enquired after your health, or made mention of things that had
happened a long time ago and that people liked to hear about.
These things reminded you of who you were, where you were,

and how, even after you had gone, there would still be this place, this earth, this happiness – all still there for those who came after you.

Chapter Six

Violet Sephotho Steals

That afternoon Mma Ramotswe went to the Riverwalk shopping centre to do her weekly grocery shop. In the past she had always done this on a Saturday morning, but had recently found the supermarket too crowded.

'It is not a good idea to shop on a Saturday morning, if you can avoid it,' Mma Makutsi advised. 'The trouble is, Mma, that Saturday morning is when men go shopping and they always slow us down – always. They cannot decide, you see, and they spend a lot of time looking for things. On a Saturday morning the supermarket is always full of men who don't know where anything is, and when they find it, they are unsure about whether it is the right thing for them.'

Mma Ramotswe had laughed at this, but realised that Mma Makutsi was right. And when she changed her shopping day to a

Friday afternoon, she found that everything went more smoothly and there was less waiting. On that particular Friday she had a great deal to think about as she browsed the aisles of the supermarket, inspecting the latest special offers. Foremost in her mind was that morning's meeting with Mr Mophephu and the story he had told her and Mma Makutsi. At the end of their interview, she had agreed to act for him, even though there was something about the case that made her feel a bit uncomfortable. But there was no doubt in her mind where her duty lay: if you provided a public service, as she did, you could not pick and choose which cases you would like to take up, purely on the basis of whether you liked or disliked the prospective client. Now, as she moved along the displays of vegetables, reaching out to test the ripeness or otherwise of what was on offer, she went over in her mind what Mr Mophephu had told her about his father and the nurse whom he had so forcefully described as a wicked woman.

She was thinking of this when she heard a familiar voice behind her. Turning round, she saw Mma Potokwani, pushing a shopping cart that was already half full with items from the bakery section – loaves of bread, pizza bases, and small iced cakes. Alongside these were some bags of peeled carrots and a large bag of onions.

They greeted one another and agreed to do their shopping together before going for tea in the café near the cinema. They had recently seen one another, of course, but they had never been at a loss for something to say to each other, and even after only a day or so there were always new developments to be discussed. They would start their shopping together at the meat counter, they decided, as Mma Potokwani needed sausages and Mma Ramotswe had beef mince on her list.

The next port of call was the tea and coffee section, where Mma Ramotswe stocked up on several boxes of redbush tea-bags, while

Mma Potokwani bought large packets of loose-leaf Tanganda Tea. After that there were a few odd purchases here and there – Mma Potokwani wanted a bag of icing sugar and Mma Ramotswe needed a jar of anchovy paste. She did not like it – it was too salty and too fishy for her taste – but Mr J. L. B. Matekoni loved having it in his sandwiches. He liked strong, salty foods, while her own taste was for sweeter things.

She started to say something to that effect as they wheeled their shopping carts back towards the checkout. 'I have a sweet tooth, as you know, Mma Potokwani,' Mma Ramotswe began. 'Mr J. L. B. Matekoni is quite different. He likes anything that has lots of salt in it. He likes—'

Mma Ramotswe felt Mma Potokwani tug at her arm. 'What is it, Mma?'

Mma Potokwani lowered her voice to a whisper. She pointed as she spoke. 'Look over there, Mma. See who's over there near the chocolate biscuits.'

Mma Ramotswe followed Mma Potokwani's gaze. For a few moments she looked at the wrong person – an entirely innocent man with a teenage son, bending forward to examine the label on a large red carton. But then she saw the object of Mma Potokwani's whispered alert. It was Violet Sephotho.

Violet was standing beside her largely empty shopping cart, reaching out for an item on the shelf before her. For a moment Mma Ramotswe held her breath. Then she turned to Mma Potokwani and said, 'I see her, Mma. I see Violet Sephotho.'

Mma Potokwani had strong views on a number of subjects. She disapproved of selfishness in any form; she disliked personal vanity; and she had a strong aversion to mendacity. Mma Ramotswe was with her on all of these, although she was perhaps a bit more tolerant than her matronly friend, and was prepared to forgive most of the failings for which she had a distaste. But for Mma Potokwani, had an ingenious chemist sought to concoct a brew of all these things that she disliked, he or she would have been unable to come up with a more perfect recipe than that embodied in Violet Sephotho.

'That woman,' hissed Mma Potokwani. 'I wonder what she's planning next, Mma Ramotswe. Something underhand, no doubt.'

Mma Ramotswe said that she had no idea. 'She will think of something, Mma,' she said. 'She has never let us down in that respect. There is always something.' She paused. 'Unless she has changed, Mma. We must always give people the benefit of the doubt. Sometimes they change.'

Mma Potokwani said that she very much doubted that. 'What do they say about leopards, Mma? Isn't it something about how leopards cannot change their spots?'

'I have heard that,' Mma Ramotswe replied. 'But I do not think it is always true, Mma. There are some people who do not change, but there are many, I think, who see that they need to change – and do so. I have seen people do that. I have seen that with my own eyes.'

Mma Ramotswe was thinking of cases in which she had helped a client to change by pointing something out. A stubborn attachment to wrong was often no more than the result of never having seen the something that was there all along, but that had been obscured. And she had heard, too, of numerous cases of people who had been changed through religious experience. A friend's cousin, a man whom she had known slightly when they were both children, was living proof of that possibility. He had been a tearaway – a ladies' man – with a passion for drinking, who had wandered into a church, almost by accident, and had done so at the very moment that the minister had been calling for any sinners in the congregation to come forward. And here and there, people had risen to their feet and had made their way to the front, to be embraced by the minister and the elders. And this man, this womanising tearaway, had felt moved to join them, and had wept tears of regret and shame as the good people put their arms around him. Sophisticated people could laugh at that, and mock it for its sentimentalism, and yet from that moment onward he had stopped abusing others, had renounced inebriation, and had returned to the wife and children whom he had previously deserted. If a man like that could change, through the forgiveness and charity of others, then anybody could change, and do so for the better.

'Violet Sephotho will never change,' said Mma Potokwani firmly. 'Believe me, Mma Ramotswe: when you are like that, you are very unlikely to change.'

Mma Ramotswe hesitated. Mma Potokwani was a very strong and persuasive character, and it was only too easy to let her dominate you if you were not too careful. Now she felt that she should stand up for the idea that you could not write people off completely. And so she said, 'I am sure that even Violet has some good points, Mma Potokwani.'

Mma Potokwani gave a wry smile. 'I doubt it, Mma. I'd like to think she had some good points, but I have yet to find them.'

'She probably just wants to be loved,' said Mma Ramotswe. 'Just like the rest of us . . .'

And it was at this point that they saw Violet reach for a packet of chocolate biscuits, glance briefly about her – though not at them – and then expertly tear open the packet, extract two biscuits, and stuff them into her mouth before returning the violated packet to its place on the shelf.

'See!' hissed Mma Potokwani. 'See that!'

Mma Ramotswe had no answer, other than to say, 'Oh, well.' And into that *oh well* was poured her disappointment over the imperfection of the world and of our human affairs. It was a small thing – the eating of two chocolate biscuits – but it was also a big thing, saying much about human nature and how in spite of everything we hoped for, in spite of all our efforts at betterment, there were still people who stole chocolate biscuits when they could well afford to pay for them. For this was not some hungry person succumbing to the temptation to snatch a bite to eat, this was a well-fed woman eating two chocolate biscuits that did not belong to her, even though she could well afford to pay the few pula needed to buy them.

Mma Potokwani found it hard to believe what she had just seen. 'Have you ever seen anything like that, Mma Ramotswe?' she asked. 'Ever?'

Mma Ramotswe shook her head. In the course of her work she had seen things that had tested her view of humanity – that had stretched her patience and capacity for forgiveness to near breaking point. Mma Potokwani, she suspected, had also seen things that were capable of distressing even those most inured to bad behaviour; and yet both of them, experienced as they were in the ways of the world, were shocked to see the naked disregard for the property of others that Violet Sephotho now showed. And what they found particularly hard to take was the brazenness of it all. Violet Sephotho had glanced around to check that she was not being observed, but there had been none of the furtiveness that can show that the perpetrator of a crime knows that what they are doing is wrong. This showed impunity: there was no other word for it.

Mma Potokwani did not consult Mma Ramotswe before she

acted. Had she done so, Mma Ramotswe might have demurred. It was not that she did not believe in the rightness of apprehending one caught *in flagrante delicto* – she did, and she would never hesitate to intervene to prevent a malefactor from harming another. This, though, was different: the crime had been committed and there was now nothing to be done about it. It was clear to her that any accusation would be met by a flat denial: Violet Sephotho would simply say that she had not eaten any chocolate biscuits, and would ask for proof, of which, of course, they had none. And would they be backed up by the supermarket manager? That was unlikely, she thought. While they would always act when they caught a shoplifter red-handed, they were wary of accusing customers of stealing. There had been an awkward case only a few months earlier in which a store had wrongly accused a woman of stealing a dress when she was, in fact, wearing an outfit that she had purchased from that same store a week earlier, and for which she had the receipt in her handbag. The situation had been made even more embarrassing by the fact that the woman in question was not only a director of the company from which the store rented its premises, but was also a lay minister in a local church. You should not accuse the Pope of stealing communion wine, Mr J. L. B. Matekoni had observed when he read a report on the incident in the *Botswana Daily News*.

None of this was in Mma Potokwani's mind as she propelled her shopping cart in Violet's direction. She was followed by Mma Ramotswe who, although not eager for a fray, felt that she should be at hand to provide witness support for her friend.

'Excuse me,' said Mma Potokwani, in a voice that Mma Ramotswe recognised as normally reserved for misbehaving orphans. 'Excuse me, Mma, but I think you have forgotten something.'

Violet Sephotho had been busy with her mobile phone. Now she turned round and stared at Mma Potokwani in astonishment.

'Are you talking to me?' she asked.

Mma Potokwani noticed the absence of the *Mma*, but one rudeness would not be met with another, and her voice was icily polite as she continued, 'It's just that I notice you have not put that packet of chocolate biscuits into your cart.' She paused, fixing the younger woman with a challenging stare. 'I wouldn't want you to forget to take it to the checkout, Mma. Imagine how disappointed you'd be when you got home and discovered that the chocolate biscuits . . .' And now came the essence of the charge – the main indictment – as solemn and as weighty as a carefully worded article of impeachment: '. . . the packet of chocolate biscuits you began to consume before payment was not there, but had been left behind in the store. You would not want that, Mma – I am sure of it. And I think that Mma Ramotswe here, who saw everything that I saw, would agree with me.'

Mma Ramotswe had been skilfully drawn in, and there was more to come.

'Mma Ramotswe,' Mma Potokwani went on, 'as you know, is a private detective. A detective, Mma. Such people have sharp eyesight – they notice things. And so if I felt, as I well might feel in the circumstances, that my eyes had deceived me, I would be able to turn to her and say, "Am I right in my recollection of what I think I have just seen, Mma Ramotswe?" That is what I could say, Mma Sephotho, if I felt at all uncertain about the evidence of my own eyes – which I do not, by the way.'

Violet Sephotho knew who they were, and she knew, too, that she had crossed swords, directly or indirectly, with them on previous occasions. Now she played for time. 'I am not quite sure who you ladies are,' she said. 'And I really don't know what you're talking about. What is all this about chocolate biscuits? Are you looking for chocolate biscuits, not that either of you large ladies should be eating too much chocolate, if you ask me.'

The insult struck home. As it was delivered, Mma Ramotswe noticed that Mma Potokwani was beginning to quiver with rage. It was a strange sight – and she could not help but think of a large jelly wobbling in a fridge.

Reaching out past Violet, Mma Potokwani snatched the opened packet of biscuits from the shelf.

'You see this, Mma,' she spluttered. 'This packet has been opened, and there will be two biscuits missing from inside. And where will they be, Mma? In your stomach – that is where. And that, Mma, is theft, and it is our duty – as citizens of this country – to report such things to the management.'

Violet stared at Mma Potokwani. Then, turning abruptly on her heel, she left her shopping cart and began to walk purposefully towards the office behind the checkout tills. For her part, Mma Potokwani seemed uncertain what to do, and in this delay lost precious seconds. By the time Mma Ramotswe spoke, Violet was almost at the door of the office.

'I think she is going to . . .' began Mma Ramotswe. She trailed off. Violet had entered the office but had rapidly re-emerged in the company of a man whom Mma Ramotswe recognised as the manager of the supermarket. Now he and Violet Sephotho were striding towards them, with Violet gesticulating and pointing in their direction.

The manager's manner was brisk and confrontational, but when he saw that it was Mma Ramotswe and Mma Potokwani to whom Violet had led him, this rapidly changed.

'These are the two ladies?' he asked Violet, in a puzzled tone.

'Yes, these are the ladies who helped themselves to chocolate biscuits, Rra,' said Violet. 'I saw them with my own eyes.'

Mma Ramotswe thought that Mma Potokwani was about to burst. She saw the buttons on the matron's blouse twist under the strain of her heaving, outraged breathing.

'Us?' cried Mma Potokwani. 'Us? You are saying that Mma Ramotswe and I ate the chocolate biscuits?'

Violet Sephotho averted her eyes from the looks of anger and incredulity emanating from the victims of her slander. 'Of course, they are denying it,' she said to the manager. 'What do you expect, Rra?'

The manager shook his head in his confusion. 'But this is Mma Ramotswe,' he said. 'And this is Mma Potokwani. These are two very respectable ladies. They are well known to me.'

'Oh, I'm sure they are respectable,' said Violet, her voice heavy with irony. 'That is often the case with shoplifting, Rra – you should know that. It is respectable people who are caught – sometimes very respectable people.' She paused, and added, 'As in this case.'

Mma Potokwani's voice rose in anger. 'I have never heard such lies, Rra. Not in ten, fifteen years, maybe more. *She* is the one who has eaten these chocolate biscuits, and *we* are the ones who saw her do it.'

The manager looked at Violet Sephotho, waiting for a refutation.

'If you believe that, Rra,' said Violet, 'then you will believe anything. Anything.'

The manager sighed. 'But Mma Sephotho, I find it very unlikely that these ladies would steal anything. I think maybe you have been confused. I think we should let this matter drop straight away.'

Violet's eyes narrowed. 'You'd like some proof, Rra? Well, look at that packet – yes, that one. Is it open? Yes, it is. Somebody has opened it. And then look inside – are there two biscuits missing? Yes, I think you will find that there are.'

The manager examined the packet that had been pressed into his hands by Violet Sephotho. Before he could say anything, Mma Ramotswe said, 'That is the very packet that this lady took from the shelf, Rra. That is the very packet from which we saw *her* take two chocolate biscuits and put them into her mouth—'

'Her untruthful, wicked mouth,' interjected Mma Potokwani.

The manager looked embarrassed. 'I am sure there is some explanation,' he said. 'I am sure that this is no more than a misunderstanding.'

Violet pulled herself up to her full height. 'Well, I have had enough of all this lying,' she announced. 'These ladies may have nothing better to do than go about the place stealing chocolate biscuits and telling lies about innocent people, but I certainly have more important things to do with my time. So I am going to leave this to you, Rra, and to the conscience of these so-called respectable ladies.'

And with that, she flounced off, swaying her hips – for the benefit of the manager, Mma Ramotswe thought, as there was nobody else there to enjoy the display.

The manager looked apologetically first at Mma Ramotswe and then at Mma Potokwani. 'I am sorry about that,' he said. 'I think there has been a big misunderstanding.'

Mma Ramotswe made a placatory gesture, but there was no such concession from Mma Potokwani. 'There has been no mis-understanding, Rra,' she said. 'But there have been plenty of lies.'

The manager hesitated, but then he showed his agreement, with an almost imperceptible nod of the head. 'I think you're right, Mma Potokwani. I have never liked that lady very much.'

Mma Ramotswe felt that nothing more needed to be said. 'In that case, Rra, we should detain you no longer. You must be very busy.'

He looked at her with gratitude. 'Yes, Mma. I do not like these scenes, and I have a lot of work to do. I would rather be doing that work than dealing with this sort of thing.'

After he had said his goodbyes and left them, Mma Potokwani turned to Mma Ramotswe and said, 'Now I have seen everything, Mma.'

'I think we should finish our shopping,' said Mma Ramotswe. 'And then we can have tea in the café. There is much to talk about.' She paused, and then added quickly, 'Not about this, of course, not about Violet Sephotho, but about other things. I have some important matters to discuss, Mma.'

The café was busy, but they found a table outside, in the open, but protected from the sun by the shadow of the building. Mma Ramotswe could tell that her friend was still seething over the incident in the supermarket, but since she did not want to revisit that rather painful episode, she lost no time in bringing Mma Potokwani up to date on the two issues that were pressing on her mind: Mr J. L. B. Matekoni's alarming plans to raise money by mortgaging the garage, and the case of Mr Mophephu and his aged father.

She dealt with the garage first, telling Mma Potokwani of how what she had thought might be depression was, in fact, something rather simpler – dissatisfaction.

'We can feel dissatisfied with something, can't we,' she said, 'without being depressed?'

'Of course,' said Mma Potokwani. 'Half the people in the world are dissatisfied with things the way they are. You ask them. You say: would you like to be living somewhere else, married to somebody other than your present spouse, doing a different job et cetera et cetera, and how will they reply, Mma? They will say – or half of them will say – "Oh yes, we are dissatisfied with all those things." Of course, for those people, nothing will ever be right. If they move into a new house, after a few years you ask them that question again and they will say, "This house is not quite right – I would like to be somewhere else." And so on, Mma.' She smiled, and shook her head. 'That is just the way people are, Mma. It is nothing to do with being depressed.'

'Well that is how I think it is for him,' said Mma Ramotswe. 'He has compared his life with the life of one of the people he was at school with – one T. K. Molefi – and he has decided that he has been a failure. And this Molefi has poured something into his ear, Mma – some potion, with the result that Mr J. L. B. Matekoni is determined to go into business with him.'

'In another garage, Mma?'

Mma Ramotswe explained about the bus company, and as she did so, Mma Potokwani's eyes widened. 'I do not like the sound of that one little bit, Mma Ramotswe,' she said. 'There are too many people who think they can have a bus company. All those minibus people – there are hundreds of them. And many of them lost their money. I have known two people in that position, Mma – no, three, now that I come to think of it. None of them has been successful. The wheels fall off . . . not really, of course, but you know what I mean.'

'Sometimes the actual wheels *will* fall off,' said Mma Ramotswe ruefully.

Mma Potokwani sighed. 'You will have to do your best to argue him out of it. What about getting Phuti Radiphuti to have a word with him. He is a businessman, and he may be able to warn him of the consequences of a risky investment.'

'I could try.'

'You must, Mma.' Mma Potokwani paused. 'And what about yoga? Have you made any progress with that?'

'I have not,' said Mma Ramotswe. 'I shall see what I can do.'

Mma Potokwani looked at her with sympathy. 'It is not easy to be married to men when they are at this stage in life, Mma. It is the male menopause, you know. I have been reading about it. Men start to behave in exactly this way at that time of life. It will pass, of course, but not before . . .'

She did not finish the sentence. Mma Ramotswe waited.

'Not before real damage is done,' Mma Potokwani concluded. 'But let us not fret too much, Mma Ramotswe. What is this other matter you wanted to talk about?'

'I have been asked to deal with a very tricky case, Mma Potokwani. And I am not sure how to tackle it. May I tell you about it? On the basis of strict confidence, of course.'

'I shall tell nobody,' said Mma Potokwani, taking a sip of her tea. Tea and juicy confidences – what could be better, she thought. It was almost enough to make one forget that terrible incident in the supermarket.

Mma Ramotswe told her about Mr Mophephu. 'I am not quite sure about him,' she said. 'I want to give him the benefit of the doubt, but there is something about him that makes me feel a bit concerned. I cannot put my finger on it.'

'You never can, with those feelings,' said Mma Potokwani. 'But they are often right, you know. Something inside you is picking up a warning signal.'

'Well, that may be so, Mma. But, anyway, whatever I feel about this man, I must do my best by him. He is my client, and I must do what I can.'

'Exactly right,' said Mma Potokwani. 'Now tell me about him.'

She told Mma Potokwani about Mr Mophephu Senior and about the farm. The moment she mentioned that, of course, Mma Potokwani knew exactly who she was talking about. 'That is old Fidelis Mophephu,' she said. 'He is a good man, I think. One of the housemothers worked for him years ago and speaks highly of him.'

Mma Ramotswe filed the testimonial away. Mma Potokwani's housemothers tended to be good judges of character, just as Mma Potokwani herself was, and she would bear this positive remark in mind.

'I wondered what it was that Mr Mophephu wanted me to do,' she said, 'and then it came out. He told me that his father is being looked after by a nurse. He said that this woman was very wicked. That was the word he used, Mma – wicked.'

Mma Potokwani interrupted her. 'I know what's coming, Mma. This nurse is trying to get old Mr Mophephu to marry her. In that way she'll get the property.' She shook her head sadly. 'It's an old story, that one, Mma: the thirty-year-old nurse marries the eighty-five-year-old man. She says it is all for love. He says the same thing. And the family say: "Ow, this nurse is a wicked woman." It is an old story, Mma.'

Mma Ramotswe said that it was not quite like that in this case. 'You are almost right, Mma, but not quite. Mr Mophephu said that his father has no intention of marrying anybody. He said that his father is no longer interested in that department. He said, though, that his father has made a will.'

Mma Potokwani rolled her eyes. 'Oh, Mma, I can see what is coming. I can see it very clearly now.'

'Yes, he has made a will. He has left most of his property – his shops and his savings in the bank – to his three children. There is no problem with that. He has more than one house, this Fidelis

Mophephu, and so he has been able to give each of them a house somewhere. They are very lucky. But then there is his farm, which is on very good land. It has a very fine house, too – you may have seen it from the road near Kgali Siding.'

'I have seen it,' Mma Potokwani confirmed.

'He has left that to the nurse.'

Mma Potokwani drew in her breath. For a few moments she said nothing, but then she exhaled in a long – and ominous – sigh. 'Mma Ramotswe, I have heard of that sort of thing happening. It is very difficult for families.'

'I am sure it is, Mma.' But even as she said this, Mma Ramotswe rehearsed her reservations. People could become very fond of those who looked after them, and there must be cases where a long-term carer was more deserving than family members, particularly if those family members were grasping. If a carer gave years of service, why should that not be recognised in this way? Why should people have a claim to property simply because they were related to the owner? Relatives could be distant, in every sense; they might rarely see the one with whom they claimed kinship, and yet if there was a prospect of an inheritance, they were quick to profess their attachment to the person who had died. She remembered attending one funeral in particular, that of a friend of her father's, where the loudest wailing came from some distant cousins who were keen to establish their claim to the property that had been left behind. They had never even met the man who had died, she was told, but since he was unmarried, and childless, and had no surviving brothers or sisters, they were potential heirs. They had not bothered with him during his lifetime, but now their grief was on public display, the forced tears trickling down their cheeks ('They have onions in their handkerchiefs,' Mr J. L. B. Matekoni had whispered to her).

It occurred to Mma Potokwani to ask how Mr Mophephu had known about the provisions of his father's will. 'Did he tell his son?' she asked. 'And if he did, why would he tell him?'

Mr Mophephu had explained this to Mma Ramotswe. 'He told me that he had been to see his father and had seen some papers in the house. There was a letter from a lawyer in Gaborone and there was a copy of the will with it. It said that the other copy, the original, was in the lawyer's safe.'

Mma Potokwani listened intently. 'That's what they do, Mma. They keep a copy in their office so that when you become late they have it there. And it also stops people from interfering with the will . . .' She left the sentence unfinished; the implication was clear.

And Mma Ramotswe picked it up. 'I think he understands that there can be no question of destroying the will. I told him that, anyway. I would never be party to something like that, Mma.'

Mma Potokwani shrugged. 'So I can't see that he can do anything. Not really. Can you?'

Mma Ramotswe hesitated. 'That's what I wanted to say to him. But I did not, Mma. It seemed to me that he may have a point, you see. If this nurse is what he says she is . . .'

'A legacy hunter,' prompted Mma Potokwani.

'Yes, a legacy hunter . . . if she has forced a vulnerable old man to make a will out in her favour, then should she be allowed to get away with it?'

Mma Potokwani had no trouble answering that. 'Of course not.' She and Mma Ramotswe saw the world in the same way – they always had. They both believed in justice; they both believed that sooner or later those who did wrong would be defeated. The trouble was that on occasion it took some time for the scales of justice to be righted by those whose job it was to do so.

Sometimes those people simply did not see what others could see; sometimes their hands were tied; sometimes they felt threatened. And all of that meant that there were times when it was left to people like them, a private detective and the matron of an orphan farm, to do what had to be done.

Mma Potokwani looked thoughtful. 'Surely there is some way of having a will like that set aside? If you are elderly and unable to look after yourself, surely the law protects you against unscrupulous people like that?' She spread her hands in a gesture of defeat. 'Otherwise, Mma, what hope is there? If the courts cannot stop this sort of thing, then what use is the law?'

Mma Ramotswe said that there could be help from the law. She had asked Mma Makutsi to ask Phuti's lawyer about this, and the lawyer had sent a message back saying that there was something called the 'rules of undue influence' that you could use to attack such documents. These rules, he had said, were made for exactly this sort of case. But you had to be able to prove that the person who had been unduly influenced could not resist, and that could be hard. There would have to be evidence.

'I have had to say to my client that I will look into it,' Mma Ramotswe said. 'I need to meet this nurse and see whether she has been up to something like this.'

'I think that is right,' said Mma Potokwani. 'You should investigate.'

Mma Ramotswe reached for the teapot. She poured a fresh cup of tea for herself and one for Mma Potokwani.

'Of course, Mma Potokwani,' she said, 'I don't really know much about nurses.'

Mma Potokwani waited.

'But I think you do,' Mma Ramotswe continued.

'You want my help, Mma? Is that it?'

Mma Ramotswe nodded. 'You were a nurse, weren't you, Mma Potokwani? You were a nurse before you became a matron?'

'A long time ago, yes.'

'That doesn't matter. I would very much like your help, Mma. I have rather a lot on my plate at the moment, what with Mr J. L. B. Matekoni and his ridiculous plan, and . . .' She stopped. For a few moments, she felt as if the burdens of life were just too much. Why could things not be simpler? She closed her eyes. Would there ever be a time when there were no problems to be sorted out? Would there ever be a time when we could all live together peacefully and without . . . and without *undue influence*?

Mma Potokwani was watching her friend. Now she reached across the table and put her hand gently on Mma Ramotswe's forearm. 'Dear friend,' she said, 'of course I shall help you. Of course I shall. And we shall start tomorrow, first thing. After breakfast, that is.'

'I would never do anything before breakfast,' said Mma Ramotswe.

And they both laughed. On that issue, they were at one, and always had been. A good breakfast was essential if one were to make any progress in dealing with any of life's issues. That, Mma Ramotswe had always said, was well known.

Chapter Seven

A Wind From the Past

Mma Ramotswe and Mma Potokwani, two traditionally built ladies, two women of Botswana, and, in their individual ways, two agents of justice, drove down the farm track leading to the house of Mr Fidelis Mophephu, retired businessman, farmer, father and grandfather, and owner of a fine herd of Brahman cattle. These cattle, gathered in a paddock near the farmhouse, were now congregating around a watering trough over which a metal windmill, ancient and cranky, turned its blades against the sky.

At the wheel of the van was Mma Ramotswe, struggling to avoid the potholes in the eroded surface of the track; at her side, Mma Potokwani, gazing at the hills behind the farmhouse, said, 'You know, Mma Ramotswe, I could live here, I think. If I could retire, I would love to be in a place like this, with my cattle, and my husband, and the sky of Botswana above my head. What more could anybody want?'

'It would be a very good place to be when you have finished working,' agreed Mma Ramotswe. 'It would be a good place to sit in the shade ...'

'Or in the sun during the winter,' said Mma Potokwani. 'When the air is cold and you need the sun. You would sit outside and think about things.'

'Yes,' said Mma Ramotswe. 'And not have to worry about anything very much. You would be at that stage in life where you are happy to let other people get on with it. You would stop shaking your head over what was happening in the world. You would grow your beans and your spinach ...'

Mma Potokwani drew in her breath wistfully. 'Spinach, Mma. I would grow a lot of spinach. It is my favourite.'

'And so good for you, Mma Potokwani. If you lived in a place like this and ate spinach every day, then you would live to be at least one hundred. Maybe more.' Mma Ramotswe smiled as she continued, 'The government might forget about you altogether and then discover that you were one hundred and ten, perhaps, and—'

'And claim all the credit,' quipped Mma Potokwani. 'They would say you have lived so long because of their wise policies.'

Mma Ramotswe caused the car to swerve suddenly to avoid what appeared to be a small crevasse in the track. 'I don't think many people can come out here,' she said. 'This track is not used very much, I think.'

'Does he not come out?' asked Mma Potokwani. 'The son? Does he not come out to visit his father?'

'Perhaps not as much as he should,' said Mma Ramotswe. 'I

don't want to be unjust, Mma, but I don't think that man likes his father very much. I did not detect any warmth.'

'Perhaps it is one of these cases when the family is waiting for the older generation to die,' said Mma Potokwani. 'That is not uncommon, Mma – particularly when the older generation has all the money.'

'That may be true,' said Mma Ramotswe. 'But I don't think we should make up our minds before we have seen what's what.'

'I would never do that,' said Mma Potokwani.

Mma Ramotswe remembered what Clovis Andersen had said about this. 'You know that book I have, Mma? *The Principles of Private Detection*? The one by Mr Andersen?'

'I have heard you talk about it,' said Mma Potokwani. And she had – quite often, in fact, and she had reflected on how useful she might have found a similar book, perhaps entitled *The Matron's Handbook*, that would give the reader guidance on the many challenges confronting the matrons of children's homes or other residential establishments. And there were many challenges in her calling: every day something arose that made her stop and think: *what do I do?* Perhaps she could write such a book herself, and make its scope a bit broader by covering the whole issue of bringing up children. She could talk about how to manage two-year-olds and their tantrums; she could talk about the teenage years, and how parents might survive those; she could deal with the issue of manners and consideration for others and how to instil awareness of those things in children in an age when there were so many voices proclaiming the very opposite message. It would quickly become a very large book, she thought, and she would never have time to write it, because her days were taken up with doing those precise things that the book would talk about; unless, of course, the message could somehow be distilled, as it probably could, into a simple piece of advice, applicable to all situations, which was perhaps even just one word – and that word was *love*.

'Clovis Andersen says somewhere,' Mma Ramotswe continued, 'I forget which page it is on, he says: *Never try to reach a conclusion before you reach the conclusion.*'

Mma Potokwani frowned. 'I am sure he is right, Mma. But what exactly does he mean?'

'I think he means that you should not make up your mind until you have looked at everything that needs to be looked at – in other words, until you have reached the conclusion of the enquiry.'

Mma Potokwani considered this. 'I think he may be right, Mma.' And then, after further thought, she said, more emphatically this time, 'That is undoubtedly true, Mma Ramotswe. I have not thought of that before – well, not in that exact way. But now that I do, I see it makes perfect sense.'

'Mr Andersen always makes sense,' said Mma Ramotswe. She had never known Clovis Andersen to be wrong – not once – and Mma Makutsi was in agreement with her on that. There were things on which she and Mma Makutsi had differing opinions, but on the relevance and essential truth of what Clovis Andersen said, they were at one. And if Clovis Andersen had been there with them in the van, he would undoubtedly have counselled caution. 'Wait until you have seen this nurse,' he would say. 'Then form an opinion – not before.' That was the wisdom of Muncie, Indiana, where Clovis Andersen lived – and it applied everywhere, it seemed to Mma Ramotswe; it was as true, no doubt, in Muncie, Indiana, as it was here on this patch of Botswana, under the gaze of that outcrop of granite hills, in front of this farmhouse at which they were now drawing up, a small cloud of dust following them, under the silence of this sky, watched by the eyes of the patient cattle at their trough.

'That,' whispered Mma Ramotswe, as they emerged from her tiny white van, 'is the nurse, Mma. That is her, you see, sitting on the veranda.'

Mma Potokwani followed Mma Ramotswe's gaze. The front veranda, running the full length of the house, had been enclosed with protective panels of fine gauze, designed to keep out flies and mosquitoes. This used to be a common feature of houses in the country, especially those on farms, where livestock could attract hordes of flies; or those near water, where stinging clouds of mosquitoes could make the evening hours an agony for the unprotected. Latterly, people had stopped bothering to build verandas, with their cool spaces, shaded from the sun, and had turned away from protective screens, seeming to prefer wide-open doorways and windows because they thought they looked more modern. They discovered, of course, that there was a reason for doing things in the traditional way of a place, which was as much the case with customs as with architecture. But Mr Fidelis Mophephu was not like this, Mma Potokwani was pleased to see: he had a shady veranda; he had mosquito screens; he had beautiful, old-fashioned cattle that would gladden the heart of any person in Botswana who knew about cattle and what they meant; and he had a tall, rather formidable-looking nurse who was not getting up from her chair on that shady veranda and coming out into the sunlight to find out who their visitors were.

'Her name is Bontle Tutume,' Mma Ramotswe said to Mma Potokwani out of the side of her mouth, and then she stepped forward and greeted the nurse in the traditional way, enquiring as to her sleep and her health while running a discreet professional eye up and down the figure of the other woman, reaching conclusions, but, out of deference to Mr Clovis Andersen, only *tentative* conclusions.

'I am the lady who telephoned you,' Mma Ramotswe said. 'I am the friend of Mr Baboloki Mophephu.'

Bontle inclined her head. 'He is the son of Mr Fidelis Mophephu.'

'Yes, so I believe,' said Mma Ramotswe. She felt a momentary irritation: of course he was the son – there was no need for her to be told that. But then she thought: the nurse is only being polite, and she smiled and continued, 'Baboloki said that if we were in the area we should drop in and see his father.'

'We were driving past,' said Mma Potokwani, helpfully.

But her comment did not prove to be as helpful as she had intended. In fact, it had the opposite effect, as Bontle turned to her and said, 'Driving past to where, Mma? I do not think this road goes anywhere. In fact, it stops down that way – over there.'

Mma Ramotswe tried not to smile. Mma Potokwani was second to none as a matron, but perhaps as a private detective she had a certain amount to learn. Mma Ramotswe quickly took over: 'We went too far, Mma. We were at Kgali Siding – you know that place where the old garage was, and then those offices. That place. But it was closed and so we drove on.'

The nurse frowned. 'What was closed, Mma?'

'The office of the people we were going to see,' answered Mma Ramotswe, wishing to bring that part of the conversation to an end before it could be subjected to further scrutiny. *Always have your cover story well prepared*, wrote Clovis Andersen. *Never make things up on the hoof.* 'But all that is neither here nor there, Mma. We hope that this is not inconvenient.'

Bontle hesitated, and for a few moments Mma Ramotswe thought that she was going to say that it was not a convenient time, but she did not. Instead, she said, 'It is always good to get visitors when you live out here.'

Mma Potokwani, who had been a bit tense after her initial unhelpful comment, now relaxed. 'I know what you mean, Mma,' she said. 'I live out at Tlokweng, at the children's home there – you may know it. And I find that I am always happy to get visitors from Gaborone. It is how I keep in touch with what is happening in the world.'

Bontle said, 'Yes, the world: there is always something happening, isn't there? People go around doing things – causing trouble, most of the time. Politicians, and so on.'

'Oh, there is plenty of that,' agreed Mma Potokwani. 'Sometimes I think how nice it would be to come across a politician who says: "I am not going to do anything. I am not going to tell you what to do." Can you imagine any of them saying that, Mma? I cannot, but I think such a politician would get many votes from people who are fed up with people shouting at one another.'

'There is too much shouting,' said Mma Ramotswe.

Bontle nodded. 'That is true, Mma. And that is why it is good to live out here. There is no shouting here.'

This exchange now reached its natural end, and a short silence ensued. During this, Mma Ramotswe continued her discreet assessment of Bontle. She was educated – that was obvious enough – and of course if she was a qualified nurse, then she would have had more years of education than she herself had enjoyed. And since she was considerably younger than Mma Potokwani, then she was probably more highly trained than the matron herself, who had completed her nursing training a long time ago, when standards were not so high, and when less scientific expertise was required of nurses. It was different now – nurses did many of the things that doctors used to do, and they needed years of training. But why, she wondered, would one need a fully trained nurse to look after just one elderly man? The sort of nursing that required, surely, was simple day-to-day care: getting him out of bed and dressed, for instance; helping him with his bath or shower, and so on. These were not things that needed much scientific training, even if they did require skills that not everybody would possess.

'You will be thirsty,' said Bontle. 'You must come in and sit on the veranda. I will make some tea.'

Mma Ramotswe accepted with alacrity. 'We are both very thirsty,' she said. 'I think I can speak for my friend, Mma Potokwani, on that, Mma.'

Mma Potokwani chuckled. 'I won't argue with you, Mma Ramotswe.'

They followed Bontle onto the veranda. It was cool, out of the sun, and the mosquito screen helped with the glare.

'This is very comfortable,' said Mma Ramotswe, as Bontle indicated the seats they were to take. Then she said, 'Is Mr Mophephu up and about, Mma?'

Bontle pointed towards the interior of the house. 'He is having his rest, but I will wake him after we have drunk our tea. I do not like him to sleep too much during the day, because that means that he does not sleep so well at night.'

'Very wise,' said Mma Ramotswe. 'My husband is like that. If he has a long sleep on Saturday afternoon, then in the evening he is wide awake.'

'And you do not want your husband to be wide awake at night,' Bontle said.

Mma Ramotswe was taken aback by the remark, which, on one interpretation, was vaguely suggestive, but when Bontle laughed and said, 'I mean, walking about the house,' she too laughed. She decided that she rather liked this woman. She had been prepared to dislike her, but so far she had seen nothing to justify Mr Baboloki Mophephu's harsh assessment. She could understand why he might be suspicious, but the whole situation, she felt, was turning out to be rather more complex than she had imagined it would be.

'No, that is true, Mma,' she said. 'My husband sometimes fixes things at night. I wake up and he is out of bed fiddling with the works of the refrigerator or replacing a washer in a tap – that sort of thing.'

'Of course, he is a mechanic,' said Bontle. 'You must expect that sort of thing.'

Mma Ramotswe smiled. 'Yes, of course, mechanics are always . . .' She stopped. How did Bontle know that Mr J. L. B. Matekoni was a mechanic? Had she, or Mma Potokwani, said anything? She did not think so.

Bontle was waiting for her to finish. 'Mechanics are what, Mma?' she asked.

Mma Ramotswe looked down at the floor. A line of small ants, disciplined and industrious, was making its way across the polished concrete surface, heading towards the inside of the house. Her eye followed it back, and she thought she saw the point at which it surmounted the top step that led down to the garden. Why did ants migrate like this? For the same reason that people did – because they thought that life would be better, that there would be better food, that there would be fewer predators, perhaps, and they wanted security for their ant children, just as we did.

She tore herself away from the ants. They were harmless, these little ones, unlike their larger cousins, the Matabele ants, that could inflict a painful bite; enough, if delivered in sufficient numbers, to paralyse a limb. She looked up and met Bontle's gaze.

'Did I tell you he was a mechanic, Mma?'

That was pure Clovis Andersen. She remembered his advice: *Do not ask about anything in general terms, because the other person may give an answer that is more suited to a totally different question. A focused question results in a focused answer.*

Bontle was unfazed. 'I don't think you did, Mma. But I know who you are, you see. You are that lady who has the No. 1 Ladies' Detective Agency. And everybody knows that you are married to the man who runs that funny little garage next door – *Racing Motors*, or whatever it's called.'

Mma Ramotswe bristled. Funny little garage indeed! 'Tlokweng Road *Speedy* Motors,' she corrected. 'It is a very good garage, Mma. I can recommend it.'

Bontle realised that she had given offence. 'I'm very sorry, Mma. I didn't mean to be rude about it. I really didn't. I like small garages. I do not like these big places where they charge you so much every time they open their mouths.'

It was another point in Bontle's favour: she had not tried to cover anything up, but had given what appeared to be a direct and truthful explanation as to how she knew about Mr J. L. B. Matekoni and then, on top of that, she had apologised in a way that made Mma Ramotswe think that she actually meant it.

There was a further surprise. 'And I think,' Bontle continued, 'that you have come to see me as a detective, Mma. I do not mind that. I am happy to answer any questions.'

It took Mma Ramotswe a moment to recover from the shock of this disarming offer. Mma Potokwani, who had reacted to the tactlessness over Tlokweng Road Speedy Motors with a barely suppressed smile, now grinned broadly. She looked at Mma Ramotswe expectantly.

It took Mma Ramotswe a moment or two to recover her composure. 'Ah,' she said, 'you have been a bit of a detective yourself, Mma.'

Bontle acknowledged the compliment with an inclination of her head. Then she said, 'It did not take much, Mma. I look out from my veranda and I see a white van coming up the track. Out of it steps Mma Ramotswe, widely known to be the owner of the No. 1 Ladies' Detective Agency, and her friend, Mma Potokwani, widely known to be a person to whom people may turn if they are in trouble.' She paused, allowing her remarks to sink in. 'So, what can one think in such circumstances, Mma, other than that there is some sort of investigation under way?'

Now it was the turn of Mma Potokwani to be taken aback. It was not just Mma Ramotswe who had been seen through: now she was exposed.

Bontle seemed to be enjoying herself. 'And then, if I ask myself a question, Mma Ramotswe, I ask myself this: who is likely to have sent a private detective to speak to me? There can be only one answer, and that is, of course, Mr Baboloki Mophephu, who does not like me, Mma, and who would love to do something – anything – to harm me.'

'Surely not, Mma,' said Mma Ramotswe. She spoke without conviction; she would register a token defence of her client only because she felt it was expected of her.

Bontle's cool command of the situation had won an ally – Mma Potokwani was now nodding vigorously. 'I can imagine that, Mma Tutume,' she said. 'Oh yes, I can just imagine that. Mma Ramotswe, you see, is a very charitable lady. You very rarely hear her say anything negative about anybody else, but in the case of Mr Baboloki Mophephu, I can tell you, Mma, she said that she did not like that man's manner. That is what she said, and if Mma Ramotswe says something like that, you can be sure that there is something very wrong.'

Mma Ramotswe looked away in embarrassment. 'Oh, Mma

Potokwani, I don't know,' she began. It was an attempt to regain control of the exchange, but it did not work. Bontle now raised her voice against any challenge.

'I am sure that is true, Mma Potokwani,' said the nurse. 'But I have nothing to hide. I do not care what that man does – the important thing is that his father, who is a very good man, is well looked after. That is the only thing – the only thing – that matters.'

She turned to Mma Ramotswe. 'So you can ask me anything you like, Mma. You can go inside the house and look in every cupboard and every drawer. You can even look under my bed, if you like, and you will not find anybody hiding there.'

Mma Ramotswe laughed. 'I have never found anybody hiding under a bed,' she said. 'I have often looked, but . . .' She shrugged, as if slightly disappointed to report such a negative result.

Bontle ignored this. 'I assume that this is to do with the will,' she said, fixing Mma Ramotswe with a cool stare.

Mma Ramotswe drew in her breath. She had not expected this. 'Yes, Mma,' she said quietly. 'That is why Mr Baboloki Mophephu came to see me. He thinks—'

Bontle's eyes flashed with anger. 'He thinks that I made Mr Fidelis leave this place to me: I know he thinks that. He thinks that I have been sitting here, plotting and scheming, and whispering into Mr Fidelis's ear: "Why not leave the farm to this nurse who is looking after you?"'

Mma Ramotswe said that she thought that was exactly what the son believed, and that it was this fear on his part that had brought him to her door with the request that she investigate. As she spoke, she wondered whether she should be saying any of this to the person who was, after all, the object of the enquiry, but then she told herself that she was actually revealing nothing:

121

everything that she said had been mentioned first by Bontle. Yet it did feel strange to her – almost as if there had been a reversal of roles, and that she was now acting for Bontle in a dispute with her employer's son.

Mma Potokwani had been listening without saying anything. Now she raised a hand. 'Did you talk to Mr Fidelis about this will, Mma? Did he say anything to you?'

Once again, the answer was immediate and, Mma Ramotswe felt, had the ring of honesty about it. 'Yes, he spoke, Mma. He said that he would like me to have this house – and the farm – when he goes. I remember his exact words. He said: "This is because I must make up for the past." That is what he said, Mma. I wasn't sure what he meant, but I think that he must have been talking about the years I have looked after him. I think that is what he meant.'

Mma Potokwani agreed. 'I can understand that,' she said. 'How long have you looked after him, Mma?'

'Ten years, Mma.' She looked down at her hands. The confident, almost challenging manner she had shown before was now replaced by a form of gentle reflection. *She is very fond of that man,* thought Mma Ramotswe. *That cannot be faked.*

'Ten years,' Bontle said again. 'Every day for ten years. Every day.' She looked at them anxiously. 'Not that I am complaining, *Bomma*. I do not begrudge him one day of that time. I do not.'

Mma Ramotswe's tone was gentle. 'That is a very long time, Mma Tutume.'

'He did not need much help at the beginning,' Bontle continued. 'But then he became more dependent. You know how it is – the body gets weaker.'

'I was a nurse,' said Mma Potokwani. 'So I know about these things, Mma.'

'Now he needs a lot of looking after,' Bontle went on. 'He likes to be independent, but it is too late for that. He is very grateful, though. He is a very polite man.'

'I'm sure you have been very kind to him,' said Mma Ramotswe.

As she spoke, a bell sounded from within the house – a faint, tinkling sound.

'That is him now,' said Bontle. 'He has a bell that he rings if he needs me. I will be getting him up now – if you would like to see him.'

Both Mma Ramotswe and Mma Potokwani nodded. 'If he is happy to see us,' Mma Ramotswe said.

'He is always pleased to see visitors.' Bontle paused. 'He is sometimes a little bit confused – his memory can be a little bit weak.'

'Whose isn't?' said Mma Potokwani, smiling.

They waited as Bontle left them to go inside. While she was away, they addressed one another in hushed tones.

'I like her,' said Mma Ramotswe. 'She is an honest woman, Mma Potokwani.'

Mma Potokwani put a finger to her lips. 'Not too loud, Mma, but yes, I think she is telling the truth.'

'I think she deserves whatever he has left her,' Mma Ramotse went on. 'If somebody looks after you for many years, then you should not just forget about them when you die.'

'Certainly not,' said Mma Potokwani. 'Of course you can understand that families feel strongly about property, but there are other people who may have a claim.'

'She is definitely not a wicked woman,' said Mma Ramotswe. 'That is pure nonsense, Mma. And I am going to tell Mr Baboloki Mophephu that. I don't care what he thinks.'

'He is probably one of those spoiled people who has always had everything he wants,' ventured Mma Potokwani. 'There are many people like that. As the country becomes richer, their numbers grow and grow.'

They heard footsteps within the house and the sound of a door being opened and closed. Then Bontle reappeared, followed by an elderly man, walking slowly, with the assistance of two sticks. When he saw his visitors he stopped, a broad, spontaneous smile crossing his face.

'I am a very fortunate man,' he said, 'to have two important ladies visiting me. I am very lucky.'

Mma Ramotswe moved forward to greet him. 'Rra, we are the fortunate ones. We know very little – you know a great deal. We are the ones who will be listening to you, Rra.'

This brought forth a laugh, deep and echoing, like a laugh one might hear in a cave.

'That is not true, Mma, I do not know very much these days. But I do know about names, and when Bontle said that there was a Mma Ramotswe who had come to see me, I thought: that can only be the wife of Obed Ramotswe. That is what I thought, Mma.'

Mma Ramotswe corrected him gently. 'Not wife, Rra – daughter. Obed Ramotswe was my father.'

She was not sure that he had heard her, as he made no mention of the correction. 'He knows cattle very well, Mma. He knows all about cattle.'

'He is late now, Rra. But yes, he knew about cattle.'

He seemed surprised. 'He is late, Mma? Your husband is late?'

'No, he was my father, Rra. And he is late.'

Mr Fidelis Mophephu shook his head sadly. 'There are so many people who are late these days, Mma Ramotswe. You say your husband is late?'

'No, my husband is not late, Rra. My husband is Mr J. L. B. Matekoni. He is not late at all. My father is the late one.'

The elderly man moved towards Mma Potokwani. 'And you, Mma – you are the sister of this lady?'

Bontle intervened. 'No, Rra. She is not the sister of Mma Ramotswe. This is Mma Potokwani, who is the matron of the Orphan Farm at Tlokweng – you know that place.'

'I wish she were my sister,' said Mma Ramotswe, smiling at Mma Potokwani. 'I can think of no better sister.'

'Is your husband late too?' Mr Fidelis Mophephu asked Mma Potokwani.

'He is not late, Rra. He is very well, I think.'

He bowed his head. 'That is a good thing to hear, Mma. There are many women these days whose husbands are now late. There are very many such ladies, and it will be difficult for them to find new husbands, I fear.'

Bontle laughed. 'Not everybody is looking for a husband, Rra. There are women who are very happy that they do not have a husband to have to look after.'

Mr Fidelis Mophephu seemed amused by this. 'We have always asked too much of women in this country,' he said. 'They hold up the sky on their shoulders. They do so much. And there are many men who never say thank you – not once, Mma Ramotswe. These men take these women for granted. They think it is their right to have somebody look after you. They really think that.'

'I have met many such men,' said Mma Ramotswe. 'But I think the number of men like that is going down, Rra. Men are beginning to learn, Rra.'

'Not before time,' said Mr Fidelis Mophephu. 'I will not be sorry when I wake up one day and find that Botswana is being run by women. I will say: about time, I think.'

Mma Ramotswe looked surprised. 'You have very modern ideas, Rra.'

125

'I am a very modern man, Mma,' he said. 'People look at me and think, "He is an old-fashioned man" – just because I use these sticks to walk.' He tapped his sticks on the floor. 'But they do not know that inside I am very modern. I am very up to date in my thinking, isn't that so, Bontle?'

'Very up to date,' Bontle agreed, smiling broadly. 'Latest outlook guaranteed – every time, Rra.'

He sat down, and his two visitors, who had risen to greet him, followed suit. For a few moments, nothing was said. Mma Ramotswe looked at Mma Potokwani, who looked at Bontle, who looked at Mr Fidelis Mophephu. Then Mma Ramotswe said, 'This is a very good house, Rra.'

Mr Fidelis Mophephu accepted the compliment graciously. 'That is true, Mma. It is a good house.'

She hesitated, but decided to go ahead. She wanted to be tactful, but there were occasions on which it was best to be direct and this, she suspected, might be one of them. 'I'm sure that you will live for a long time yet, Rra, but none of us lives forever.'

'Thank goodness,' Mma Potokwani interjected. She sighed. 'I would not like to live forever. I would get very tired, I think. And seeing the same people day after day for all time—' She broke off. 'Although I wouldn't mind seeing you every day, Mma Ramotswe – I was not thinking of you.'

Rather to her surprise, Mr Fidelis Mophephu responded to the humour in this remark. 'You had to say that, Mma,' he chuckled. 'Otherwise, Mma Ramotswe would have thought that you would not want to see her every day until the end of time. Hah!'

Mma Ramotswe laughed. 'You are right, Rra.' She waited a moment or two, before continuing, 'But I was wondering whether your children will live here when you eventually – and

126

that will not be for many years, I think – become late, as we all will do eventually, one way or another.'

He was not offended. 'I have left the farm to this lady here,' he said, nodding towards Bontle. 'It is what I have to do.'

Mma Ramotswe wondered why he should have said he had to do it. Did this suggest that somebody had forced him to make the will? Was this the 'undue influence' mentioned by Phuti's lawyer?

She tried to make her question sound casual. 'But why would you have to do it, Rra?' she asked.

Mr Fidelis Mophephu seemed surprised by the question. He answered now with the air of one who was stating the obvious. 'Because you must look after the wife you have left,' he said.

Mma Ramotswe exchanged glances with Mma Potokwani. 'Wife, Rra?'

Mr Fidelis Mophephu made a quick gesture with his right hand – as one might do in dismissing a minor error. 'Yes. Wife. I mean Bontle. This lady.'

Mma Ramotswe smiled. 'Of course, I see. You want Bontle to have it. You said *wife*.'

'I meant Bontle,' he said. 'I have given a lot of property to my children. They do not need everything.'

Mma Potokwani said that she thought this was entirely reasonable. Bontle, quite correctly, in Mma Ramotswe's opinion, did not express a view, but stared out across the paddock towards the hills while this delicate conversation took place. And Mr Fidelis Mophephu, it seemed, was tiring of the subject. He wanted to talk about Obed Ramotswe, whom he remembered from Mochudi days.

'Your father – you said he is late, Mma . . .'

Mma Ramotswe felt relieved that he now seemed to have grasped that Obed Ramotswe was her father. 'Yes, he is late, Rra.'

'Your father was a very good man, Mma Ramotswe. He's late, you say?'

'That is true, Rra. He has been late for some time now.'

'That is a great pity. There are many other people who deserve much more to be late than him, Mma – I can tell you that.'

Mma Ramotswe suppressed a smile. Perhaps we all had our lists of those, she thought, but she did not want to think along those lines.

'I bought some cattle from him, you know. It was a long time ago. He had some of the best cattle in the country.' He paused. 'They said that his cattle respected him. That is what people said, Mma.'

Mma Ramotswe always felt a very particular pleasure when somebody reminisced about her father's cattle. It did not happen very often now, as those days were slipping away into a past of which we were losing sight, but when it did occur, as now, she was strongly moved by it. She looked at Mr Fidelis Mophephu with affection. This was the old Botswana incarnate – the courtesy, the moral attention, the feeling for cattle. She lowered her eyes. She did not want to question this man any further; she did not want to intrude. And Mma Potokwani felt the same: she looked at her watch, and caught Mma Ramotswe's eye. 'I think, Mma . . .' she began.

'We must get back to town,' said Mma Ramotswe. 'I have enjoyed our talk so much, Rra.'

He smiled at her. She saw that his eyes were rheumy, as if they harboured dreams unspoken.

Bontle whispered to him gently – something about his pills. Mma Ramotswe rose to her feet. In the paddock, the metal vanes of the windmill pump turned slowly – responding to a wind from somewhere altogether elsewhere; a wind from the past, perhaps, if there could ever be such a thing.

Chapter Eight

Tea Is Required

While Mma Ramotswe and Mma Potokwani were visiting Mr Fidelis Mophephu, Tlokweng Road Speedy Motors was itself receiving a visit of some importance – from a valuer acting on behalf of the Commercial Division of the First Standard Bank, the bank with which Mr J. L. B. Matekoni had had an account ever since he had set up in business. It was also the bank that looked after the deposits, such as they were, of the No. 1 Ladies' Detective Agency, and its senior manager, Mr Tennyson Mogorosi, was on good terms with both Mma Ramotswe and Mma Makutsi. He knew Phuti Radiphuti too, as Phuti had provided the bank with office furniture for its branches throughout the country and the two men had also served on a church poverty relief committee together. 'Tennyson Mogorosi is a good man,' Phuti had said when Mma Ramotswe had spoken to him on the telephone about Mr J. L. B. Matekoni's doubtful bus proposition. 'I am sure he will at least listen to me if I speak to him about your concerns, but you must remember that business is business and I am not sure if a bank manager can pay too much attention to what a client's wife – or husband – might say about a proposed transaction.' He paused. Even as he spoke, he was changing his mind. What Mma Ramotswe was asking for was impossible, and so he now continued in a less uncertain tone, 'In fact, Mma, it is out of the question, I'm afraid. You cannot have this sort of interference, I think.'

Mma Ramotswe persisted. 'Could I not warn him, Rra? Could I not just say to him that I may not be involved in the garage business, but I am the wife and if the husband loses all his money in a foolish investment, then it is the wife who will suffer as well?'

Phuti was hesitant. 'I do not think that banks work that way, Mma. They cannot discuss their clients' affairs with another party.'

'But I am not another party, Rra,' exclaimed Mma Ramotswe. 'Since when is a wife "another party"?'

For a few moments, Phuti said nothing. Then, hesitantly, he said, 'I understand why you are concerned, Mma Ramotswe. Business is a risky . . . well, a risky business, I suppose, if you know what I mean.'

Mma Ramotswe waited. Then Phuti continued, 'A bus company might not be too bad a proposition, you know. You shouldn't write it off just like that.'

Mma Ramotswe did not sigh, but she might have. She did not want to hear this and she wondered whether it was not simply a matter of men closing ranks. And there was something else to consider: Phuti was a mild-minded man, she had always thought that, but perhaps there was a side to him that she had not seen before – a risk-taking side.

The discussion had ended there, and there would be no attempt made to sway the bank's decision. As a result, when the bank received an application for a loan on the security of the business premises of Tlokweng Road Speedy Motors, Mr Tennyson Mogorosi, having satisfied himself that the loan application was for a bona fide business purpose, had approved it in principle, subject to the property offered as security being of sufficient value. To ascertain whether this was the case, the bank had instructed one of its valuers, Mr Kabelano Tefo, to make an appointment to value the garage.

Mr Tefo was a slight man in his mid-thirties, dressed in a dark, shiny suit, and wearing a pair of thick pebble-lensed glasses to correct his long-standing myopia. When he arrived at the garage, Mr J. L. B. Matekoni was working with Fanwell on the fuel system of a delivery van.

'There is a man with glasses,' said Fanwell, tapping his employer on the shoulder. It was a habit of his, this tapping, and it irritated Mr J. L. B. Matekoni, who frequently found greasy fingerprints on his shirt and had to explain to Mma Ramotswe that these were not his, but Fanwell's.

Mr J. L. B. Matekoni knew immediately who their visitor was. Wiping his hands on a piece of the blue paper towel he kept for the purpose, he stepped forward to greet the valuer. 'You are very welcome to look around, Rra,' he began. 'Everything is as you will see it . . .'

Mr Tefo made a fussy, impatient gesture. 'That is why I am here, Rra. I am instructed by the bank to make a valuation of the premises and the business.'

Mr J. L. B. Matekoni nodded. 'Here it is before you,' he said. 'It is not a large place – as you can see.'

Mr Tefo pursed his lips before he spoke. It was a curious

mannerism, and it made him look as if he thoroughly disapproved of what he saw.

'I can see that,' he said. 'You are right, Rra: this is a small place.'

Mr J. L. B. Matekoni remained cheerful. 'It is not like those big garages – all flashy showrooms and so on. Hah! This is a proper garage. We fix cars. That is what we do. We do not play music or show films of new cars. We do not connect computers to cars to see what is troubling them. We use our hands.'

Mr Tefo frowned. 'It sounds a bit old-fashioned, Rra. I go to . . .' And here he named a car dealership that did all the things that Mr J. L. B. Matekoni had just excoriated.

Fanwell, who had been following the conversation from a few yards away, said, 'You will pay those people a lot, Rra. They are not cheap. You would save money if you came to Tlokweng Road Speedy Motors.'

Mr J. L. B. Matekoni gave his assistant a discouraging glance. 'There are many different ways of doing the same thing. People should be free to choose.'

Mr Tefo was looking at the building's façade. 'So, is this the front?' he asked.

Mr J. L. B. Matekoni looked surprised by the question. 'Yes, it is the front, Rra. It is in the front, you see. The back is over there – behind the front.'

Mr Tefo took a notebook out of his pocket and made a brief note. He gazed through his thick spectacles. 'I see that you have an extra wing on this building. You have the garage over on this side – where all the mess is – and then you have . . .' He waved towards the office of the No. 1 Ladies' Detective Agency. 'Then you have that extension. Is that the toilet?'

Fanwell gasped. Not only had there been a disparaging reference to mess – and what *real* garage was not messy to some degree at least? – but the office, the nerve centre and headquarters of Botswana's only private detective agency, had been casually referred to as a *toilet*.

Mr J. L. B. Matekoni would have reacted in the same way, had he not been so shocked. All he could do was stare in disbelief at Mr Tefo.

'No, Rra,' he said eventually. 'That is the office of the No. 1 Ladies' Detective Agency. You will see their sign – if you look.'

Mr Tefo peered myopically in the direction indicated by Mr J. L. B. Matekoni. 'What is it doing there, Rra?'

'It is part of our premises,' he said. 'The garage leases it to the agency.'

Mr Tefo was silent for a few moments. Then he asked, 'This No. 1 Ladies' What-not What-not – what does it do?'

'No. 1 Ladies' Detective Agency. It provides services to people who have problems in their lives.'

Mr Tefo raised an eyebrow. 'That's just about everybody, Rra.'

Mr J. L. B. Matekoni thought this might be a joke, and he grinned weakly. 'Yes, we all have problems, don't we?'

Mr Tefo made another note in his notebook. As he did so, he said, 'Yes, we all have problems. I have irritable bowel syndrome. Do you know about that, Rra.'

Mr J. L. B. Matekoni shook his head. 'I am sorry to hear that, Rra.'

Mr Tefo pointed to the open door of the garage. 'I would like to see inside, please.'

Mr J. L. B. Matekoni led him into the garage. He warned him of the inspection pit. 'You have to be careful in a garage like this. We have a pit and you don't want to fall into it.'

'It is a good size, this building,' said Mr Tefo. 'Very nice, I think. Yes, very nice altogether. Commodious.'

It was the first friendly remark he had made, and Mr J. L. B. Matekoni reacted warmly. 'Yes, it is a good building, Rra. It would be worth a lot on the open market – not necessarily as a garage, but as . . . well, anything, really.'

'We call it general commercial property,' said Mr Tefo. 'And there is always a demand for that so close to town – even if it is filled with mess. If this went on the market, it would get a much better price as something other than a garage – a beauty salon, perhaps – something like that.' He laughed, adding, almost suggestively, 'There are lots of ladies, you see, who are interested in looking beautiful. Watch out, men, I always say.'

For a few brief moments Mr J. L. B. Matekoni imagined himself the proprietor of a beauty salon, with Fanwell and Charlie as his chief assistants. Somehow it did not seem right.

Mr Tefo pointed to the door that led into the agency office. 'I should like to view the extension,' he said. 'Will we be interrupting anything?'

Mr J. L. B. Matekoni shook his head. 'My wife runs the agency, but she is out of the office on business. There is only her assis—' He stopped himself. He had made that mistake many times before. 'There is only her colleague, Mma Makutsi. I have told her that you might need to have a look round.'

'Let us go in then,' said Mr Tefo.

Mma Makutsi looked up from the file in front of her. There had been a mistake in the calculation of fees, and it seemed that the agency had undercharged the client. That was awkward, but not as potentially embarrassing as would be a discovery that they had overcharged. The disparity would have to be ignored, especially since the error was hers, and not Mma Ramotswe's. Now she saw Mr J. L. B. Matekoni at the door, along with the man he had said was coming to value the premises – for insurance purposes, she imagined. That was wise. At the Botswana Secretarial College they had stressed the importance of regular revaluations of office property. 'Never be underinsured,' the lecturer had said, and Mma Makutsi could hear her now; she had been the vice-principal, and she spoke in a thin, rather pedantic voice. She was right of course, and years later, remembering what had been said, Mma Makutsi had passed the advice on to Phuti, who had readily agreed with her that under-valuation was a bad mistake.

Mr Tefo started off on the right foot with a traditional greeting to Mma Makutsi. But there it stopped, and the encounter rapidly went downhill.

'What is this place?' he enquired, gazing around the office through his powerful spectacles.

Mr J. L. B. Matekoni glanced nervously at Mma Makutsi. She had not reacted well to Mr Tefo's question, and he had seen that familiar flash of light from her large round glasses. To the practised eye, that was a warning sign.

Mr J. L. B. Matekoni hurriedly suggested tea. 'It is very hot this afternoon,' he said. 'Do you think you could make some tea, Mma Makutsi?'

Mma Makutsi nodded in a perfunctory way. She would make tea because it was polite to offer a visitor tea, but she would not have people coming into her office and saying, 'What is this place?' There were limits, and one had just been transgressed.

'This place, Rra,' she said, as she crossed the room to switch on the kettle. 'This *place* is the office of the No. 1 Ladies' Detective Agency. Has Mr J. L. B. Matekoni not told you that already?'

Mr Tefo wrinkled his nose. He ignored the question. 'It is not very big,' he said, looking about him with the air of one who had been expecting something altogether different.

Mma Makutsi stopped in her tracks. She stared at the visitor.

'This is an office, Rra. We are not keeping cattle in here. We are not building aeroplanes. It is an office. You do not need much floor space for that.'

Once again, Mr Tefo seemed not to pay any attention to what she had said. He was tapping the floorboards with the toe of his shoe. 'This floor probably requires replacement,' he said, making a note in his notebook. 'Termites get at floors, you know. One moment, you have a floor – the next, your floor has disappeared. I have seen that happen.'

Mma Makutsi flicked the switch of the kettle with rather more force than was necessary.

'There are no termites here, Rra.'

Now Mr Tefo appeared to notice her. 'You cannot say that, Mma. Termites are very small. They move about. They are always there in the background, looking for something to eat.'

Mma Makutsi's spectacles caught the light from the window. There was a dangerous flash.

'Does our insurance cover termite damage?' she asked Mr J. L. B. Matekoni.

He shrugged.

She turned to Mr Tefo. 'Well, Rra, perhaps you can answer that. Does your cover include termite damage?'

'Nothing to do with me,' replied Mr Tefo.

Mma Makutsi's eyes widened. 'But you are the insurer,' she said.

'I am from the bank,' said Mr Tefo curtly. 'I am here to value these premises as security for a loan.'

Mma Makutsi caught her breath. 'We are borrowing money?'

Mr J. L. B. Matekoni shifted from foot to foot. He was about to say something when Mr Tefo interjected. 'There is a loan to cover the cost of investing in a bus company. That is what this is about.'

The electric kettle began to hiss. In silence, they waited for the tea to be made. Then Mr Tefo turned to Mr J. L. B. Matekoni. 'I don't think this office adds substantially to the valuation. It doesn't detract from it, of course, but it doesn't change the fundamental picture.' He paused. 'Not that you need worry, Rra. I think that the value of the entire building is very easily sufficient to cover the proposed advance.'

Mr J. L. B. Matekoni shot another anxious glance in Mma Makutsi's direction, but she said nothing. 'I am very pleased to hear that,' he muttered.

Mma Makutsi was passing a cup of tea to Mr Tefo. Her lips were set in a thin line. She looked at the valuer over the top of her tea cup. Her eyes narrowed.

Tea was drunk in silence. Mr Tefo moved about the room, peering into corners, observed in all his movements by Mma Makutsi. When he had drained his tea cup he put it down on Mma Ramotswe's desk, from where it was ostentatiously and disapprovingly retrieved by Mma Makutsi and placed on top of a filing cabinet.

'I think that I have all I need to make the valuation report,' Mr Tefo announced.

Mr J. L. B. Matekoni inclined his head. 'That is good, Rra.'

'So you will be hearing from the bank,' Mr Tefo went on. He paused, and looked at Mma Makutsi. 'Thank you, Mma, for allowing me to have a look round.'

Mma Makutsi struggled. She did not want to appear churlish, and so eventually she responded, muttering something that could have been *It was no trouble* but that could equally have been something else, possibly *It has been a lot of trouble*. Mr J. L. B. Matekoni was not sure what it was, but he was relieved that the difficult encounter was drawing to an end.

Mma Makutsi watched through the window as Mr Tefo walked

back to his car and drove away. Then she went to the door that led into the garage. Mr J. L. B. Matekoni was standing by an open toolbox, gazing down at it as if uncertain what to do.

Mma Makutsi drew in her breath. 'This is a very foolish thing you are doing, Mr J. L. B. Matekoni,' she said. 'This is not going to end well.'

He turned round. 'I'm sorry, Mma Makutsi,' he said, his voice remaining even, 'but this is my business.'

She stared at him, unused to the tone of quiet resolve with which he had spoken to her. Was there something wrong with him? Perhaps this was that depression from which he had suffered once before, returning now and propelling him down this ridiculous course of action. He was like a schoolboy who has seized on a wild idea and decided to persist in spite of all advice to the contrary.

She did not attempt to argue. She knew that Mma Ramotswe had already spoken to Phuti; now she would speak to him herself, and urge him to do whatever he could to dissuade Mr J. L. B. Matekoni from becoming the agent of his own ruin. And then it dawned on her. That was it! That was what lay at the heart of this reckless scheme: the male menopause. She should have thought of it before this, she told herself, and yet even so, the making of the diagnosis would not change anything. Male menopausal behaviour was beyond rational argument – the only thing you could do was watch the tragedy unfold and hope that at the end the consequences would not be too severe, the damage too irreparable.

Mma Ramotswe dropped Mma Potokwani off at the Orphan Farm before returning to the office. She had errands to run, and had thought that she might not bother to go back to the agency that day, but there were one or two pressing matters that she needed to discuss with Mma Makutsi. Prominent amongst these was the finalisation of the trading accounts for that half of the year – not a major task, as there were relatively few outgoings and correspondingly few receipts, but one that she wanted to get out of the way. After years of scraping along just on the right side of profitability, the agency now generated slightly more revenue, but once Mma Ramotswe had paid salaries to Mma Makutsi and Charlie, and taken her own drawings, there was very little left to invest in the business – twenty thousand pula at the most. Had there been shareholders, they would have been clamouring for that, but there were none, and so Mma Ramotswe was able to fund odd improvements here and there – a new telephone, a reconditioned filing cabinet, the occasional advertisement in the *Botswana Daily News*.

She could tell immediately from Mma Makutsi's demeanour that all was not well.

'Is everything all right?' she asked, not expecting anything but the reply that Mma Makutsi now gave – which was a stern shaking of the head.

'You are going to have to do something,' Mma Makutsi said. 'I do not like to tell you what to do, Mma, but I cannot stand by and let this happen.'

Mma Ramotswe knew, of course, what it was that Mma Makutsi was talking about.

'This bus company?'

Mma Makutsi expelled air past her lips in a long, low sound – like a distant train, thought Mma Ramotswe; to be specific, like the locomotive of the old steam service on the Bulawayo to Cape Town line, stopping at Mahalapye, releasing steam into the noonday air. It was a sound that presaged an outbreak of disapproval, determination, and resolution, all at the same time.

'Yes, Mma,' said Mma Makutsi. 'This bus company. The man from the bank was here this morning – the valuer. He was a ridiculous man, Mma. If you saw him in the street, you would hardly notice him. And yet he stood right here, Mma – right in the middle of our office – with his notebook and looked about him as if there was a bad smell in the room.'

'And there was no smell, Mma?'

Mma Makutsi was dismissive. 'There was definitely no smell.'

'Ah.'

'He was valuing *our* office,' continued Mma Makutsi, with the air of one imparting grave news. 'It was not just the garage – it was the entire building.'

'Oh dear.'

Mma Makutsi shook her head. 'You told me that you had mentioned this Molefi business to Phuti. What did he say?'

'I asked him whether we might be able to speak to the bank. He said they would not consider it to be any of our business.'

'And did he say anything about his own views?' asked Mma Makutsi. 'I have not discussed it with him yet.'

Mma Ramotswe hesitated. She did not want to become involved in a potential disagreement between husband and wife. 'He was cautious, Mma.'

Mma Makutsi pursed her lips. 'He didn't write off the whole idea out of hand?'

Mma Ramotswe shook her head. 'I wouldn't say that, Mma.'

'Men!' exclaimed Mma Makutsi. 'They're all gamblers at heart.'

Mma Ramotswe thought this was going a bit far. 'Surely not all of them, Mma? There are many careful men around.'

Mma Makutsi did not seem convinced. 'And now Mr J. L. B. Matekoni will go and borrow money to buy buses and when the buses fail – as they almost certainly will, Mma – then the bank will come and take our office and that will be that, Mma. That will be that. The end.' Occasionally Mma Makutsi would say *the end* in order to emphasise a point. And the effect was indeed emphatic: there was not much you could add if somebody said *the end* like that.

Mma Ramotswe did not know what to say. She feared that Mma Makutsi's pessimistic view of the likely fate of the nascent bus company was probably justified. There were too many bus operators, and it was not a field that anybody could enter without substantial backing. An existing transport company might be able to do so, having the funds to buy a fleet of new vehicles, but not a tiny operation of the sort envisaged by Mr J. L. B. Matekoni's friend, Mr T. K. Molefi. He was speaking of only one bus at this stage – but where could one go with only one bus? The timetable of such a company would provide limited reading, she thought.

Mma Makutsi raised a finger. 'There is only one thing that we can do, Mma – only one thing. We must all put our foot down. All together – at the same time. If the No. 1 Ladies' Detective Agency refuses to pay rent, if Fanwell threatens to find another job, if I no longer make tea for Mr J. L. B. Matekoni when he comes in here at teatime, then perhaps he will see sense. *The end.*'

Mma Ramotswe pointed out that the agency currently paid no rent – Mr J. L. B. Matekoni provided the office rent-free. 'You do not normally pay rent to your husband, you see,' she said.

This did not deter Mma Makutsi. 'Well, you could say that if you did pay rent, then you would no longer pay it. That would show him.'

'And Fanwell would find it hard to get another job,' Mma Ramotswe continued. 'Jobs are tight at present. We cannot expect him to put his career at risk.'

Mma Makutsi had no answer to that, nor to the next objection raised by Mma Ramotswe – that Mr J. L. B. Matekoni was perfectly capable of making his own tea.

'Then I shall tackle Phuti about this,' said Mma Makutsi. 'I am not going to give up easily on this one, Mma. There are times when you have to realise that if men are allowed to go their own way, then ruin awaits them. This is one such time, Mma – this is definitely one such time.'

There was much that Mma Ramotswe wanted to say to this. She wanted to say that however strongly Mma Makutsi felt about Mr J. L. B. Matekoni's folly, she should proceed with caution. People had to be left to make their own mistakes, even if the rest of us could see quite clearly the dangers that lay ahead. It was his life and his garage, and while Mma Makutsi had the right, as a friend, to express her views on the things he wanted to do, she should remember that she was dealing with a grown man, who had a lot of experience of the world, and who might resent being dictated to by others. She would have liked to say this to Mma Makutsi, but somehow she felt she could not, for fear of exacerbating what was already a tense situation. And at the back of her mind was the thought that if she stopped Mma Makutsi from trying to intervene, and the proposed investment proved to be disastrous, she herself might be blamed for standing by and not doing enough to prevent it. So she bit her lip and said, 'Whatever you can do, Mma – I'm sure it will be helpful.'

Mma Makutsi gave a nod to indicate that this is what she wanted – and expected. 'Now, Mma,' she said, 'we should look at the accounts. I have checked the figures and I think our profits are continuing to rise.' She paused, and fixed Mma Ramotswe with a reproachful stare before continuing, 'It would be a pity if an unwise business venture should cause this situation to be turned on its head. Just an observation, Mma. Just an observation.'

Mma Ramotswe might have taken offence. She might have sided with her husband, as loyalty, from one way of looking at things, might require of her. And yet she remembered that she and Mma Makutsi had been through a great deal over the years, and when all was said and done, Mma Makutsi would do anything for her, and she would do the same for Mma Makutsi. That was what counted. And so, if Mma Makutsi felt that she had to issue a dire warning, this would be done through love, and through love alone. With this in mind, she said to Mma Makutsi, 'Oh, Mma, I am very worried. I am very worried indeed, and I am grateful to you.'

And Mma Makutsi said, 'Mma Ramotswe, you are my sister. And sisters share their worries. We will put a stop to this loan nonsense in one way or another and then all will be back to normal once again and we shall all be happy. That is what will almost certainly happen.'

Then she said, 'And now would you like some tea, Mma? It is some hours since I have had a cup of tea.'

Mma Ramotswe said yes. This was exactly the sort of occasion when tea was required. In fact, it was hard to think of *any* situation in which tea was not helpful in the way that only tea could be. And sitting down to tea with Mma Makutsi would give her the chance to tell her all about her visit to Mr Fidelis Mophephu and her conversation with him, and with Bontle. There was a lot to talk about – and a lot to think about too.

Chapter Nine

A Man With Lots of Money

That evening Mma Makutsi took particular care with the preparation of dinner. Phuti Radiphuti was not a man of sophisticated tastes when it came to food, and there was little point in offering him anything that he had not eaten as a boy. In the early days of their marriage, Mma Makutsi had purchased a large cookery book entitled *Food Adventures of the World*, and begun to hone her cooking skills on various recipes she found in this book. Her intention was to impress her new husband and to expand his culinary horizons, but the eventual effect proved to be exactly the opposite, and Phuti, a cautious eater before the beginning of these food adventures, was soon even more conservative in his views. As elaborate creation followed elaborate creation, the face that Phuti showed at the table became longer and longer. In the past, Mma Makutsi had seen him tackle his dinner with vigour and enthusiasm; now he was more likely to play with his food, shifting it about his plate with his knife and fork, and only occasionally taking a rapidly swallowed mouthful.

'You must eat up, Phuti,' Mma Makutsi urged him. 'You must keep up your strength. You need it for your work.'

Phuti averted his gaze, staring at the pasta and cheese sauce on the plate before him. There was a strong smell of garlic – something he was not particularly fond of – and the cheese was of a sort that he had not tasted before.

'This is a very popular Italian dish,' said Mma Makutsi. 'They eat it in places like Rome.'

Phuti gazed at his plate. 'It is very . . .' He struggled to find the right word. 'It is very cheesy, Mma.'

Mma Makutsi nodded. 'Cheese goes very well with pasta.'

Phuti lifted a strand of pasta with his fork. He thought of the Pope, seated at his dining table in Rome, contemplating a large plate of pasta.

'You see?' said Mma Makutsi.

'It is very good,' said Phuti, without a great deal of enthusiasm. 'The Italians—'

'Yes,' interrupted Mma Makutsi. 'The Italians eat a lot of this dish. They like pasta very much.'

'And garlic,' added Phuti.

'They are very fond of garlic,' Mma Makutsi confirmed. Now she warmed to her subject. 'There are recipes in my book from all over the world, you know, Phuti. We can try some Chinese dishes. You like rice, don't you? That is what the Chinese like to eat. With pork and a sauce that is sticky and very sweet. That is what they like over there.'

After a week, Phuti summoned up the courage to tell Mma Makutsi that much as he admired her adventurous spirit in these matters, he wondered whether it might be possible to return to the food that people in Botswana customarily ate, which was not covered in exotic sauces, nor laced with palate-searing peppers, nor served in tiny, highly coloured portions.

'I would never criticise you, Grace,' he said. 'You know that. But my poor stomach has had enough adventures. It is a very ordinary stomach. It has no degrees or diplomas. It does not want any surprises. It only wants the things we have always liked in Botswana: the beef, the sorghum porridge, the sausages, the spinach. It likes fried eggs and bread with margarine. It likes fat cakes. It likes fried potatoes too. That sort of thing.'

She had been mortified, and in spite of herself, in spite of being the most distinguished graduate of her year in the Botswana Secretarial College, in spite of her ninety-seven per cent in the final examinations of the college – notwithstanding all that, she felt herself becoming tearful, and wiped at her eyes with the threadbare lace handkerchief that she had so treasured in the indigent years of her spinsterhood; but she had pulled herself together because she was, after all, Grace Makutsi from Bobonong. Yet he had seen the effect of his words and had put his arm about her and apologised.

'I shall eat whatever you want to cook,' he whispered. 'I am a very happy man. I have a wife now who has all these recipes at her fingertips, who is a clever detective and can do anything. I am the most fortunate of men.'

'But I am the one who is fortunate, Phuti,' she said. 'I was a nobody person with nothing. You did not mind that my family was very poor. You did not mind my greedy uncles who tried to get more and more cattle out of you. You said nothing, when you could have said so much about their grasping requests.'

Phuti made a dismissive gesture. 'They were just doing their job,' he said. 'That is what uncles do in such cases.' He paused, looking at her with concern. 'And you must never say that you were a nobody person. That is simply not true. It does not matter where you are born or who your people were. That is never important. What matters is what is inside you.'

She lowered her eyes. He was right. And yet she still felt embarrassed that she had tried to impress him in this way, and all the time he had found the food she served him unappealing, even inedible. She had learned, though, and how else could you feel your way into a marriage except by telling one another what it was that each person wanted. Phuti wanted the traditional food of his people, and she would give it to him. It would be plain, and copious, and it would be the same thing, day after day. Yet that is what men liked, it seemed, especially traditionally minded men like Phuti Radiphuti. There might be more modern men who would enjoy the variety that *Food Adventures of the World* promised, but she was not married to one of them. They could eat their Chinese and Italian dishes to their heart's content, but Phuti would from now on be served the plainest of fare.

So it was that on that evening, when Mma Makutsi had delicate business to discuss, she took care to serve exactly those dishes that would on any table in Botswana be considered to be the most traditional and yet the most desirable of food. There was pumpkin soup, followed by beef cut in thin pink slices and doused in rich gravy. There were fried potatoes and spinach covered in melted butter; there were beans. And when his plate had been wiped clean of gravy with thick slices of bread, there were doughnuts filled with apricot jam – the dream dessert of any child; and most men, she reflected, were, in a sense, still boys. That last thought came to her not in any unkind or dismissive way, but in fondness. What woman, on looking at the man she had taken to her heart, would not wish to cherish the boy within – the vulnerable, the imaginative, the playful boy who lurked behind the most masculine of male countenances?

At the end of the meal, as Phuti sat back in his chair, replete and in exactly the receptive mood that Mma Makutsi wanted him to be in, she said, 'You're going to have to do something, Phuti. I know you say that the bank will not speak to us about Mr J. L. B. Matekoni's business. I know that. But we cannot let him ruin everything – not only for himself, but for Mma Ramotswe too. If the bank gets a bond over the office of the No. 1 Ladies' Detective Agency too, then where will we be if this bus company goes broke?'

Phuti sighed. 'You will be in a very difficult position. Mma Ramotswe will be—'

'She will be finished,' interjected Mma Makutsi, wagging an admonitory finger. 'They will both be reduced to nothing, Rra. Mr and Mrs Nothing – that's who they will be.'

'Oh, I don't know ...'

Mma Makutsi was firm. 'Well, I do, Rra. And that is why you have to do something, Phuti. We cannot let this happen.'

Phuti shrugged. 'I think you might be overestimating the risks involved. What if this business proposition that Mr J. L. B. Matekoni is looking at turns out to be a good one? What if the business plan this man has makes sense? This could be a great opportunity for Mr J. L. B. Matekoni, and perhaps the rest of us should not do anything to interfere with it.'

Mma Makutsi made a dismissive gesture. 'Molefi's business plan will not make sense, Rra. If it did, then why is he not taking it to some company that already runs this sort of venture? Why is he bringing it to a man who knows nothing about buses?'

'You cannot say that about Mr J. L. B. Matekoni,' Phuti

countered. 'A bus is a vehicle, and there are very few people in Botswana who know more about vehicles than he does.'

'Of course a bus is a vehicle. Of course it is. But there is a difference between knowing how something works mechanically, and knowing how to run a bus company. There is a big difference, Phuti. I know what a table is and how it works, but I could not run a furniture company half as well as you.'

This had not been intended as flattery, but it had that effect. 'I am sure that you would run the Double Comfort Furniture Store very well, Grace,' he said. 'You are very good at everything.' And he almost said, 'You got ninety-seven per cent, let's remember . . .' but before this or any other reciprocal compliment could be paid, Mma Makutsi had moved on to make another, more telling point.

'But the real issue is this, Phuti: Mma Ramotswe is very, very worried. Her business is at stake too, you see. This is not just a risk that Mr J. L. B. Matekoni is taking – he is forcing her to take the risk too. And is that fair, Rra? Can you really say that something like that is fair?'

It proved to be exactly the right approach for her purposes. As a man of traditional, not to say conservative views, gallantry was part of Phuti's character, and he paused and frowned as he replied to her point. 'Yes, that is true, Mma. I had not thought of that. A man should not make his wife suffer.'

'Of course not,' said Mma Makutsi quickly. 'I know he may not mean it, but there can be no doubt about it: this scheme will make Mma Ramotswe very unhappy.'

Phuti was silent, and Mma Makutsi watched him. She knew that her husband, for all his gentleness – he rarely raised his voice and was always considerate of others – was still an astute businessman. And had he not had a good measure of business acumen, he would never have managed to make the Double Comfort Furniture Store the success that it was. Now she watched him as he went over pos-sibilities in his mind, and she saw him lift up his head, as people will do when they have an idea and are about to reveal it.

'You have something to suggest, Phuti?' It was the pumpkin soup and the beef, she thought; it was the doughnut with apricot jam; it was all of these things that had put him in the mood to think of some way of saving their old friend from the conse-quences of his folly.

Phuti smiled. 'I have thought of something,' he said. 'There is one possible way. It might just work. Maybe.'

Mma Makutsi could barely contain herself. 'And what is that?'

Phuti drew in his breath. 'This T. V. Molefi person ...'

'T. K.,' Mma Makutsi corrected. 'He is T. K. Molefi.'

'This T. K. Molefi probably doesn't mind too much where he gets the investment from.'

Mma Makutsi considered this. 'Probably not. Money is money, whatever pocket it has been in.'

'Exactly,' said Phuti. 'That's the thing about money – it all looks the same, doesn't it? It all says "Bank of Botswana" on it and how many pula and so on, and has a picture of some cattle or a diamond mine or whatever. It is all very much the same, I think.'

Mma Makutsi listened politely. She was not sure where this was going, but she did not want to put Phuti off his stride. So she restricted herself to saying, 'That is all very true, Rra.'

Phuti rubbed his stomach in a satisfied way. His expression was benign: the meal, thought Mma Makutsi, was working just as she had hoped it would.

'So,' Phuti continued, 'if somebody else were to come along and offer to invest a sum of money rather larger than anything Mr J. L. B. Matekoni might raise, then ...' He left the sentence unfinished, but the implications were clear.

'He would take it,' said Mma Makutsi firmly. 'A man like that would go for the bigger chance. He would be unscrupulous.' She knew next to nothing of Mr T. K. Molefi, and she realised that she had no grounds to dismiss him so completely, but the battle lines had been drawn and she knew which side she was on.

'I think he would,' said Phuti. 'I would, if I were in his shoes.'

Mma Makutsi sighed. 'But who would make such an offer, Rra? He must have asked other people and been turned down. That's why he ended up with Mr J. L. B. Matekoni, who is not the most obvious choice, surely.'

'But you don't know that, do you?' came Phuti's retort. 'And what if I knew somebody who could be interested? What if I spoke to that person and put him in touch with this Molefi? What then?'

Mma Makutsi's eyes widened. 'You know somebody, Phuti?'

He nodded. 'I know somebody who would love to hear of this. He is one of those people who likes to back business propositions that nobody else wants. He's a bit of a gambler, I suppose. And he has lots of money – although he loses a large amount of it every year, he still has big reserves. His father was a big cattle trader over the border. Also up in Angola and Zambia. Cattle, cattle, cattle. He left him more money than he knows what to do with.'

Mma Makutsi frowned. 'But would you not feel bad if he took this up and the whole thing came to nothing?'

Phuti assured her that he would not feel in the slightest bit guilty. 'He will not even notice it if the investment proves worthless. That's not the way he looks at things. Firstly, he can afford to lose what would be a small enough sum for him, and secondly, the whole point about this – for him at least – would be the enjoyment of the risk. He likes danger. He would thank me for the introduction – I can tell you that, Grace. He would thank me – whatever happened.'

Mma Makutsi hesitated. There was something about what was being suggested that made her uneasy. Phuti might have explained that this would not amount to practising a deception on his acquaintance, but was this not doing something under-hand behind Mr J. L. B. Matekoni's back? It was, she felt, but then she thought again, and she decided that there were times when you had to save friends from themselves. You had to. And that might mean resorting to tactics that were perhaps less than open, but that nonetheless were meant to save another from the consequences of their folly. This, surely, was just such a case, and so she said to Phuti, 'I think this is a very good idea. I think you should do it. Mma Ramotswe would thank you, Rra. She would thank you for fending off a big disaster.'

Phuti looked uncertain. 'Perhaps she would, Mma, but may I suggest something? Don't tell Mma Ramotswe about this – at least not yet. We would not want word of this to get to Mr J. L. B. Matekoni because . . .' He looked at her severely. 'Because that's the way friendships are ruined.'

Mma Makutsi put a finger to her lips. It was the universal sign of discretion, of confidence, of conspiracy, and Phuti, with a smile, and in response, touched the side of his nose with his forefinger – another universal sign, this time a knowing one which suggested that things might possibly happen that were best not spoken about.

Chapter Ten

People Who Deserve
to Be Spanked

It was one of those decisions you make when you are driving, when you are going in an accustomed direction – to work, perhaps – and you suddenly decide that you will go in another direction altogether in order to do something you had not planned to do but that now seems the right thing to do. It was like that for Mma Ramotswe when, the following morning, she set off for work in her white van, her radio tuned to a discussion of a new plan that the government was hatching to help drought-afflicted farmers. Mma Ramotswe thoroughly approved of helping farmers – as did the entire population of Botswana, she imagined. Mind you, she thought, everybody approves of government schemes to get money to people in need – who would not?

The problem, of course, as Mr J. L. B. Matekoni had once pointed out, is that no government has an endless supply of money.

'The general public thinks that there is a special well of money,' he said, 'and that all the Minister of Finance has to do is to lower a bucket and pull the money out. But there is no such well, Mma Ramotswe. It does not exist.'

She agreed, even if a bit sadly. It would be good if there could be an end to need in this world; it would be good if people did not have to worry about what would happen to them if their crops failed, or if their cattle got sick and died, or if they lost the jobs on which they, along with a number of hungry mouths, depended. Those in power – those who held the public purse strings – could go some way towards alleviating the suffering that went with all of those things, but they would never be able to answer every call for help. Simply being human involved a risk of suffering – that, she realised, was inevitable, and it was also something about which one might be able to do little. Yet the rich, she reflected, could do a bit more, if only they would stop to think of those less fortunate than themselves. Some of them did, of course, and they did what they could to help the poor, but others, it seemed, had hardened their hearts and were indifferent to the plight of their less fortunate brothers and sisters. For that is what we are, thought Mma Ramotswe; we are brothers and sisters, whoever we are and whatever we do, and we should never allow ourselves to forget that.

And it was this thought, sparked by the discussion on Radio Botswana, that led to her turning left rather than right at the end of Zebra Drive and heading, not to the office of the No. 1 Ladies' Detective Agency on the Tlokweng Road, but towards the suburb of Phakalane, where the unashamedly plush houses of those rich people she had been thinking about were to be found. There was more money on those well-paved streets than anywhere else in the country, and it was on display in the form of large electric gates, ornate front doors, and highly polished and impractical cars that would not last minutes on the sort of tracks that Mma Ramotswe's tiny white van took in its ancient and rattling stride.

She did not have a plan, but in Mma Ramotswe's experience it was not always necessary to have a plan. Sometimes, instead of having a plan, one might harbour a *hunch*, and there had been many occasions during her professional career when a hunch had proved to be more productive than a carefully considered plan would have been. In fact, no less an authority than Clovis Andersen had said something about this in *The Principles of Private Detection*. He had written, she recalled, that *it is not a bad idea to follow your nose, even when your nose has not bothered to tell you why it's pointing in a particular direction. Do not be ashamed to act on impulse: beneath the impulse there may be a very good idea waiting to get out. Let me give you an example.*

But then, for some unexplained reason, Clovis Andersen had failed to give the promised example, and had gone on to talk about some other topic altogether. Mma Ramotswe had noticed this, as had Mma Makutsi, and they had discussed the omission at some length.

'Mr Andersen has many ideas in his head,' said Mma Makutsi. 'I know how he feels. I have many ideas in my head – not all the time, Mma, but very often – and when that happens, I sometimes find that I forget about what I was going to say and go on to say something new. That can happen, you see, and you cannot blame Mr Andersen for that.'

'That is certainly true,' said Mma Ramotswe. 'But perhaps it would be best if he wrote down his ideas as they came to him, so that he would have a list and he would not forget to give examples – for example.'

Mma Makutsi considered this. 'That is possible, Mma Ramotswe, but remember that the ordinary rules do not apply to somebody like Mr Andersen. He is what you call a creative person, and you cannot apply ordinary rules to creative people. That is not the way it works.'

Well, thought Mma Ramotswe, as she drove out towards Phakalane, I have a hunch that I might be able to find out something about those people I heard about at the Orphan Farm. And she thought of the young girl, and of what the housemother had said, and of the burning sense of injustice that had come over her when she heard of the child's experiences. How could people do that sort of thing? How could anybody tolerate slavery in this modern age, when all its horrors and cruelty were meant to have been consigned to the past? And it was slavery that still lurked among us – or something so close to slavery as not to make much difference. People might not use the actual word, but if you were trapped in a relationship with your employer from which you could not escape because you were too young, or too weak, or too frightened to insist on your rights, then what better word existed to describe your plight than that simple term, slavery? Of course, in most cases the state would not tolerate such arrangements, and Botswana had, for the most part, a good record when it came to human rights, but these things happened everywhere. There was slavery in places like London and New York and Paris, Mma Ramotswe had read – it existed in corners where the authorities might not see it or may be unable to act. It thrived on the fear its victims felt and on the ruthlessness of those who exploited them. It could exist as much under the sun and in the light as under the cover of darkness. It seemed always to be there – like a disease that was impossible to eradicate.

What could she possibly do? She could go to the police – she had her contacts – and tell them what she had heard, but she knew they would ask for proof, and she had none. The police, quite understandably, could not act on the basis of the suspicions that somebody might have about somebody else. That was not the way the world worked. And yet, now that she had decided that she would do something, she would not walk away – she had never done that before in the face of a wrong that was crying out to be righted, and she would not start now. Mma Ramotswe was too modest to consider herself brave, but that was what she was. She was a brave woman, and however boastful men might be about their deeds of heroism, when it came to bravery, women could hold their heads up as high as could men, higher perhaps – not that these things should ever be measured.

She knew which house it was, as she had driven past it once with Mma Makutsi, who had pointed it out and said, 'That is the house of those very rich people, Mma – you know the ones. He is the one who bought all that land and built all those buildings. I call them the Pula-Pulas because they have so much money and are so pleased about it. Those ones.' And she had looked at the house, and wondered how one family could use all the space it must have contained. Perhaps they had so many possessions that all those rooms would be needed for cupboards in which to store all the things they owned. Probably there were large rooms for entertaining all the friends they had, because rich people, in Mma Ramotswe's experience, were never short of people ready to call themselves their friends. And these friends would expect to be entertained well if they paid a visit – a cup of tea would never be enough, she imagined: a full meal was the least people would expect if they called on a wealthy household; a full meal

157

and a present perhaps, a joint of beef or a bottle of whisky or some other gift that would confirm the high regard in which the recipient was held. Mma Ramotswe smiled as she thought of the Pula-Pulas – the Money-Money family – and their circle. Such friends, of course, were very much in attendance as long as things were going well, but if misfortune arose, then would they be so much in evidence? She thought it unlikely. There were many formerly rich people who complained of a lack of invitations and loneliness.

She had no idea what she was going to do, but as she approached the house she saw that a short distance down the road, at the edge of the plot of land on which the house had been built and which was now surrounded by a whitewashed wall, was an area of yet-to-be developed scrubland. This was typical of the scrub that surrounded a growing town in that part of Africa – a sort of dusty no man's land, not quite bush but not yet urban. Studded with acacia trees, it was criss-crossed with paths of the sort that seem to go nowhere, but that must be used by somebody to get from one place to another. A lone goat, detached from its herd, was nibbling on the lower leaves of a young thorn tree, standing on its rear legs, as goats will do, to enable it to reach the shoots it was after. A few scraps of detritus – an empty potato crisp packet, a ripped white plastic bag, a punctured tin of some fizzy drink, and a few other little eyesores – reminded the passer-by of the human traffic that went that way.

Mma Ramotswe saw that there were several substantial acacia trees at the edge of this land, right at the point where the road ended and where the white wall of the fence turned a corner. In a shady spot beneath one of these trees were several flat-topped rocks, arranged in a rough circle, one of them darkened on one side, as if it had been used as a cornerstone for a fire. Rocks like

these might be thought by a casual observer to be of no conse-
quence, but Mma Ramotswe knew better. These were rocks on
which people would sit and talk, protected from the sun by the
branches of the tree above, and placed in such a position that
whoever was sitting on one of these rocks could speak freely,
without being in any danger of being overheard. These rocks,
for all their simplicity, were an essential part of the conversation
by which people kept in touch with each other and shared their
thoughts about the issues of the day. These were not rocks to be
taken lightly.

She parked the van by the side of the street and picked her way
across the patch of stones and weed that separated the rocks from
the roadside. Once under the shade of the tree, she seated herself
on one of the rocks and looked about her appreciatively. She liked
sitting like this, close to the earth, close to the very soil of her
beloved Botswana. Here, unmediated by any structures contrived
by man, you might see and feel what the land was trying to say to
you. *Please send me rain, please do not cover me with concrete, please
be gentle in how you walk across my surface ...* And all of these
messages would be whispered against a background of screeching
cicadas and all the other sounds made by the tiny creatures with
whom we shared the world.

Mma Ramotswe closed her eyes so that she could not see the
sky, the great, empty sky of Botswana above her, but somehow
she could feel it, a warm hand upon her upturned brow; and
she could hear it too, for the sky had a sound that it made to
those who were prepared to listen to it. It was the sound of the
wind, a soft, rustling sound; it was the sound of hot air rising;
it was the sound of clouds forming somewhere far away, a soft,
cotton-wool sound.

She allowed her thoughts to wander. She thought of the

office, but only briefly, imagining Mma Makutsi at her desk, as she would be by now, shuffling though her papers and looking at her watch. She would be wondering why Mma Ramotswe was not there, but would not be worried, as she often arrived late if she did some shopping beforehand or had some other tasks to perform.

She thought of Mr J. L. B. Matekoni and his worries about not amounting to much, and her heart gave a leap. It was so unfair that a man of his nature, a good man who was beloved of so many, should feel that he had failed in business, and in life. How wrong that was – how completely back to front.

She thought of her father, the late Obed Ramotswe, of whom she thought every day without fail, and whom she could imagine sitting with her on one of the other rocks, telling her some story about great cattle of the past. That made her smile. If her father had ever written a book, it would have been called *The Great Cattle of the World*, or *Great Cattle I Have Known* – something like that. And there would have been no shortage of people who would love to read just such a book, because people loved their cattle and knew that cattle had their life stories, just as we did.

'Mma?'

Mma Ramotswe opened her eyes. A woman was standing a few yards away, looking at her with concern.

'Are you all right, Mma?'

Mma Ramotswe began to stand up, but the woman signalled for her to remain seated and made her own way towards one of the other rocks.

'I am all right, Mma. I was just thinking. Daydreaming, you see.'

The woman smiled. 'I thought that maybe you were ill. I once came across somebody having a heart attack sitting on that very rock. She got better, but they had to call an ambulance.'

Mma Ramotswe shook her head. 'I think my heart is still beating, Mma.'

The woman laughed. 'You'd know if it wasn't, Mma.'

Mma Ramotswe studied the new arrival. She might have arrived on one of the paths, or from one of the nearby houses. She wore a housecoat in a faded pink, and old, serviceable shoes. That was enough to rule out her being somebody who lived in one of these houses, and at the same time enough to confirm that she was, in all probability, a domestic servant.

'Do you work around here?' asked Mma Ramotswe.

The woman nodded. 'In that house.' She nodded in the direction of the large house behind them. Then she added, 'My name is Alice, Mma.'

'And mine is Precious,' said Mma Ramotswe.

'Where are you from?' asked Alice.

'I live in Gaborone. There is a street called Zebra Drive. I live there.'

Alice took this in. 'And your village, Mma?'

Mma Ramotswe pointed over her shoulder. 'Mochudi.'

Alice said that she had known people from Mochudi, but she had forgotten their names.

'I don't think it was me,' said Mma Ramotswe, and they both laughed.

'I am the housekeeper for that place,' Alice volunteered. 'Those people who live there ... He's a very big man – you may have heard of him.'

'I know who he is,' said Mma Ramotswe. 'I do not know him, though.' She thought of the nickname that Mma Makutsi had coined for them – the Pula-Pulas. *Pula* meant rain and the good fortune rain brought, of course, but here, doubled this way, it sounded different – and rather apt, in the way that childish nicknames often did.

'Don't bother,' said Alice. 'He is not very nice. He would not pay any attention to ordinary people like us.'

Mma Ramotswe sighed.

'God will catch him eventually,' mused Alice. 'He will catch him and give him a good spanking.'

'That would be good,' said Mma Ramotswe. She believed in justice, although she might have put it a bit differently from the way in which Alice did.

Mma Ramotswe hesitated. Things were turning out exactly as she had hoped they would – rather better, in fact. She had hoped that, seated at this strategic intersection, she might bump into somebody who knew something about what went on behind that tall white wall, but she had not imagined it would be somebody at the very heart of the household – and one who was clearly disaffected. In Mma Ramotswe's experience, the very best informant in any circumstances was the disgruntled employee, although there were also cases, of course, in which the disgruntled employee was the obvious suspect.

'I think that you do not like these people very much,' Mma Ramotswe ventured. 'Have you worked for them for a long time?'

'Six months,' Alice replied. 'And the moment I can find another job, I'm off.'

'How did you get the current post?'

Alice pointed towards the other side of town. 'I had friends over that way who knew that they were looking for somebody. They put me in touch with his manager. He has a manager, you see, who runs everything – house, car, garden, orders from the stores and so on. He is a very ill-mannered man. And he is lazy, too, Mma. You never see him do anything himself – it is always "You do this, you do that". That is the way he speaks. I have even heard him speaking like that to his own wife – Mrs Manager, I call her. He says, "You make my dinner now-now. You make sure my shoes are repaired today itself – no delay. You clean up the mess." And so on. And she says, "Yes, big husband, whatever you want." It makes me sick, Mma – it really does.'

'There is much that is wrong in the world,' said Mma Ramotswe quietly. That was true, and yet she was not one to mention this fact too often, as its repetition tended to bring despair rather than resolution to do something about it. It was the right thing to say in the current circumstances, though, as she wanted to encourage Alice.

It worked, as she could see that Alice recognised her as a kindred spirit. 'I think we see things the same way, Mma,' Alice said. She paused, and then continued, 'What about you, Mma? What do you do?'

This would have to be handled carefully. 'I am an enquiry agent,' said Mma Ramotswe. People could be put off by the word *detective*, whereas *enquiry agent* sounded not dissimilar to a host of innocent occupations, such as import-export agent, or customer service agent. And yet it did express what she did – it was not untrue.

Alice looked puzzled. 'What enquiries? Missing people? Cheating husbands?'

She had understood perfectly, and so Mma Ramotswe said, 'Yes. I'm actually a private detective. I run the—'

Alice gave a shriek of surprise. 'No. 1 Ladies' Detective Agency? That place on the Tlokweng Road?'

'That is me,' admitted Mma Ramotswe. 'There is another lady, Mma Makutsi, and we have a part-time young man. That is the agency.'

'I have walked past that place once, with my cousin,' said Alice. 'She pointed it out. She said that you are very good at your job and have solved many people's problems.'

'She is very kind,' said Mma Ramotswe. 'We do our best. Sometimes we can help people; sometimes we have to say that there is nothing we can do.'

Alice looked thoughtful. 'I do not have any problems,' she mused. 'Except one – which is how to get a new job.' She paused. 'You don't know anybody who needs a housekeeper, do you, Mma? I am a very good cook.'

Mma Ramotswe shook her head. 'I wish I could help you, Mma, but I do not. I am sure something will turn up.'

Alice looked glum. 'I hope so – otherwise I shall have to keep working for these people over there.' She gave a toss of her head in the direction of the white wall and the house beyond.

Mma Ramotswe saw her opportunity. 'They must employ other people, Mma – a big house like that.'

The answer came quickly. 'Yes, they do. But they are very mean. They employ a lot of people – here in town and at their farms. But they treat them very badly.'

Mma Ramotswe drew in her breath. She had not imagined that she would get so easily to the heart of the matter, but that was where they were.

'Tell me more, Mma.'

'They use people who have no family,' said Alice. 'People who are alone in the world. Weak. People with no work permit, from up north – Zambia, Malawi. They tell these people that if they complain, the police will arrest them for being illegal. Or young people who have been kicked out of the house by their parents and have nowhere to go. People like that have nowhere else to go and so they put up with it.' She fixed Mma Ramotswe with a challenging stare – as if she expected her to gainsay what she had said. 'I am not making this up, Mma. I have seen it with my own eyes.'

'I did not think you were making it up,' Mma Ramotswe

assured her. 'I have seen this sort of thing before. It is very bad.' She waited for a few moments before continuing, 'And are there some of these people there now? Still there?'

Alice nodded. 'There is a teenage girl and her brother. He works in the garden. He is not quite right in the head, Mma. He cannot count or read anything. But he is a nice boy. He is fourteen, or thereabouts – I do not think he knows how old he is.'

'And they do not want to go away?'

'They are frightened to. The boy can't do anything by himself, and the girl is terrified of the wife. She has threatened them in some way. They will not speak to me about it. The girl just shakes her head and turns away if I try to speak to her.'

Mma Ramotswe asked about the wife. Where was she from? What was she like? Was she worse than the husband, or were they both equally bad?

'She is about as bad as he is,' Alice replied. 'She is a bit different, though.'

'In what way?'

'She is a gossip. She is always looking for bad things to say about other people.'

Mma Ramotswe clicked her tongue in disapproval. 'That is not very nice, Mma.'

'That's what I think. Her tongue is very sharp. And she's very superstitious. You know how some people are? She is always worried about signs.'

Mma Ramotswe waited.

'She always pays a lot of attention to her horoscope. She gets a magazine that has horoscopes in it – she loves that sort of thing. And good luck charms and so on – she has plenty of those. I think she might even go to see a witch doctor sometimes. There are still people who do that sort of thing.'

'She really believes in all that, Mma?' she asked.

Alice nodded. 'She is a big believer, Mma.'

Mma Ramotswe looked at her watch. It was later than she had imagined, and she had remembered that she had an appointment. She was reluctant to leave her new friend, but she had learned something very important, and already an idea was forming in her mind.

'I am going to have to go, Mma,' she said to Alice. 'I was only resting for a few minutes, but now time is getting on and I must go.'

'I have enjoyed talking to you, my sister,' said Alice. 'But I must go too, as I am meant to be on duty and that woman makes a big fuss if I'm late. She is very mean. I had to go to a funeral the other day and she docked my wages for the time I spent away. Can you imagine that, Mma?'

'Perhaps God will spank her too,' said Mma Ramotswe.

Alice laughed. 'If He does, she will not be able to complain. There are many people, Mma, who deserve a good spanking – and she is one of them.'

'Perhaps we should all keep a list,' said Mma Ramotswe.

Alice laughed. 'A very good idea, Mma.' And then she added, looking shrewdly at Mma Ramotswe, 'I can tell that you are a very wise lady, Mma.'

Chapter Eleven

A Good Name for a Bus

Mma Ramotswe smiled to herself as she negotiated the last turning in the road that led to the office of the No. 1 Ladies' Detective Agency. It was now ten o'clock, which meant that she had lost two hours of the working day: lost, but not wasted. Although her meeting with Alice had been unplanned, it had been more productive than she could reasonably have expected. Not only did she have a contact within that large, secluded house – a contact who would be only too happy, she imagined, to help – but she had a vital piece of information about the mistress of the house who was, if Alice were to be believed, a most unpleasant person. To learn unpleasant facts about pleasant people could at times be painful; to learn such facts about unpleasant people usually had the opposite effect, giving rise to the warm feeling that comes with the confirmation of a prejudice.

There were other matters to think about, of course – prominent among which was the case that she was currently investigating: that of Mr Mophephu and his controversial will. She knew that she would have to get back to work on that matter, and yet she did not relish the prospect. This was not because the enquiry had stalled – it had, in fact, barely begun – rather it was because she did not feel enthusiastic about doing anything to help the particular client at whose behest she was acting. In this, she knew she was wrong: her professional duty was clear, as Clovis Andersen pointed out in his ethics chapter. *It is not for you to pick and choose your clients,* he wrote. *Humanity is made of crooked timber and you must accept that many of those who consult you will be imperfect. You must do your best for everybody who engages you, whether or not you like them. That is what we call professionalism, and it is very important.*

She may not have liked the implications of this, although she could see that Mr Andersen was, as ever, essentially correct. What she did like, though, was his choice of words: the crooked timber of humanity. That was a very arresting expression, and she thought that it really did describe how people actually were. All of us had our quirks, our little ways, that were the equivalent of the knots or bends one found in wood. You had to accept that and work with what you had, even if you would prefer it to be otherwise. So she had to find out if there was any truth in the allegation that the nurse, Bontle Tutume, had exercised undue influence in getting Mr Fidelis Mophephu to change his will in her favour. Mma Ramotswe was not sure exactly how to proceed, but she thought that the next step in that case would be to convene a meeting with Mma Potokwani and Mma Makutsi. If two heads were better than one, then three heads would be even better in throwing light on what might be a rather difficult path ahead. Mma Makutsi had met neither the nurse nor Mr Fidelis Mophephu, but she had met Mr Baboloki Mophephu in the office and she would undoubtedly have views on the case. The three of them could discuss it and come up, she hoped, with some sort of plan.

That was what Mma Ramotswe was thinking as the office and Tlokweng Road Speedy Motors swung into view. But her thoughts were interrupted, quite abruptly, by a sight that made her think of something altogether different but equally – if not more – problematic. There, parked beside the garage, occupying the place where Mma Ramotswe normally left her van, was a large bus.

She drew up in a different, less shady place, and stepped out of the van. The bus was being worked upon by two figures in blue overalls, now recognisable as Fanwell and Mr J. L. B. Matekoni. The young mechanic was wielding the business end of a spray-paint device, while a few feet away stood a noisy, thudding compressor. Mr J. L. B. Matekoni was standing at the front of the bus before an open engine compartment, a large toolbox at his feet. Fanwell saw her first, and must have said something to Mr J. L. B. Matekoni, who looked back over his shoulder and gave her a cheerful wave.

Mma Ramotswe walked over towards them, her heart heavy with dread. It was too late. The deed had been done.

Fanwell pointed to the side of the bus. Running across an expanse of the coachwork was a paper form out of which letters had been cut. The form had then been taped to the side of the bus and paint sprayed across it. Even before Fanwell removed the paper, which he now did, Mma Ramotswe had been able to make out the inscription that had just been painted on the bus. *The Joy and Light Bus Company.*

Mr J. L. B. Matekoni walked over to meet her.

'Well,' he said. 'It has arrived. The first bus.'

She surveyed the aged vehicle. It was not a bus in the first flush of youth. 'So I see,' she said, struggling to make her voice sound normal.

'It is a very fine bus,' said Mr J. L. B. Matekoni. 'It requires a certain amount of mechanical work – but no more, really, than one would expect in the case of a vehicle of its age.'

She was uncertain what to say, but eventually she asked, 'How old is this bus, Rra?'

Mr J. L. B. Matekoni looked down at the ground. This was a sign of embarrassment; it was what he always did when put on the spot.

'Oh, it is maybe twenty or thirty years old. Something like that.'

Mma Ramotswe drew in her breath. 'But Rra, there is a big difference between twenty and thirty.' She gave him a plaintive look. 'Ten years, in fact. There is ten years' difference. Surely the vehicle registration documents must say when it was first on the road.'

Mr J. L. B. Matekoni continued to study the ground. 'Ah yes,' he said at last. 'Yes, you're right. I think it is closer to thirty than to twenty.'

She looked at him, and he shifted his weight uncomfortably from one foot to the other.

'In fact,' he considered, 'since you ask, I think it is thirty-five years old. Yes, it is thirty-five years old.' Now he looked up, as if pleading with her. 'I don't think that is too old for a well-made vehicle, Mma. In those days, they knew how to make buses. Buses today are . . .' He shrugged. She knew his views on modern vehicles. '. . . held together by glue,' he said. 'They're made of disposable bits and pieces.'

The look in his eyes was enough to make her relent. 'I am sure that it is a very solid vehicle,' she said. 'Look at its tyres. They are very big, aren't they, Rra? Those tyres would be good on a bad road.'

He responded with relief. 'Oh, I am glad you like this bus, Mma Ramotswe. I was saying to Fanwell only a couple of minutes ago – this is a good bus: it has that feel about it.'

He looked at Fanwell for confirmation, and the young mechanic nodded. 'There is nothing wrong with this bus,' he said. 'Or there won't be, once we have fixed all the things that ...' He floundered, before continuing, '... all the things that are wrong with it.' Then he added, hurriedly, 'Not that there are all that many things wrong, I think. Just some. Just three or four ... or five. Small things, mostly, like brakes and so on.'

'All of those things will be attended to,' said Mr J. L. B Matekoni. 'I have written them down here – on a list. We shall go through them one by one and fix them.'

'And I shall finish this very soon,' said Fanwell, pointing to the newly painted lettering. 'You'll see, Mma Ramotswe, that I have put the name of the bus company on the side of the bus. Nobody will look at this bus and wonder who owns it. They will know immediately.'

Mma Ramotswe read the inscription aloud. 'The Joy and Light Bus Company. That is quite a name, isn't it? Who chose that, I wonder?'

Mr J. L. B. Matekoni answered. 'That is the name that my friend Mr T. K. Molefi chose. He wanted to call it the Joy Bus Company but I said that we should add the word *light* because joy and light often go together.'

Fanwell joined in. 'It is a name that will give people confidence. It will also make them feel better. People like joy and light, too, I think. You wouldn't want to call a bus company the Bad Dreams Bus Company or Slow-Coach Buses or something like that.'

Mr J. L. B. Matekoni laughed. 'I remember once seeing a bus going by with the name The Big Seat Express on it. I did not think that was a very good choice.'

Fanwell looked puzzled. 'Why not, Boss? Wouldn't people think they might be comfortable sitting in a bus with that name?'

Mr J. L. B. Matekoni glanced at Mma Ramotswe. He looked embarrassed, but he need not have: a smile was playing about her lips. 'I do not think so, Fanwell,' he said. 'But that is another matter. This is the Joy and Light Bus Company – there can be no argument about a name like that.'

Mma Ramotswe now asked the question that she had wanted to pose right at the beginning. 'Does this mean that everything is arranged? Has the bank already said yes?'

She was dreading the answer, and felt immediate relief when Mr J. L. B. Matekoni shook his head. 'It is not yet final, Mma. It will be soon, but there is a lot of paperwork to do. They said it might take a week or two. But T. K. had already bought the bus and so I said that we could start work on it.'

A week or two ... That still gave them time. 'So you have signed nothing? Not even a promise?' Her question had a worried edge to it, and it sounded more anxious than she had intended.

'I have signed nothing,' said Mr J. L. B. Matekoni.

'Paperwork, paperwork,' said Fanwell, dismissively. 'There is always paperwork for everything. If you ever get to heaven, then I think there is paperwork that you have to fill out before they let you in.'

Mr J. L. B. Matekoni laughed at the joke. 'But now we must get on, Fanwell. You must finish the paintwork and then you can

172

help me with the brakes. They are the most important thing: if you start, you have to be able to stop.'

How wise, thought Mma Ramotswe. She felt that the observation might have some bearing on the situation that Mr J. L. B. Matekoni was creating for himself, but she was not sure exactly how that might be. Perhaps she would speak to Mma Makutsi about it and see whether she could see the connection.

Inside the office, Mma Makutsi greeted Mma Ramotswe with a mournful stare.

'Have you seen what is going on out there, Mma Ramotswe?'

Mma Ramotswe crossed the room and tossed the keys of her van onto her desk. 'I have seen it, Mma. I have seen everything.'

Mma Makutsi shook her head. 'I was very surprised, Mma. It was here when I arrived, and that means it must have been brought round very early, maybe even when it was still dark.'

'Like a thief in the night,' said Mma Ramotswe.

'Exactly. It would have been just like that, I think.'

Mma Ramotswe mentioned that Mr J. L. B. Matekoni had said that he had not finalised any contracts. 'I don't think the bank has paid the money yet,' she said. 'And I don't think that Mr T. K. Molefi has given him any shares yet. I think that none of this has happened – just yet.'

'But they have started work on the bus,' pointed out Mma Makutsi. 'It's as good as agreed, Mma – otherwise would they do that work on the bus? I do not think so.'

Mma Ramotswe wondered whether they would just have to make the best of the situation. When there were things that you could not change, then there was a strong case for accepting things as they were and working from there.

Mma Makutsi looked thoughtful. 'There is something called

mitigation of damage,' she said. 'Have you heard of it, Mma? I think perhaps you have not.'

It was not intended to be a belittling remark, but that was the way it came out. Mma Makutsi had a tendency – rarely manifest, but occasionally surfacing, to assume that Mma Ramotswe's comparatively short period of school education meant that she would be unaware of matters that she, Mma Makutsi, would know all about, having undertaken what she described as *tertiary studies*. These tertiary studies had all been at the Botswana Secretarial College, not necessarily one of the great institutions of learning, but one of which Mma Makutsi was inordinately proud and which she was ready to defend against any critical imputation.

'We learned all about mitigation of damage at the Botswana Secretarial College,' she continued. 'It is what you do when a bad situation develops. You take steps to make sure that it does not become worse. That is what we call mitigation of damage.'

Mma Ramotswe was tolerant. 'I had not heard that important name for it,' she said quietly. 'But I think that I have been mitigating damage all my life. That is what everybody does. I think it is quite natural, Mma, even if some of us have not heard the term "mitigation of damage".'

Mma Makutsi pursed her lips. She seemed to be framing a retort, but obviously thought better about it. Instead, she said, 'I have spoken to Phuti, and he has had an idea.'

Mma Ramotswe seized on this. 'To stop him? Does Phuti think he might be able to do something?'

Mma Makutsi looked about her, as if to confirm that nobody else was listening. 'This is very confidential,' she said.

'Of course, Mma. I shall not say anything.'

Mma Makutsi was relishing the moment. 'I know that you have been very worried, Mma Ramotswe. I imagine that you have not been sleeping well – with all this worry. It often affects one's sleep, you know.'

Mma Ramotswe played along. It did not matter if there had to be a prolonged build-up – as long as there was positive news at the end of it. 'You are right, Mma Makutsi. I have been tossing and turning, tossing and turning. You know how it is. And you turn on the light, in the hope that your worries will go away, but they do not. Because when you turn on the light, you see Mr J. L. B. Matekoni lying there, deep in sleep, in spite of the fact that he is the cause of all your worries. So you end up worrying even more, and you put the light out again.'

Mma Makutsi looked sympathetic. 'It is what we women have to do, Mma Ramotswe. We have to worry. We have all those worries on our shoulders while the men are just sleeping away – as if there was nothing to worry about.' She shook her head sadly. 'It is not easy being a woman, Mma. It is not easy.'

Mma Ramotswe agreed. But then she said, 'And I think, to be fair, Mma, it is also not always easy to be a man. In fact, it is hard for some men, I think, and they cannot talk to people about their worries in the same way as we can. We can speak to our friends. We can go up to them and start crying, and they will comfort us and let us tell them about our worries. And that helps, of course. But can men do that? I don't think it is as easy for them to do that sort of thing. Men do not like to cry on their friends' shoulders.'

Mma Makutsi conceded the point. 'Yes, you are right, Mma. I am glad that I am not a man. I have never wanted to be one, but if somebody came to me and said that I could have the choice, I would say, "No thank you! Not me. I am a woman and I do not want to be anything else." And I think that Phuti would not be pleased if I told him one morning that I had decided to be a man.'

Mma Ramotswe laughed. 'He might be surprised, I think.

But the most important thing is happiness, isn't it? If somebody would be happier being something else, then I think you should not be unkind to those people. There is no need to be unkind to people who are unhappy inside themselves. There is room for everyone. Everyone should be able to find somewhere on this earth to sit down.'

Mma Makutsi hesitated. 'Perhaps you are right, Mma.' She adjusted a pile of papers on her desk – a sign that the subject was about to be changed. 'About this bus company nonsense ...'

Mma Ramotswe encouraged her. 'You must tell me, Mma. I am very eager to hear.'

Mma Makutsi told her of her conversation with Phuti the previous evening. As she spoke, a broad smile broke over Mma Ramotswe's face. 'That sounds like a very good idea,' she said, when Mma Makutsi had finished. 'And is he going to see this person soon – the person who might want to invest?'

'Today,' said Mma Makutsi. 'Once he has decided to do something, Phuti likes to act quickly. He is Mr Quick-on-the-Draw, you know. If he thinks it is a good idea to do something, then he likes to get it done that very day.'

'That is very good, Mma. If you sit about thinking of things you are going to do, then you will never do them.'

Even as she said this, Mma Ramotswe thought of those things about which she had been thinking for some time and that she had yet to do something about. She had to reorganise the kitchen – she had been thinking about that for months; she had to clear out Mr J. L. B. Matekoni's wardrobe and get rid of some of his old shirts; she had to write to an old friend in Molepolole who had recently been unwell and who was now recuperating, but who was said to need cheering up. She needed to return her library book. She needed to have the heel of one of her office shoes fixed. All of these tasks had been outstanding for some time, but that did not prevent her admiring rapid and decisive action in others.

'Yes,' Mma Makutsi went on, 'Phuti will see this man at lunchtime and tell him about Molefi's business. He says there is a good chance that he will want to be involved because he can't resist this sort of speculative investment. He sounds very foolish to me, but sometimes these foolish people are very successful. They go for the schemes that nobody else wants, and then suddenly everything works, and they become very rich. Phuti says that there are many cases of that sort of thing happening.'

Mma Ramotswe thanked her. 'I thought that you might be able to help, Mma. So many times you have saved the day – I have stopped counting them, in fact.'

Mma Makutsi basked in the praise. 'I do my best, Mma,' she said primly. 'That is all I can do. But I am happy if what I do proves to be useful to others.'

Mma Ramotswe looked at her watch. 'You know, Mma Makutsi, I am very excited about this news you have given me. I am so excited, in fact, that I shall not be able to settle here in the office. Would you be interested in driving down to Lobatse to interview one of Mr Baboloki Mophephu's sisters? We have to do something about that enquiry, and perhaps now is the time to do it. It will take our minds off bus companies and loans and so on.'

Mma Makutsi required no persuading. 'I would very much like to do that,' she said. 'I shall make a flask of tea and we can drink that by the side of the road.'

'And I have two fat cakes in the van.'

'Then we have everything we need, Mma,' said Mma Makutsi.

'Except her address,' said Mma Ramotswe. 'But I think

177

we shall find her. We know her name is Maisie – Mr Baboloki Mophephu told me that. And we know that she is the headmistress of a junior school.'

'Then we have found her already,' said Mma Makutsi.

Chapter Twelve

Secretarial Reminiscences

The first primary school they went to was not the right place, but Mma Ramotswe enjoyed a fairly lengthy conversation with the school secretary about the rains – or lack of them; the difficulty of making ends meet with prices being what they were; and about the latest film showing at the local cinema – a film that the secretary said she was hoping to see again, having enjoyed it so much the first time. The second visit, she said, would be made with a friend who had been obliged to leave halfway through their first visit because she had eaten something that disagreed with her and she was feeling distinctly queasy. Mma Makutsi then entered the conversation with a question about the filing system the school office employed, and with one or two other secretarial reminiscences that Mma Ramotswe was not really interested in, but to which she listened with her customary politeness. At the end of this, the question was asked as to where they might find a primary school in the area that was presided over by a lady whose first name was Maisie. This query was answered directly.

'She is the principal of the Community No. 4 Primary School on Pilikwe Road,' said the secretary. 'That is not far from here. Do you know that road?'

Mma Ramotswe did.

'She is a very pleasant lady, that one,' said the secretary. 'Sometimes with school principals they just look at you – almost down their nose – and you can see them thinking: this person is just a secretary. She is not like that.'

Mma Makutsi bristled. 'Oh, I know what you mean, Mma. I know very well what you are talking about! That sort of thing used to happen a lot. It is not so common today, I think, but there are still people who do not know how much everything depends on secretaries. They just do not know it.'

This brought hearty agreement. 'You are very right, Mma,' said the secretary. 'We must be vigilant.'

Mma Ramotswe was not sure about this vigilance. Did it mean that secretaries should be permanently on the lookout for slights of one sort or another? It seemed to her that there were a lot of people doing that these days, and she was not sure whether it made people behave any better. If you accuse people of not liking you, then that, she felt, was the quickest way of making them not like you. Love was the answer, of course, to this, as it was to so many other problems. Love the people who did not love you; treat with courtesy those who did not show that courtesy to you, and they would realise what wrong they were doing. That was what she did, and she had found that in almost every case those who showed arrogance, or unkindness, or sheer malice, could be shamed into regret, and through regret came change. Of course, it did not always work. There were some occasions in which confrontation was necessary, and harsh words had to be spoken because some people seemed impervious to the pain they caused. But it was better to avoid such showdowns if one possibly could. There was always more than one way of bringing in a harvest.

Mma Makutsi was smiling at the secretary. 'May I ask you something, Mma? Where did you do your secretarial training?'

Mma Ramotswe glanced at her watch, not entirely discreetly, but even if she spotted this, Mma Makutsi was not ready to bring the conversation to an end.

The secretary gave her answer. 'I was at the Botswana Secretarial College,' she said. 'That is in Gaborone. You may have heard of it.'

Mma Makutsi interrupted her. 'Mma, I was there too! I was there! We are both graduates of the same college.'

Mma Ramotswe wondered whether the two would embrace each other, so warm was this exchange becoming; but they did not. They were wreathed in smiles, though, as the inevitable *Do you remember?* conversation got under way. Dates were exchanged, and it was established that Mma Makutsi had been at the college exactly a year before the school secretary enrolled. Most of the staff members had been the same, though, and their mention unlocked a stream of anecdotes and reminiscences. Did Mma Makutsi remember the lecture that the principal gave every year to the graduating class, and was there, in her year, a standing ovation at the end? She did, and there was. And did she remember the way that the head of the accountancy department used to talk about double-entry book-keeping in a hushed voice, as if he was discussing the secrets of a high-security laboratory? She did. And then Mma Makutsi said, 'We had somebody very well known in our year. Even in those days she was up to no good.'

The secretary put her hand to her mouth. 'Oh, Mma, I think I know who you're talking about. You do not need to give me the name. It's Violet Sephotho, isn't it?'

Mma Makutsi nodded grimly. 'That is the person I had in mind, Mma. She would have graduated by your time, though, wouldn't she? Not that she graduated with any distinction. Barely fifty per cent, in fact. She just scraped a pass, because she spent all her time thinking about men. All her time, Mma. Every single minute, as far as I could work out. And painting her nails at the same time.'

'They were still talking about her, though,' said the secretary. 'Her reputation hung about – like a bad smell, if I may say so, Mma.'

'That is a good way of describing it,' said Mma Makutsi.

The secretary looked thoughtful. 'You mention her graduation. You know, the year before I was there – which must have been your year – they said there was a student who got ninety-seven per cent in the final examinations. Can you believe it, Mma?' She paused. 'Did you know her, Mma?'

Mma Ramotswe held her breath. Had a choir of angels passed overhead and launched into a chorus of hosannahs; had the sun halted in its arc and beamed down for a while with redoubled vigour; had the very earth stopped spinning and nature itself fallen silent, one could not have conjured up an atmosphere of greater moment. She turned to Mma Makutsi and watched the expression of sheer delight spread across her face.

'Actually, Mma,' Mma Makutsi said, her voice quiet and modest, 'actually I was that student. It was me – as it happens.'

'You, Mma?' exclaimed the secretary.

Mma Makutsi nodded. 'Yes, it was me. I haven't thought about it for a while, though.'

Mma Ramotswe gasped. That was simply untrue. It was completely untrue. Mma Makutsi thought about her ninety-seven per cent virtually every day, as far as Mma Ramotswe could ascertain. But even if there was a time when blatant untruths should be corrected – just to keep the record straight – this was not one of them.

Mma Ramotswe cleared her throat. 'I really don't want to break this up,' she said. 'But we need to go to see this principal.'

Mma Makutsi dragged herself away from the conversation with her new friend and they went back to the van, which was parked directly outside the school office.

'A very interesting lady,' said Mma Makutsi as they drove away from the school. 'And it is good to find connections with other people, isn't it, Mma? That's important in this country, I think.'

'It is,' said Mma Ramotswe. She agreed with Mma Makutsi about that. Connections with others were what made life bearable. If we were alone, she thought, it would be hard to carry on in the face of all the disappointments and difficulties that were strewn across our path. Loneliness went against the grain in Africa, where the traditional view was that we were all brothers and sisters, in spite of everything; bound by a web of kinship, not only to the living, but to the dead too. Brothers and sisters to each other – however frustrating, inconvenient and noisy that could be.

Sitting in her office at the Community No. 4 Primary School, Maisie Mophephu – she still used her original family name – looked quizzically at her two visitors. She had received them courteously and had ordered tea; now she wondered what brought these two ladies from Gaborone, one traditionally built and wearing a colourful red dress, the other somewhat less generously proportioned and wearing less colourful clothes, apart from a pair of bright green shoes with a contrasting blue bow on each toe. They were what she might describe as 'statement shoes', even though Mma Mophephu could not be expected to know that Mma Makutsi's shoes, alone amongst the shoes of Botswana, were inclined, from time to time, to make utterances – or seemed to do so, even if it was obviously impossible for shoes ever to say anything.

Mma Ramotswe liked the look of Maisie Mophephu. She had already been predisposed to a positive reaction in the light of what the secretary at the other school had said, but now, throwing a discreet and yet evaluative glance at the woman behind the desk, she decided that she very much liked what she saw. The principal was neatly dressed in a dark brown trouser suit, and wore a small Botswana pin flag in her right lapel. Mma Ramotswe approved of that. She had never been one for aggressive patriotism, but she was very much in favour of professing love of one's country. There was no suggestion in such sentiment that other countries were less important – what it did show, though, was that one had a certain feeling for those amongst whom one lived. They were one's people, and had a claim on you, and you on them. It was all about community and the sense of belonging.

Mma Mophephu cleared her throat. 'I have a slightly sore throat, *Bomma*,' she explained. 'It comes from working with children. They are walking reservoirs of infection – as I suspect you know. You pick up every cold going if you work in a school.'

Mma Ramotswe laughed. 'I know what you mean, Mma. I have a friend who is a matron in a children's home. She says that if one child gets a cold, the rest of them have it the next day, and the staff too. She says there is no way round it.'

Mma Mophephu looked interested. 'That isn't a lady called Mma Potokwani, by any chance?'

'It is,' Mma Ramotswe replied. 'She is a very old friend of mine.'

'And mine too,' contributed Mma Makutsi.

'I have heard of her,' said Mma Mophephu. 'People speak highly of her.'

'They do,' said Mma Ramotswe, adding, 'I would not like to get on the wrong side of her.'

Mma Mophephu grinned. 'Ladies like that are very important,' she said. 'We need more of them – to stand up for children.'

There was a short silence.

'You may be wondering why we are here,' began Mma Ramotswe.

'I was, yes, Mma. I thought maybe it had something to do with getting a place for a child in our school. But then, I thought, no; there is something else you want to discuss.'

Mma Ramotswe was direct. 'We are from the No. 1 Ladies' Detective Agency, Mma. We are making enquiries.'

Mma Mophephu raised an eyebrow. 'My goodness: this is very interesting. I don't think I have met a private detective before. You are the first, I think.'

'We are not here to investigate *you*,' said Mma Ramotswe.

Mma Mophephu laughed. 'That is a big relief.'

'Our client is your brother, Baboloki,' said Mma Makutsi. 'He has approached us, and that is why we are here.'

This disclosure had an immediate effect. Mma Ramotswe noticed that at the mention of her brother, Mma Mophephu tensed. After a moment or two, though, she relaxed again, even if she now seemed slightly guarded in her manner.

'Why has my brother been to see you?'

'It is to do with your father's will,' Mma Ramotswe replied.

Mma Mophephu frowned. 'My father is not yet late, Mma. Why is Baboloki talking about his will?' She wrinkled her nose,

185

showing her distaste at an inappropriate and premature interest in something that should not be talked about while their father was still alive.

Sensing this, Mma Ramotswe said, 'I understand how you feel, Mma. I know that there are often arguments over property once somebody has become late; I do not think those arguments should start while people are still alive.'

Mma Ramotswe now told her of the concerns that Baboloki had raised. 'He thinks that this nurse who is looking after him has got round him in some way. He thinks that she has persuaded him to leave her the farmhouse – and the farm too. He thinks she is very wicked.'

Mma Mophephu's eyes widened. '*He* thinks *she's* wicked? Hah! That's very funny, Mma. It's the other way round, if you ask me. My brother is my brother, and he will be my brother until we both are no longer here, but I am sorry to say, Mma, he is not a good man. I would not necessarily describe him as completely wicked, but I think he is one of those people who are a bit wicked. I would not trust him.' She sighed. 'And it gives me no pleasure to say that. It makes me sad, Mma.'

Mma Ramotswe waited. Mma Mophephu looked as if she was about to add to what she had just said.

'And as for the nurse, I am very grateful to her. She has been wonderful with my father – for years, Mma. She has been patient. She has looked after him so well.' She paused. 'I think that if it had not been for Bontle, my father would no longer be with us, Mma. He never took proper care of himself – ever. And why should he not reward her?'

'I suppose one might expect family members to resent property going outside the family,' Mma Ramotswe suggested.

Mma Mophephu shook her head vigorously. 'Not in this case,

Mma, no. I can tell you something that you may not know – my father is a very wealthy man. He has always had a lot of property. A few years ago he gave much of it away – to me, to my sister in Gaborone, and to Baboloki himself. Baboloki got a much bigger share than we did. He got the stores – and there are a lot of them. He got a farm up north. He got a storage yard and warehouses up in Francistown. He got many, many things, Mma.'

'And did you and your sister object to that?' asked Mma Ramotswe.

'No, we did not, Mma, because we all had more than we needed. If my father chose to favour Baboloki because he was a man, then that was up to him. We may not approve, but it is the sort of thing that men of that generation do. They often favour sons. We did not want to argue with an old man.'

Mma Ramotswe thought about what she had been told. Mma Mophephu's attitude was very generous, and the opposite, she felt, of Baboloki's grasping. She was about to commend her, when a thought occurred to her. She looked at Mma Mophephu. 'What was your mother's name, Mma? And is she late now?'

Mma Mophephu seemed surprised by the question. 'My mother? She is still alive, Mma. And she is happy – I think. She lives with a younger sister. There are many nephews and nieces near where they are, and they are kind to her. She was the first wife of my father. I am only a half-sister of Baboloki and Betty, as he may have told you.'

'And her name, Mma? The name of your mother?'

'Bontle.'

Mma Ramotswe caught her breath. For a few moments, she said nothing. Then she asked, 'Were they divorced?'

Mma Mophephu looked uncomfortable. 'They were not divorced, Mma.' She hesitated. Then she continued, 'She was a traditional wife. He married her according to customary law. She was his village wife, you see. Then he left her and married a second wife under civil law.'

Mma Makutsi groaned. 'Oh, Mma, those are very difficult situations. That is still going on, I think. And it causes big problems.'

Mma Mophephu nodded her agreement. 'In my view it is quite wrong. The law says that you can only marry one person, but people use these customary marriages as a backdoor to polygamy. I'm afraid that my father was careless. His village wife was his secretary a long time ago. Then he drifted away from her and started an affair with Baboloki's mother. She insisted on a proper civil marriage, but there was still this other wife in the background. My father more or less forgot about her. He made support payments – he did not let her go without, but she was the forgotten lady, I'm afraid.'

'That is very sad,' said Mma Makutsi.

'Yes,' said Mma Mophephu. 'But I can tell you that I think my father always felt a bit guilty about it.'

'And your mother is called Bontle?' asked Mma Ramotswe.

'Yes, as I told you. She is Bontle ... Of course, the nurse is called Bontle too, but she's a different Bontle. It is a common enough name.'

Mma Ramotswe raised a hand. 'I just want to think about something for a moment,' she said. Suddenly everything made sense – or looked as if it might.

Mma Mophephu and Mma Makutsi both watched her as she wrestled with her thoughts.

'It occurs to me,' said Mma Ramotswe at last, 'that your father has been confused. He is an old man now and I think he may get things mixed up.'

'He certainly does,' said Mma Mophephu. 'He's all right much of the time, but then he can get things really back to front.'

Mma Ramotswe looked out of the window as she spoke. It always helped her to get things in order to stare at the branches of an acacia tree. It was like studying clouds as they moved across the sky: the effect was a calming one, and everything made more sense when she felt calm. There was such a tree directly outside the principal's window, and she fixed her gaze on it now – the delicate leaves against the sky, the branches like arteries, the twigs like veins. From somewhere within the school there came the voices of children singing.

'I'm coming to the conclusion,' said Mma Ramotswe, speaking very slowly and deliberately, 'that your father may think that the nurse is your mother. I think he thinks the nurse is his wife – he said as much when I spoke to him. I didn't pay much attention to it, as I thought it was just a slip of the tongue, but I think that he meant to leave the farm to the Bontle who had been his village wife.'

Mma Mophephu was staring at her in open astonishment. 'What did he say, Mma?'

'I remember his words very clearly,' replied Mma Ramotswe. 'I asked him why he had left the farm to Bontle, and he replied, "Because you must look after the wife you have left." Those were his exact words. That is what he said, and I remember it very well, Mma. And then he went on to say, "Wife. I mean Bontle. This lady."'

Mma Mophephu sat motionless. 'Oh, Mma, do you think so?'

'Yes,' said Mma Ramotswe. She had convinced herself of something that until a few moments ago had been no more than hypothesis. Now she was sure of it.

They spoke to one another for a further twenty minutes. Each of them had her questions; each of them had something that she wanted to say. Then a bell rang, and Mma Mophephu announced that she would have to go to take a class. 'Even a principal has to teach from time to time,' she said with a smile. Then she added, as she rose from her chair, 'May I ask you a favour, Mma Ramotswe? Do you mind not discussing this with my brother just yet? I would like to talk to my sister about it, and then perhaps you will be able to meet both of us in Gaborone – Betty and me.'

'That's exactly what I was going to suggest,' said Mma Ramotswe.

Mma Mophephu showed them out. As they walked back to the van, they heard, drifting from the classrooms, the high-pitched buzz of children's voices. Just like the sound of cicadas, thought Mma Ramotswe, and smiled at the comparison.

'You're smiling at something,' said Mma Makutsi. 'What's so amusing?'

Mma Ramotswe looked up at the sky. 'Oh, this and that, Mma Makutsi.'

'Ha ha.'

It was such a tiny sound – almost inaudible, but it was definitely *ha ha*. Where had it come from? Mma Ramotswe found herself looking down at Mma Makutsi's green shoes with the blue bows. Impossible, she thought. But then she thought: a lot of things that are impossible become possible when you look at them again, when you believe in them hard enough, when you want them to be true. But not talking shoes. That did not apply to talking shoes, for which there must be some other explanation – imagination, perhaps. That's what it was: imagination.

She glanced at Mma Makutsi, and saw that she was looking down at her shoes. But by then they had reached the van, and it was time to get in and drive back to Gaborone.

Chapter Thirteen

I Would Have Liked to Have Been a Director

Over the next three days, Mr J. L. B. Matekoni and Fanwell worked almost exclusively on the bus. They had now moved it into one of the two work-bays in the garage, although its length meant that only the front section was under cover, the rear remaining exposed to the sun. Fanwell had painted not only the lettering along the side, but had touched up the front and completely resprayed the roof, which had been blistered by years of neglect. 'It was mostly bare metal up there,' he explained to Mma Ramotswe, as she stood and surveyed his handiwork. 'There was even a bit of rust. I have ground that down and it is all now in tip-top order.'

Her feelings about the whole matter were unchanged, but she

did not want to put too much of a dampener on the young man's enthusiasm, and so she praised his deft touch with the spray gun and the paintbrush. Fanwell beamed with pleasure. 'I am pleased that you like it, Mma,' he said. 'Perhaps I shall do more spray work in the future.'

Mma Ramotswe gazed at the bus. It was certainly looking good, but there still seemed to be a lot of mechanical work going on, and there was a growing pile of greasy engine parts stacked near the garage door.

'It looks as if you have removed a lot from the engine,' Mma Ramotswe observed to Mr J. L. B. Matekoni. 'Do all those bits and pieces have to go back in?'

'I have already replaced some of them,' he said. 'And I shall clean up the others and fit them back in. A bus is a complex piece of machinery, Mma. It is not like that van of yours, you know.'

'But it is very old,' she said. 'You have often said to me that machinery cannot go on forever.' Such remarks, of course, had been pointedly made, and had been prompted by Mr J. L. B. Matekoni's desire to replace the tiny white van with something more modern. Mma Ramotswe had always resisted the suggestion that she might drive a newer vehicle; this ancient bus might prove an ally in that campaign of resistance.

'It is an old bus,' said Mr J. L. B. Matekoni, 'but once we have renewed what needs renewing, it will go for another five years without too much trouble. These old vehicles have stout hearts, Mma Ramotswe. They are like those old people you meet in the remote villages – people who have been sitting under the same tree for nobody knows how long – people who remember way, way back. It's like them. They go on and on, and these buses can do the same.'

She smiled at the analogy. She wondered, though, what it was that led to this longevity – in those old people in the villages and in these old vehicles on the road. Was it the way they were built?

She asked him, and he smiled as he gave his answer. 'I think that the secret is not to be in too much of a hurry. If you drive a truck or a car too fast, they get exhausted – just as people do. And then they start to go wrong – just like people. But if you take it slowly, then you can go on and on. That applies to cars and people, you know. Same thing, Mma Ramotswe.'

'And will this bus be driven slowly, Rra?'

He shrugged. 'That will depend on the driver. If we get a good, responsible driver, then he will not push it too fast.'

She winced at his use of *we*: he already thought of himself as being part of the company. But she kept her feelings to herself. This was a situation that had to be played very carefully, and there was still a possibility that Phuti's intervention might avert disaster.

She asked whether Mr T. K. Molefi had said anything about a driver.

'I think he has a brother-in-law who wants to do it,' said Mr J. L. B. Matekoni.

Mma Ramotswe drew in her breath. 'His brother-in-law, Rra?'

'Yes. I think his brother-in-law works in that hardware store out in the industrial sites. He said something like, "My brother-in-law has always wanted to drive a bus."'

Mma Ramotswe's eyes narrowed. 'But, Rra, driving a bus is not an easy thing. You need a special licence, don't you?'

'He can take the test. It isn't too difficult. There was somebody I was at school with who was hopeless at everything, but who managed to pass his bus-driver's test first time.'

'But Mr J. L. B. Matekoni,' she protested, 'driving a bus is a very responsible job. You have all those lives in your hands. If you drive a bus over a cliff, then there will be trouble.'

Mr J. L. B. Matekoni frowned. 'Botswana is a very flat country, Mma. There are no cliffs.'

'But there are some busy roads. And there are dangerous drivers on these roads – same as everywhere else. There are people who go far too fast. There are people who talk and wave their hands about when they are driving—'

'Like Mma Potokwani,' interjected Mr J. L. B. Matekoni. 'I have been in her minibus with her and I have found myself praying, praying, praying. I know she is your friend, Mma, but you can't deny that she is a very erratic driver.'

Mma Ramotswe was loyal. It was true that Mma Potokwani used her hands to emphasise a point while she was driving, but somehow she had avoided being involved in even a single minor accident. Mma Ramotswe had wondered about this in the past, and had come to the conclusion that the steering of Mma Potokwani's small, creaking minibus was so stiff and unresponsive that it remained on the same course when the driver took her hands off the wheel. In theory, on a straight road, the minibus would not wander from its pre-ordained course until considerable force was used to turn the wheel.

'She has not had any accidents,' said Mma Ramotswe. 'Maybe she should be called a safe unsafe driver, if there is such a thing, Rra.'

Mr J. L. B. Matekoni looked doubtful.

She decided to take a chance. 'Are you still committed to all this, Rra? Do you still want to be involved financially? You have done a very good job on the bus – both of you – and I have been wondering whether you might not say that this is enough.'

Mr J. L. B. Matekoni wiped his hands on a piece of blue paper towel. 'I am still very keen, Mma Ramotswe,' he said. 'This is my big chance, you know. I think that in this life we get only one big chance, and you have to be ready to take it.' He paused. 'Look at you. You took your big chance when you opened the No. 1 Ladies' Detective Agency all those years ago.'

'But, Rra—'

He cut her off. 'No, Mma, it's true. Back then there were probably plenty of people who said, "Don't do this foolish thing – whoever heard of a detective agency in Gaborone?" There would have been people like that, Mma. They call them doubting Thomases. There are many doubting Thomases in this town. They are everywhere.'

She thought: am I a doubting Thomas? Is that how I sound?

'I just don't want you to lose all your money,' she said quietly. 'Once there is a bond on these buildings, then it has to be paid back to the bank. They will want regular payments. Where are those going to come from?'

She did not have to wait for a reply. He spoke as if the answer was obvious. 'From the profits of the bus company, of course.'

She bit her lip. She would have to be more direct now. 'Has he agreed to a specific share? Has Molefi told you how much you can expect each month?'

Mr J. L. B. Matekoni shrugged. 'That is a detail, Mma. That can be agreed in due course. I can rely on T. K. to sort that out.'

She stood her ground. 'Oh yes, Rra? And will the bank say the same thing about the repayments? Will they say, that is just a minor detail and we can decide in due course how much money you pay back each month? I do not think so, Rra. I do not think that is the way banks operate.'

In her view, this was an unanswerable objection. Yet Mr J. L. B. Matekoni appeared impervious to any warning – to any logic, it seemed. Mr T. K. Molefi, he said, was a trustworthy business-man. You would not find somebody unreliable being asked to give a lecture at a business seminar. And, quite apart from that, they had known one another at school. If you could not trust people with whom you had shared those early years, then whom could you trust?

'The fact that you have sat in the same classroom is no guarantee of anything,' Mma Ramotswe pointed out. 'Look at Mma Makutsi.'

'What about her, Mma?'

'She was in the same class at the Botswana Secretarial College as Violet Sephotho. Yes, Rra – Violet Sephotho, no less. Does that mean that Mma Makutsi can trust Violet? I think not, Rra. I think definitely not.'

'That is different, Mma.'

She sighed. She and Mr J. L. B. Matekoni never argued, and this conversation was getting perilously close to being an argument; indeed, to being a row. So she said, 'I must get back into the office, Rra. Perhaps we can talk later.'

He returned to his mechanical task, and she went back to her desk, to contemplate the uncertainties of the life ahead. Living under a burden of debt would be alien to her – she had never been indebted – and she was not looking forward to it. The bus company would not be a success, no matter how much she wanted it to work. Small companies rarely made it: that was a fact of economic life, and it seemed to her that the chance of a bus company succeeding when it had only one bus were remote indeed.

She looked across the room towards Mma Makutsi, who was busy with correspondence.

'Mma Makutsi,' she said, 'has Phuti heard yet from that man?'

Mma Makutsi shook her head. 'He said it would be a few days before we heard anything. But he was definitely interested in it, Mma. There is still a chance.'

*

That afternoon, Mma Ramotswe dozed off during the invariably soporific hour that followed lunch. That meal, taken at her desk, had consisted of a bowl of soup from a flask, a bread roll in which a thick slice of cheese had been inserted, and an apple, which, being over-ripe and bruised, had to be abandoned after a single bite. From her side of the office, watching the apple being tossed into the bin, Mma Makutsi observed that had Eve done that in the Garden of Eden, then human history might have been rather different. Feeling drowsy, Mma Ramotswe found it difficult to say much to this, other than to point out that she thought there probably was never an actual Garden of Eden, and that such stories were never intended to be taken literally.

'Oh, I know that, Mma Ramotswe,' said Mma Makutsi. 'But if there *had* been a Garden of Eden, then I think it was probably in Botswana. Up in the Okavango Delta, I think, Mma. If you look at that place now, it is just like the Garden of Eden, I think.'

'Possibly,' muttered Mma Ramotswe. Her eyelids felt heavy. It was far too warm; no wonder she felt so sleepy. She would get a fan for the ceiling one day, although sometimes those fans just stirred up the hot air and did not really make it any cooler. An air conditioner would be more effective, but they used up a lot of electricity and they were not good for the planet. There were places, after all, that were meant to be hot, especially in the hot season, and perhaps it was best just to accept that, as we accepted other facts about who we were and where we lived and . . .

She was vaguely aware that Mma Makutsi had more to say, and indeed was saying it.

'Of course, they say that everyone came from Africa originally. I was reading that everyone – and I mean everyone, Mma

Ramotswe – started off up there in Kenya somewhere. There is a big valley there, and that was where we began. Then we moved north. We are all related to one another – all people are distant cousins, you see. French people, Russian people. American people. Malawians. Everyone.'

She did not see Mma Ramotswe's eyes close.

'It could have been Botswana, of course,' she continued. 'Kenya is not all that far away and it is possible that it all started here. Perhaps even in Gaborone itself. Right here. And then these ancestors moved their cattle up north. If they had cattle, of course – I'm not sure that they did. They were hunters, I think, and so they would not have had cattle. Cattle came later . . .'

She stopped. A car had drawn up outside and Mma Makutsi stood up at her desk to get a better view.

'Mma? Are you asleep?'

Mma Ramotswe battled to open her eyes. She could hear Mma Makutsi calling her. Sleep was like a blanket covering her. It was too hot to be awake, and there was no reason why she should not drift off again. Mma Makutsi did not have to wake her – there was no need.

But then, 'Mma Ramotswe, you must wake up. It must be that person. It's that Molefi. He has come.'

Mma Ramotswe was quickly awake.

Mma Makutsi was giving a running commentary. 'He is right outside, Mma. He is looking at the bus now. Mr J. L. B. Matekoni is with him.'

Mma Ramotswe rose from her chair. 'I am looking forward to meeting this T. K. Molefi,' she said.

Mma Makutsi was not going to be left out. 'I am too,' she said, moving quickly towards the door.

Mma Ramotswe felt that she had to restrain her. 'I think we

should be a bit careful, Mma,' she said. 'We do not want to make matters worse than they are.'

Mma Makutsi stopped where she stood. She looked at Mma Ramotswe as if she was about to argue, but she evidently thought better of it. 'No, Mma, you're right. We should be careful. People like this Molefi . . .' She did not finish, but the message was clear: she had the measure of Mr T. K. Molefi even before meeting him.

They went outside, and saw that Mr J. L. B. Matekoni and Mr T. K. Molefi were standing near the front door of the bus, with Fanwell in attendance. As the two women emerged from the office, Mr T. K. Molefi turned and looked in their direction. Then he turned to Mr J. L. B. Matekoni, who said something to him and pointed to the front of the bus.

They made their way to where the men were standing, and were greeted politely by Mr T. K. Molefi.

'You are Mma Ramotswe, I believe,' he said, reaching forward to shake her hand. 'You are the well-known detective person, I think, Mma.'

It was a disarming beginning. 'That is me, Rra,' said Mma Ramotswe. 'But I do not think I am well known.'

'And this is Mma Makutsi?'

Mma Ramotswe was momentarily taken aback. She was not surprised that he might have known that she was the wife of his old friend, Mr J. L. B. Matekoni, but how did he know about Mma Makutsi? Of course, the mention of her name had its effect on Mma Makutsi, who, having been ready for a confrontational meeting, was all of a sudden beaming with pleasure.

'I was just admiring the work that has been done on the bus,' Mr T. K. Molefi said. 'It all looks very good indeed – especially the signage.'

He turned to face Fanwell, who seemed to grow several inches taller under the compliment.

Then Mr T. K. Molefi said, 'I need to talk to you, Mr J. L. B. Matekoni.' He turned to Mma Ramotswe. 'And you might care to join us, Mma. And you, Mma Makutsi.'

They looked at one another.

'Right now?' asked Mma Ramotswe.

Mr T. K. Molefi nodded. 'If you don't mind, yes. Could we?' He gestured in the direction of the agency.

'We can certainly talk in the office, if you like,' said Mma Ramotswe.

'That would be very good,' said Mr T. K. Molefi.

Mma Ramotswe had noticed his good manners. Mma Makutsi, it seemed, had done the same thing, and now they exchanged a look that said, in effect, *One can be wrong*. And they exchanged another such look when, at the door into the office, Mr T. K. Molefi stepped aside and invited the two women to go through the doorway ahead of him.

'This is a very fine office,' he remarked as he entered, adding, 'I would feel very confident if I were a client of this agency – I can tell you that, Mma Ramotswe!'

Mma Ramotswe and Mma Makutsi were by now almost purring with pleasure – in spite of everything. Mr J. L. B. Matekoni, by contrast, looked anxious, and spent some time adjusting the barely detectable crease in his trousers once he had sat down.

Mr T. K. Molefi lost no time in getting to the point. 'You may know,' he said, addressing Mma Ramotswe and Mma Makutsi, 'that I have been planning a commercial project with Mr J. L. B. Matekoni here.'

Mma Ramotswe inclined her head. 'We had heard something about it, Rra. It had been mentioned. A bus company, I believe.'

'Yes, indeed,' said Mr T. K. Molefi. 'The Joy and Light Bus Company. You will have seen that name on the side of the bus out there.'

Mr J. L. B. Matekoni was still adjusting his trouser crease. Mma Ramotswe watched him with concern: if his fingers were greasy, as they usually were, he would leave black marks on the material. This was a problem with men's clothes. They picked up marks, even if the man was working in an office. It was inexplicable.

Mr T. K. Molefi cleared his throat. 'Unfortunately, there has been a change of plans.'

Mma Ramotswe and Mma Makutsi stared at him wide-eyed. Mr J. L. B. Matekoni froze. He was looking at the floor, and his gaze did not shift.

'Yes,' Mr T. K. Molefi continued breezily. 'My business plan has shifted. I would have very much liked to have you as a partner, Mr J. L. B. Matekoni – after all, we go back a very long time, and that counts for something in my book.'

Mma Ramotswe did not reveal her thoughts. She was thinking: yes, that counts for a lot – until a better offer comes in. But she did not say this: she felt only relief, and she could see from Mma Makutsi's expression that her relief was shared.

But not by Mr J. L. B. Matekoni, of course. He now raised his downcast eyes and fixed his gaze on Mr T. K. Molefi. 'But we had an agreement, Rra. I was to invest—'

Mr T. K. Molefi cut him off. 'We did not actually agree, Mr J. L. B. Matekoni. Not in so many words. We had a spoken draft memorandum of understanding. You could put it that way. It was only a draft. I had not signed anything. You had not signed anything. No money had changed hands.'

Mma Ramotswe's sense of relief grew larger. 'I think it is true that agreements should be in writing,' she said. 'That is because the details are only sorted out once things are in writing.'

Mma Makutsi now rallied to the cause. 'You are right about that, Mma,' she said. 'Until something is in writing, it is just smoke in the air. Puff.' She blew into the air, to demonstrate the point.

Mma Ramotswe glanced at Mr J. L. B. Matekoni. He looked as if he was struggling to comprehend what was happening. 'You said,' he began. 'You said that . . . And then we have spent all that time on the bus.'

Mr T. K. Molefi raised a finger. 'The company will pay for the work done on the bus. Of course, we shall pay for that, Rra. You must give me the bill.'

Mr J. L. B. Matekoni gave Mma Ramotswe an anguished look. Instinctively, she reached out to put an arm around his shoulder. 'There will be many other business opportunities,' she whispered. 'This one . . . Well, he has somebody else who is taking the risk. It is better that way, I think.'

He looked miserable. He shook his head. Mma Ramotswe looked for the words to console him, but they eluded her.

Mma Ramotswe drove Mma Makutsi home that afternoon. They left the office early, putting a sign on the door that said 'Gone Home' – a sign they sometimes used when it was too hot to remain in the office, or when there was no work to do, or simply when they both felt – as they occasionally did – that it was a good idea to go home and look at their gardens, or tidy the house, or simply go to sleep until it became a bit cooler.

They travelled in silence at first, and then Mma Makutsi said, 'Well, Mma Ramotswe, that seems to be that.'

It was unarguably true. That, indeed, was that, and Mma Ramotswe did not disagree. But the fact that that was that should not preclude at least some observations as to why that had become that, and so she said, 'I am relieved, of course. I am certainly much relieved, Mma Makutsi. And thankful, too. We have had . . .'

'A narrow escape,' Mma Makutsi provided.

'Yes, a narrow escape. And it is all thanks to your Phuti and this foolish friend of his.'

Mma Makutsi felt uncomfortable about describing their rescuer as foolish. 'He is adventurous, maybe,' she said. 'I do not think we should call him foolish.'

'Perhaps not,' conceded Mma Ramotswe. 'I was just thinking of a saying I know. It is "A fool and his money are soon parted". Have you heard that saying, Mma?'

Mma Makutsi had. But sometimes these sayings, she warned, sounded good, but were too broad, or too narrow, or simply not right once you had a close look at them. 'There is one thing puzzling me,' she said. 'And that is why Mr T. K. Molefi should have wanted to talk about this with us, as well as with Mr J. L. B. Matekoni. Did you notice how he suggested that we should all be there for when he made his announcement?'

Mma Ramotswe noticed that Molefi had become Mr T. K. Molefi – and she was not entirely surprised. He had proved to be a most charming man, and she, like Mma Makutsi, rather regretted the poor view she had had of him before she had actually met him. There was a lesson there, she thought – one on which even Clovis Andersen might have something to say. He did talk – somewhere – about the importance of not making up one's mind about people until one had looked at them carefully. Perhaps they should both read that section of *The Principles of Private Detection* again.

But there was the question posed by Mma Makutsi to be considered, and so she said, 'I think that he wanted our support. I think he wanted us to be there so that it would be easier for him to give Mr J. L. B. Matekoni this bad news.'

Mma Makutsi considered this. 'I think you might be right, Mma.' She paused. 'This Molefi is perhaps a tricky man after all.'

He had become Molefi once more, and that was what he remained until Mma Makutsi got out of the van at her front gate. As she did so, a car pulled up immediately behind the van.

'That's Phuti,' said Mma Makutsi. 'He said he was going to be coming home early today.'

Phuti Radiphuti stopped the engine of his car and got out. He walked over towards his wife, planted a perfunctory kiss on her cheek, and then bent down to address Mma Ramotswe through the open window on her side of the van.

'It is good to see you, Mma,' he said.

'And you, Rra. I hope you are well.'

Phuti gestured towards Mma Makutsi as he replied, 'I am well because I am well looked after, Mma Ramotswe.'

Mma Makutsi rolled her eyes. 'You must not believe men when they say things like that.' But she was clearly pleased.

'I just wanted to say sorry,' Phuti continued. 'I am sorry that I was unable to help you over this bus business. I did my best.'

Mma Ramotswe frowned. 'But you did help us, Rra. Your friend has done exactly what you wanted him to do. He has made a much bigger offer, and Molefi has accepted.'

Phuti drew back. 'No, Mma, that cannot be. He called me at the office fifteen minutes ago – just before I left – and told me that he would not be getting involved. He said that he had too many other things on the go. He had been tempted, he said, but had decided against it.'

Mma Ramotswe glanced at Mma Makutsi, who seemed as puzzled as she herself was.

'But we have just seen Molefi,' Mma Makutsi said. 'He told us himself. He said that his business plan had changed.'

Phuti shook his head. 'I do not understand this,' he said. 'Perhaps this Molefi is not telling you the truth. Perhaps—'

He did not finish. Mma Makutsi now burst out, 'No, Rra, I do not think he was lying.'

'Then how did—' Phuti began, only to be cut off once more by Mma Makutsi.

'Somebody else,' she said. 'It must be somebody else. There are other people with more money than sense.' She paused. 'There are plenty of people like that.'

Phuti thought about this. 'I suppose so,' he said at last. 'But it is a bit odd, don't you think?'

Mma Ramotswe said that she did think it was odd, but she had been in practice as a private detective long enough to know that strange things happened, and sometimes these strange things were very strange indeed.

Phuti returned to his car, and nosed it up the driveway, waving to Mma Ramotswe as he went past. Mma Ramotswe looked at Mma Makutsi. 'It is very puzzling,' she said. 'But you know something, Mma? It makes me feel a bit better. I was beginning to feel guilty that we had ruined Mr J. L. B. Matekoni's plans. Did you see his face when Molefi broke the news?'

'Oh, I saw that,' said Mma Makutsi, sounding quite miserable. 'And I felt the same as you, Mma. I felt that I had spoiled things for an old friend.'

'But we didn't, did we?' Mma Ramotswe said. 'It was not our fault after all.'

'It is what they call the act of a third party,' pronounced Mma Makutsi. 'That is the term they use.'

'Who, Mma? Who talks about third parties?'

Mma Makutsi waved a careless hand. 'That is what they say in business circles. And lawyers, I think. Lawyers talk a lot about third parties.'

Mma Ramotswe looked about her, at the scattered houses, and, beyond them, the expanse of open bush, criss-crossed by paths, along which third parties, she reflected, might make their way, bound on the errands that only third parties know about. It was a world of third parties, just as the business people and the lawyers said. It was a world that seemed always ready to surprise us, to present us with situations in which what we thought had happened, had in fact not happened. It was that sort of world, and we should always be prepared to be reminded of that.

'Do you feel a bit better?' asked Mma Makutsi.

'I think I do,' Mma Ramotswe confessed. 'But then, I think of poor Mr J. L. B. Matekoni and his plans for something that will never be.'

Mma Makutsi gave what comfort she could. 'He has you, Mma. Remember that. And he has Motholeli and Puso and Tlokweng Road Speedy Motors and ...' She tried to think of other things in Mr J. L. B. Matekoni's life, but she could not, and so, as tactfully as she could, she stopped, took a step back, and waved to her friend as the van drove off.

It was while she was driving away from Mma Makutsi's house that Mma Ramotswe had her idea. It was the second idea on this particular subject that had come to her when driving. The first had involved that exploratory trip that had led to her meeting with Alice, the housekeeper of the people known by Mma Makutsi as the Pula-Pulas. A ridiculous name, she thought, but Mma Makutsi often hit the nail on the head with her pithy remarks, and now, in Mma Ramotswe's mind, the Pula-Pula family is what they were. She thought now of Mma Pula-Pula, whom she had not met. She thought of what she represented. She thought of the young people whom they used – for there was no other name for it. They used them. And then she thought that she would pay an unscheduled visit to Mma Pula-Pula. Why not? There were evil people in the world – we all knew that – and for much of the time they got away with it because they were rich and powerful and could act with impunity. But every so often, one might be able to sneak up on these people and poke them in the stomach – as Mma Makutsi might say. Why not now?

She answered this question by turning the van round in somebody's gateway and heading off in the opposite direction – to the enclave of large houses and their surrounding walls. As she did so, she thought of what lay ahead and found herself smiling. She was not frightened of these people, for all their wealth and influence, and she thought that there was a chance – a remote chance – that her idea might work. Superstition was a very powerful thing, and those who lived in its grip were often far weaker than others might imagine. That was generally true, she thought, but now she might just put the proposition to the test.

It did not take her long, as the traffic going in that direction was light. When she arrived, her tiny white van looking quite conspicuous and out of place in this suburb of sleek vehicles, she found that the gate of the house had been left open. Without hesitation, she swept up the short driveway that led to the house and parked under a suitable-looking tree. To do so, she had to infringe on a well-maintained, lush kikuyu-grass lawn – did these people not know about the water shortage? Did they not care?

She stepped out of the car, adjusted her dress, and took a deep breath. She was a citizen of Botswana. She had the right to be anywhere she chose to be. She had no reason to apologise for being here, standing before this imposing mansion, her van parked on its expensive lawn. No, she had no reason to have to justify any of that.

There was a bell at the front door. That was significant. Most people were happy just to let people knock, or call out, as was polite. The Pula-Pulas had to have a bell, which she now rang, jumping slightly at the loud and rather alarming sound it produced. She took another deep breath. She was entitled to ring that bell, no matter how intimidating it was.

Alice came to the door. She looked at Mma Ramotswe in momentary confusion, and was about to say something – to express the surprise she must have felt – when Mma Ramotswe raised her finger to her lips. Alice understood, and immediately composed herself. She greeted Mma Ramotswe in the traditional manner. Then, with a toss of her head back towards the cool interior of the house, she asked, 'You are here to see her, Mma?'

'Yes, I would like to see her, Mma. I have something very important to tell her.'

Alice's eyes widened. A smile flickered across her lips. 'Very important, Mma?'

'Very,' Mma Ramotswe confirmed. 'A matter of number one importance.'

Alice nodded. 'I shall go and fetch her,' she said. 'You may wait in this room, Mma.'

She led Mma Ramotswe across a wide and highly polished parquet floor towards a sitting room. This was furnished with ungainly, over-upholstered armchairs covered in expensive-looking material. Mma Ramotswe sat down gingerly: one might disappear altogether in such chairs; one might disappear and not be found for days.

And then Mma Pula-Pula appeared. She was a very short

woman, dressed in a loud red trouser suit, and wearing large round glasses of the sort favoured by Mma Makutsi. Mma Ramotswe found herself thinking of how Mma Makutsi would approve of the glasses, even if she would almost certainly disapprove of the red trouser suit. In spite of her limited stature, Mma Pula-Pula had about her a strong, confident air of authority. But it was not authority of the sort that one would encounter in a school principal or a magistrate or somebody of that sort: this was the authority of the bully. Mma Ramotswe sensed that immediately.

'You have come to see me, Mma. Who are you, please?'

'My name is Mma Ramotswe.'

The woman was looking at her, summing her up. The conclusion of the evaluation was apparent in the cursory, almost rude, tone of what followed.

'What do you want to see me about? I am very busy, you see.'

Mma Ramotswe remained calm. She smiled. 'I am the owner of the No. 1 Ladies' Detective Agency,' she began. *Try to tell the truth*, Clovis Andersen had written. *The truth always makes you strong.*

Mma Pula-Pula was not impressed. 'I have never heard of that.'

'Well, there is no reason why you should have heard of us, Mma. We are not very important.'

She wondered whether the other woman would go so far as to concur with that self-effacing description, but she said nothing, and continued to stare at Mma Ramotswe, clearly waiting for further explanation.

'In my particular work, Mma,' Mma Ramotswe continued, 'we come across unexpected things. We hear confidences. We discover facts. We lift up stones and look underneath them.'

She was being watched. She was being listened to now.

'And I have come across something that made me very concerned,

Mma. I learned of something that might affect you, and although I do not know you, I thought I should come here to warn you.'

Her words had an immediate effect.

'Me, Mma? Might affect me?' The anxiety behind this response was palpable.

Mma Ramotswe lowered her voice. 'You have some young people here, I think, Mma . . .'

Mma Pula-Pula stiffened. 'So?'

'You have some young people working for you who have a relative.'

Mma Pula-Pula's eyes narrowed. 'So? We all have relatives.'

'But this relative, Mma, is an unusual one. Many people who have such relatives would not speak about it. They are people who . . . who, shall I say, move at night. They are people who use . . .' She paused. Her words were having the precise effect she had hoped for. 'Well, I know nobody likes to talk about this, because it has no place in our modern Botswana. No place at all, Mma.'

Now Mma Pula-Pula was quite still. Her confident manner had entirely disappeared.

'This relative, whom I came across in the course of investigating something else altogether, has heard what has happened to these young people. He heard that somebody – and this can't be you, Mma; it must be somebody else – was making use of them. You know what I mean, Mma. Making them work and not paying them properly. That is terrible when that happens, Mma. You have probably not seen that sort of thing happen, but in my business, Mma, we come across it from time to time.'

Mma Pula-Pula opened her mouth to say something, but evidently thought better of it.

'This relative,' Mma Ramotswe continued, 'has, I am sorry to say, Mma, put a curse on the person who has been doing these

things. Now I know, Mma, that it can't be you, but I learned that
there has been some sort of mistake, and that you must have been
mistaken for somebody else. But he has put the curse on you, I
think, and once these things are done . . .' She shrugged, as if in
the face of some greater fate, the operation of which was beyond
mere human control.

'Oh,' said Mma Pula-Pula.

'Yes,' said Mma Ramotswe. 'It is very bad. These people who
use *muti* in this way are very backward. They are stupid. But it
is important for their victims to know that they are being tar-
geted. That brings it out into the open, which is always helpful.
Shine a light on dark things, people say. That is what they say,
isn't it, Mma?'

No answer came.

'And yet,' Mma Ramotswe continued, 'even if there is no basis
to this nonsense – this so-called witchcraft – it's amazing to see
how sometimes it appears to work. I cannot understand that, but
it seems to have an effect.' She paused. 'There was a woman who
had a curse put on her and she lost all her fingernails, Mma. It
was terrible. And another man who was also the victim of one of
these people grew fatter and fatter and had to be moved about on
a wheelbarrow, Mma, because he could no longer walk. That was
also terrible. It was very sad. I don't believe it can have had anything to do with a curse, but it just seems such an extraordinary
coincidence, don't you think, Mma?'

Again, there was no answer. But when Mma Ramotswe looked
into Mma Pula-Pula's eyes, she saw not only horror, but fear.

'Of course,' said Mma Ramotswe, 'if the young people in question were to be found a good place, then it would all blow over,
and nobody would be harmed.'

She stopped. Mma Pula-Pula was staring at her with the air of a supplicant. 'Is there . . .' the small woman began, but then trailed off. She looked miserable.

'I don't believe in all this sort of thing,' said Mma Ramotswe. 'I am not superstitious, Mma.'

'Nor am I,' said Mma Pula-Pula, but so weakly, and so unconvincingly, that Mma Ramotswe barely heard her.

'There is a lady out at Tlokweng,' Mma Ramotswe now said. 'She is called Mma Potokwani. You may have heard of her. She runs that place for children – for young people. She looks after them very well. Her name is Mma Potokwani, Mma. Mma Potokwani.'

Mma Pula-Pula nodded. 'I shall remember her name, Mma.'

'Good,' said Mma Ramotswe, rising to leave.

Alice saw her out, accompanying her out to the van.

'Superstitious people are very easy to deal with,' Mma Ramotswe said as they went outside, her voice lowered.

Alice giggled. 'Oh, Mma, that is excellent. I do not know what you have done, but I think you have done something very good.'

They reached the van.

'And you have parked on her lawn,' said Alice, clapping her hands together. 'Oh, Mma, you are a very fine woman. You are one of the best ladies in Botswana, I think.'

Mr J. L. B. Matekoni was late home, arriving only a few minutes before Mma Ramotswe was ready to serve his dinner. He washed his hands and then appeared, in silence, at the kitchen table. She had prepared beef stew, but even that did not seem to lift his spirits.

She looked at him. She looked at this good, kind, uncomplaining man whom she had married and who, in her eyes, and the eyes of so many other people, represented all that was fine about their country. She looked at him and she wanted to weep. Mr J. L. B. Matekoni did not deserve to be unhappy. Nobody deserved to be unhappy, she thought, if we were with charity, but those like him, who spent their time simply working hard, doing a job that had to be done, keeping things going – they, in particular, did not deserve to be unhappy. And yet life was not always a matter of just deserts.

'You must not worry too much,' she said, her voice quiet, faltering because of the emotion she felt. 'You must not worry too much because one plan has not worked out. There will be others – perhaps.'

He nodded – but not with a great deal of conviction, she thought. 'I would have liked to have been a director of a bus company,' he said. 'It would have been something.'

Yes, she thought, it would have been something. And that was what most of us wanted in our lives: something. But we could not always have it, for any one – or more – of a number of reasons: because there was not enough to go round; or because opportunities came at the wrong time, when we were unprepared for them; or because what we wanted would not be good for us. There was inevitable disappointment in everybody's life, but knowing that disappointments were inevitable did not necessarily make them any easier to bear. So she served his meal and they ate in silence. She had felt relief, and with good reason, that their security had not been compromised by a risky loan, but there were some victories that, for all they saved the day, were hollow nonetheless. This, she thought, was one of them.

Chapter Fourteen

Mma Know-it-all and
Mma Hippopotamus

Maisie Mophephu telephoned Mma Ramotswe to ask whether she and Mma Makutsi might meet her at the home of her sister Betty, formerly Betty Mophephu but now Betty Leseyane. She did not give them much notice – she proposed meeting that day at noon, explaining that her trip to Gaborone needed to be arranged hastily, as her duties as a school principal were not ones that she could easily reschedule. 'Every day,' she said, 'something goes wrong and requires me to put it right. It happens without warning, every single day, Mma – I am not exaggerating. People come to me about this, that, and the next thing – all the time.'

Mma Ramotswe thought: how many of us can say the same about our own days? Most of us, she suspected. But she was understanding, and sympathised with Maisie and her feelings about the burdens of her office.

'It would be very good if people stopped being people,' she said. 'But they will not do that, will they?'

Mma Makutsi was listening in on this telephone call. She usually answered the phone in the office, and could switch calls through to the telephone on Mma Ramotswe's desk. Mma Ramotswe had grown used to Mma Makutsi's being very slow to hang up at her end – this gave her the opportunity to hear a good part of, if not the complete, conversation between any caller and Mma Ramotswe. She did this now, and when Maisie suggested a meeting of the four of them later that day, Mma Makutsi signalled her assent by an enthusiastic nodding of her head.

'Well, you probably heard that,' said Mma Ramotswe, once she had rung off.

'I did not have time to transfer the call entirely,' said Mma Makutsi. 'So yes, I heard that, Mma. And I am free to go to that meeting.'

The meeting was to take place at Betty's house, which was in a part of town called the Village – not all that far from the Tlokweng Road and not more than a fifteen-minute drive in Mma Ramotswe's tiny white van. This they parked under a tree near the gate of an older house – one of those shady, practical buildings that the Botswana Housing Corporation had built fifty years earlier for the civil servants of the nascent state. They had aged well, these houses, because they respected the climate: their tin roofs reflected the heat of the sun, their dark verandas provided precious shade, their polished concrete floors repelled hungry termites, and their generous yards encouraged pawpaw trees, jacaranda, and rockeries for Kalahari succulents.

They were ten minutes early, but Mma Ramotswe decided

that rather than wait in the van, they would go in. 'I like these places,' she said, as they made their way along the path to the front door. 'They are not showy. There are so many houses now that are showy, Mma Makutsi. These houses are simple.'

Mma Makutsi agreed. 'It is best to live in a simple house,' she said. 'Although a large house is also a good thing.' She thought for a moment. 'A simple house that is also large, perhaps.'

'You do not need your house to be too large,' said Mma Ramotswe. 'Because then people will talk about how you have more than you need. They will be envious and they will spread stories about you.'

'People are always envious of other people,' Mma Makutsi observed. 'They do not like others to have more than they have. It is a feature of human nature, I think.' She paused. They had reached the front door, and they could hear voices drifting out from the inside of the house.

'That is Maisie,' whispered Mma Ramotswe. 'That is her voice.'

Mma Makutsi listened. 'And that will be her sister. Listen.'

They were not deliberately eavesdropping, but the conversation between the two sisters was loud enough for them to make out exactly what was being said.

'Those women,' Maisie was saying. 'I don't know what they'll think.'

There was a brief silence. Then the other woman's voice said, 'Who knows? The one with the glasses calls the shots, I think. Mma Know-it-all. The other one – Mma Hippopotamus – is really just a friendly aunty.'

Mma Makutsi froze. Then she turned to Mma Ramotswe and gripped her forearm. From her large round glasses, a flash of light signalled danger.

Maisie spoke next: 'He's been asking for it. For years, I think.'

'I feel no guilt,' said the other voice. 'Look at me – do I look guilty? I don't think so.'

Mma Ramotswe turned, and signalled to Mma Makutsi to follow her. Together they retraced their steps down the path.

'Are we leaving?' whispered Mma Makutsi.

Mma Ramotswe shook her head. 'No, we shall walk back up the path, but we will need to make a noise so they think we have just arrived. Then they will not think we have overheard them.'

Mma Makutsi was seething. 'How dare they!' she muttered. 'Mma Know-it-all. Mma Hippopotamus? Friendly aunty?'

Mma Ramotswe managed to smile. 'People who eavesdrop very rarely hear anything good spoken about themselves. I was taught that as a little girl. I think it's true.' Then she added, 'There is nothing wrong in being a hippopotamus.' She was about to add, 'Or a know-it-all,' but stopped herself.

'They are up to something,' said Mma Makutsi. 'They are trying to trick us.'

'So it would seem,' said Mma Ramotswe. 'But let's just see.'

They went back up the path, talking loudly so as to give warning of their approach. As they neared the house, they saw a movement beyond the open front door, and then a woman appeared and waved to them.

'There you are,' she said. 'We were just talking about you.'

Mma Makutsi gave Mma Ramotswe a meaningful look.

'Yes,' said Mma Ramotswe. 'Here we are. We're a bit early, I think – I hope you don't mind.'

The woman, who introduced herself as Betty, said that she did not mind at all. 'We can have tea on the veranda. My sister and I have something to discuss with you. We will need to start straight away, as she has to get back down to Lobatse and does not have much time.'

Mma Ramotswe said that they understood. 'It is a very demanding business, being a school principal.'

They were shown to chairs set about a table on the veranda. A teapot and tea cups were waiting for them, along with a plate of digestive biscuits. As they sat down, Maisie joined them from inside the house. She greeted them effusively – too effusively, thought Mma Ramotswe.

Tea was poured.

'I shall not waste your time,' said Betty. 'My sister and I have been talking.'

'I am sure you have,' said Mma Makutsi, pointedly.

Mma Ramose threw a cautionary look in Mma Makutsi's direction.

'And we have reached a conclusion about what has happened,' Betty went on. 'We think that you were right about our poor father mistaking the nurse for Maisie's mother. He is always getting things mixed up now.'

Mma Ramotswe waited.

'And we are agreed on one thing,' said Maisie. 'We think that Bontle – that is, the nurse – deserves to be rewarded for all the years she has looked after Daddy. We think that she should get what the will says she should get, even if he thinks he is leaving it to my mother.'

'Yes,' interjected Betty. 'That is what we think. Maisie's mother is very old now. She is married to a man whom we—' She broke off, looking to her sister for support.

'She is married to a man we do not like very much,' Maisie said. 'She married him twenty years ago. He spends his time with bar girls half his age, you see, and he has not made her happy. But she sticks with him.'

218

'Maisie looks after her,' said Betty. 'She has everything she needs. But if she were to get any property from our father, there is no doubt that her husband would take it and spend it on those bad women. It is one of those cases, Mma Ramotswe, where it is best to keep any assets well away from somebody who would lose them very quickly.'

Mma Ramotswe raised an eyebrow. 'So you think we should not try to change anything?'

Betty nodded. 'Yes, that is exactly what we think, Mma. If we go to a lawyer and say that there is a misunderstanding in the will that our father has made and that he did not have the ability to make it—'

'Because he was confused,' interjected Maisie.

'Yes, because he was confused. If we do that, then Bontle, the nurse, gets nothing, and the house and the farm go into our father's general estate – most of which is going to go to our brother.'

Maisie explained that their father had made an earlier will and that this will would come into effect if the new will were to be overturned on grounds of lack of capacity. 'Under that earlier will,' she said, 'our brother was left the house and farm – along with a lot of other things.'

'So we do not want this new will to be disturbed,' said Betty. 'It gives the nurse what she deserves and it stops our brother getting everything. He already has far more than he needs.'

'And you?' asked Mma Makutsi suddenly. 'What about you? I don't want to seem a know-it-all, but I have been wondering: what about you?'

Mma Ramotswe caught her breath at Mma Makutsi's boldness. She waited for a reaction, but the two sisters seemed not to have noticed the deliberate taunt.

'It makes no difference to us at all,' said Maisie quickly. 'We have already been given a lot of property by our father. He did that some years ago. If we went back to the old will, we would probably get more anyway – but that is not the point. What we are proposing leaves us no better off, but it stops things being wasted by my useless stepfather, and at the same time it prevents our greedy brother from getting much more than he really needs.'

Mma Ramotswe raised a hand. 'This is very complicated,' she said. 'I need to think about it.'

'Even a hippopotamus needs to think before she gets into the water,' muttered Mma Makutsi.

'What was that?' asked Betty.

'Nothing,' said Mma Makutsi. 'I was just thinking.'

They looked at one another. Mma Ramotswe stared up at the ceiling. Then she looked out over the garden. Eventually, she said, 'You are asking us to mislead our client. That is what you have in mind, I think.'

Betty and Maisie exchanged glances. 'You could put it that way,' said Betty.

'On the other hand,' Maisie said, 'you might say that we are asking you to approve of something that brings about a just result.'

'Possibly,' said Mma Ramotswe.

'Definitely, Mma,' insisted Maisie. 'Look at it this way. Your client has lied to you. He has told you that the nurse is a wicked woman. He has said that she has tried to trick our father into leaving the farm to her. That is simply not true, Mma Ramotswe. That is a big lie. And if he has lied to you, then I think you no longer have a duty towards him.'

'You do not,' said Betty, forcefully.

'If you do nothing,' Maisie went on, 'then you have just done nothing. You haven't told any lies. You just say that there is no

evidence of this undue influence you mentioned. And there
is not. You are not telling a lie. Then you leave nature to take
its course.'

'Justice will be done,' said Betty. 'Everybody will be happy –
apart from our brother, who is never happy with anything that
does not make him richer.'

Mma Ramotswe looked at the two sisters, first at Betty, and
then at Maisie. She looked them directly in the eye, and she
saw that neither of them flinched. Then Betty said something
that made Mma Ramotswe feel that they were being completely candid.

'We were worried that you would not let us do this, Mma. We
thought you might be on our brother's side.'

Mma Ramotswe raised a hand. 'Let's not argue,' she said. 'I
will be truthful with you. I heard you say some things that were
uncomplimentary ...'

Betty gasped. 'We were just—'

Mma Ramotswe stopped her. 'No, let's be honest with
one another.'

Maisie put a hand to her mouth, and then took it away. 'I am
very sorry, Mma Ramotswe. We said some unkind things. Please,
will you forgive us?'

Mma Ramotswe looked at her. 'Yes,' she said. 'Of course I
am happy to forgive you. And I will tell you, too, that I fully
understand why you want to do what you have proposed. It is
a fair result. It is a good result.' She paused. 'I shall tell your
brother that we found no evidence of undue influence. That is
true, isn't it? The nurse has not tried to get him to make that
will. It was his decision. I shall tell him that the nurse is not a
wicked woman, as he says she is, but that she is a deserving lady.
I shall tell him that if the matter were to go before a court, I

would not hesitate to give evidence that when I saw your father he said that he wanted to leave the farm to Bontle – and that he pointed to the nurse when he said that. I can say that in complete honesty, because that, I think, is what he really wanted – in a way.'

Betty clapped her hands. 'We are very lucky that you are such a fair-minded woman, Mma,' she said. She glanced at their tea cups. 'And I think your cups need refreshing.'

A few minutes later, two young children emerged from inside the house, to stand, inquisitively, in the doorway, staring at the visitors.

'These are my two youngest,' said Betty. 'They are not yet at school.'

She called the children over to her side. 'You should say *dumela* to these two aunties,' she said.

The children obeyed. They were respectful.

Mma Ramotswe smiled at them, as did Mma Makutsi.

In the van, on the way back to the office, Mma Makutsi said, 'It is good to see children like that, Mma. So many children these days are so rude. Not those ones.'

'Only other people's children,' said Mma Ramotswe, without really thinking of what she was saying. 'Our own children are always very well behaved.'

It was a subject on which she might have said more, but she did not. She was still thinking of what they had achieved at the meeting. She thought the result was the right one, and that the cause of justice had been served. She hoped that was the case, anyway, and that, she supposed, was the way it would always be. You hoped that what you did was for the overall good, but you could never be sure. Sometimes there were doubts, and those doubts could persist, but often you really had no choice.

You had to feel your way through the complexities of this life and hope, just hope, that you got it right more often than you got it wrong. And sometimes, of course, you did not have to do anything at all.

Chapter Fifteen

I Am Feeling a Bit Happier

Mma Ramotswe was accustomed to surprises, given the nature of the work she did. You will be looking for one thing, she observed, and then something quite different comes to light. Or you succeed in finding what you are looking for, and then you see that right beside it is something even better – something you should have been looking for in the first place. But in spite of this experience, she was not ready for what happened almost exactly a week after that crucial visit from Molefi when Mr J. L. B. Matekoni's hopes had been so suddenly punctured.

She and Mma Makutsi had been out together on a piece of minor business – a visit to a shop in which anomalies in the stock-taking system had been revealed. Employee dishonesty had been suspected, but they had been able to trace deficits to a fault in the recording of orders, and had lifted the cloud of suspicion that had settled over the heads of the people who worked in the business. Mma Ramotswe was pleased with this outcome, as trust, she said, lay at the heart of every successful business, and it was so easily lost through suspicion and accusation.

When they were still some distance from the garage, Mma Makutsi suddenly called out, 'There is another bus, Mma! Look, right there. There is another bus.'

She was right. Parked outside Tlokweng Road Speedy Motors was a large bus, similar in style to the one on which Mr J. L. B. Matekoni and Fanwell had worked before.

Mma Ramotswe was silent as she parked the van. Was this another hare-brained bus company scheme, born of frustration over the failure of the last? She looked at Mma Makutsi to see if she could shed any light on what was happening, but she simply shrugged.

And then she saw him. There was Mr T. K. Molefi, conferring with Mr J. L. B. Matekoni and Fanwell in the workshop of the garage.

The two women went over to join them.

'Mma Ramotswe!' exclaimed Mr T. K. Molefi. 'And the charming Mma Makutsi!'

Mma Ramotswe tried to smile. Mma Makutsi pursed her lips. She was impervious to this sort of false charm – she knew about men like Molefi, who said one thing and then did another.

Now Mr J. L. B. Matekoni spoke. 'T. K. has come to talk to me.'

'So I see,' said Mma Ramotswe.

'I have come with a business proposition,' said Mr T. K. Molefi.

Mma Ramotswe gritted her teeth. Mma Makutsi visibly bristled.

'Yes,' he continued, 'I have come to ask Mr J. L. B. Matekoni to provide all mechanical services to the Joy and Light Bus

225

Company. We have been going for one week exactly, Mma Ramotswe, and the response has been overwhelming.' He paused. 'Overwhelming, Mma. So much so that I have already acquired four other buses. All old ones, but I know how good Mr J. L. B. Matekoni is at fixing up these old vehicles.'

Mma Ramotswe glanced at her husband, and saw his delight. It was there, all over his face, unmistakable. His expression was not that of one who thought of himself as a failure.

'And young Fanwell here is going to paint something special,' went on Mr T. K. Molefi. 'Not only is he going to put the name of the company on the side . . .'

'The Joy and Light Bus Company,' said Fanwell, pointing to the side of the bus. 'In big letters.'

'Not only that,' said Mr T. K. Molefi, 'but I have asked him to paint underneath "Maintained, for your safety, by Tlokweng Road Speedy Motors".'

Mr J. L. B. Matekoni was beaming with pleasure.

'And I have asked my old friend to be on the board of the company,' said Mr T. K. Molefi. 'No investment will be needed . . .' He turned to Mr J. L. B. Matekoni. 'Just your wisdom, old friend. That is what we need most of all.'

Old friend. Mma Ramotswe thought of these words. They were so powerful. To call another *old friend*, when it was true, when one had known the other for a long time, right back into the years of childhood, was one of the warmest, most touching things one could say of another. *Old friend.*

She looked at Mma Makutsi. Mma Ramotswe was as confident as she could be that as far as Mma Makutsi was concerned, Molefi was once again Mr T. K. Molefi. And Mma Makutsi's expression confirmed this. Mr T. K. Molefi had been completely rehabilitated.

Always be ready to admit that you have been wrong, Clovis Andersen wrote. He was right, Mma Ramotswe thought: he was right about being wrong.

One month later, on the day of Mma Ramotswe's birthday, she and Mma Potokwani met for lunch at the President Hotel. Mma Potokwani was in town to do some shopping and, remembering what day it was, had suggested the lunch as a way of celebrating the birthday.

'You must let me pay,' she said. 'It is your special day, and so I shall pay for lunch.'

'You are too kind, Mma Potokwani. And I think even if I say no, you will insist. You are not an easy lady to argue with.'

Mma Potokwani laughed. 'I prefer it if people do not argue with me,' she said. 'And by and large they don't.'

They sat at a table near the veranda parapet, protected from the direct rays of the sun by a canvas awning, but sufficiently in the open to allow them to see what was happening in the square below. And that was life, really – people walking; people talking; people buying things from those who had erected stalls about the square; people laughing at jokes that those looking on from afar could not hear.

'Oh, there is something I wanted to tell you,' said Mma Potokwani, as she began to tuck into the plate of curry and rice she had helped herself to from the all-you-can-eat buffet. 'You know that child you met at Mma Molebatsi's? The one who had been exploited by those people?'

Mma Ramotswe nodded. 'I remember her, Mma.'

'Well, a remarkable thing has happened. Two other children appeared from the same place. Another girl, who had been kept as a sort of indoor domestic – unpaid, as far as we could make out – and a teenage boy who had been working as a gardener. The boy had been very badly treated. Anyway, they turned up at the Orphan Farm – dropped off from a truck that did not linger.'

Mma Ramotswe toyed with a small pile of desiccated coconut that she had added to the side of her plate of curry. She had a helping of sliced banana, too, and was thinking about why it was that these things went so well with curry.

Mma Potokwani was watching her. 'We are going to look after these children,' said Mma Potokwani, 'but I find myself wondering how they managed to get away and why there is no attempt to recover them.' She paused. 'You wouldn't know anything about that, would you, Mma?'

She knew, of course, that Mma Ramotswe would know everything about it, and it did not take much cajoling to get her to reveal what had happened. And, as she listened to the story that her friend now told, she began to smile, her smile becoming broader as the story reached its climax.

'So it worked!' she said when Mma Ramotswe had finished.

'It was like magic,' said Mma Ramotswe, with a laugh.

'You are a very cunning lady,' said Mma Potokwani.

'I am not sure that I would like to be called cunning,' protested Mma Ramotswe.

'Well, perhaps I should say mischievous.'

'I am not sure I like that either,' said Mma Ramotswe.

'How about outrageous?' asked Mma Potokwani.

They both laughed.

'Happy birthday, anyway,' concluded Mma Potokwani.

And then, later on in the lunch, she said, 'And there's another thing I might mention, Mma.'

Mma Ramotswe waited.

'That good man – Mr J. L. B. Matekoni's old friend . . .'

'Mr T. K. Molefi?'

'Yes, him. He got in touch the day before yesterday to offer us the use of one of his buses from his company, the Joy and something . . .'

'The Joy and Light Bus Company.'

'Yes, that's it. He has offered the occasional use of one of his buses – free – to take the children on outings.'

'He is a kind man, I think,' said Mma Ramotswe.

'He is,' agreed Mma Potokwani. 'But you know, Mma, most people are kind – if you give them the chance.'

'I would like to think that's true, Mma Potokwani.'

'I think it is, Mma.'

Mma Ramotswe looked at her now empty plate. Should she have a second helping of curry? Or would it be her third?

Mma Potokwani must have read her thoughts. 'Third,' she whispered. 'But why not?'

That evening, Mma Ramotswe and Mr J. L. B. Matekoni held a private celebration after the children had gone to bed. They sat on the veranda and watched fireflies dancing in the darkness. They talked about the sorts of things they liked to talk about when there were no important decisions to be made and when the conversation could wander comfortably along uncluttered shores.

'I am feeling a bit happier,' said Mr J. L. B. Matekoni. 'Things are going well at the garage and that rash I had on my leg has cleared up.'

'That is very good,' said Mma Ramotswe. 'You cannot be completely happy if you are bothered by a rash.'

'No,' said Mr J. L. B. Matekoni.

He took a sip of his cold beer.

'The Joy and Light Bus Company has bought another bus,' he said.

Mma Ramotswe smiled encouragingly.

'They are doing really well,' Mr J. L. B. Matekoni continued. 'They will have eight buses by the end of the year, I hear. It is a very successful company.'

'So, there are lots of passengers?'

'Hundreds,' said Mr J. L. B. Matekoni. 'People like them, and they are being very well run by T. K. They are starting several new routes. There will be a lot of mechanical work for me, I think, although I will not forget my old clients.'

Mma Ramotswe was happy, and all that she could think of to say was, 'Ah.' There were times, she thought, when *ah* said everything that needed to be said.

He smiled at her. He loved his wife. She was everything to him.

Mma Ramotswe looked thoughtful. 'The important thing is to carry on doing what you're doing,' she said. 'And not to do what you think other people think you should do. You should do what you do as well as you possibly can.'

'That is true,' said Mr J. L. B. Matekoni.

'And you should do it with love,' she added.

A firefly came into view against the warm darkness. Then it went off, darting and dipping erratically – out into the night, a tiny pinpoint of light, which, at the end of the day, is all that is needed.

Alexander McCall Smith is the author of over one hundred books on a wide array of subjects, including the award-winning The No. 1 Ladies' Detective Agency series. He is also the author of the Isabel Dalhousie novels and the world's longest-running serial novel, *44 Scotland Street*. His books have been translated into forty-six languages. Alexander McCall Smith is Professor Emeritus of Medical Law at the University of Edinburgh and holds honorary doctorates from thirteen universities.